1

The Book Club.

First published in 2017.

All rights reserved.

Text: © Jim Ryan
Image: © Jim Ryan

The events and characters portrayed in this book are fictitious. Any similarity to real persons, living or dead, is coincidental and not intended by the author.

For Mike – thanks for the happy memories.

Prologue

The group said their goodbyes to one another and made off in different directions, the summer sun still hovering above the horizon, not yet wanting to call the day over.

The woman looked at her husband as they slowly walked home with the low sun on their faces, neither of them in a great hurry to get home and see what havoc had been caused in their absence. Hopefully the babysitter wouldn't be in tears this time and the cat would still have her whiskers.

'So, what did you really think of the book?' she asked him.

'Load of rubbish. I only read it all the way through as I was on the night shift last night bored rigid and needed something to pass the time. That said, I think the book slowed time down to a standstill, it was that painful.'

'So why did you say it was thought provoking then?' she said, stepping out of the way as a jogger made his way past them.

The man scratched his beard. 'It was. It made me think it was a load of crap. Honestly, one of our boys could have done a better job.'

'Whose suggestion was it again?'

'Who do you think? The Ice Queen's, after she read a review in some newspaper. Not sure why we all voted for that recommendation.'

'That explains a lot then. That's several hours of my life I won't be getting back. Why do people keep choosing these awful books?'

'God knows. I've been trying to get rid of the last two that we read by selling them on eBay, but no one wants them.'

She chuckled dryly. 'No surprises there then really.'

'I'll take them to the charity shop instead,' he said with a sigh.

The two of them continued ambling along the pavement, the man nodding at a chap who was watering his garden as they walked past, the smell of freshly cut grass filling the evening air.

'What's the next one called?' The woman asked, whilst pulling out a packet of pre-sliced carrot sticks from her floral handbag, and crunching down on one.

The man checked the back of his hand, where he had written the name of the book down in the absence of a scrap of paper to use.

'"*The Winding River*", which sounds a little bit more promising I suppose. Hopefully it will only be a quid or so on Kindle.'

'Mmm.'

'But if this one is rubbish, I'm going to quit the Book Club and join the Morris Dancing group instead.'

One

Harry

As he stood in the kitchen stirring his coffee, Harry watched the aging tabby cat, Clover, as she yawned and opened one eye lazily. He guessed that as the children weren't around yet, she must have breathed a sigh of relief, before readjusting herself on top of the warm clanking boiler that was in the corner of the kitchen.

Screwing up his face as he tried to remember what shift he was on tomorrow at the police station, Harry heard an explosive thud, thud, thud coming down the stairs. He decided to pick up his mug and temporarily retreat into the small utility room, which was used more as a junk room than serving any practical use. Just as he was safe inside the room, he heard the kitchen door fly open, crashing quickly into the sideboard behind it, causing the already chipped mugs to rattle together.

Harry knew without being in the kitchen that regardless of her advancing years, the cat would have leapt down and shot out through the kitchen door into the conservatory. From there, he knew she would zig-zag expertly around the pile of washing and scattered toys, before vanishing out through the hole where the cat flap had once been in the outside door to the garden; quite possibly breaking the current land speed record as she did so.

Blowing on his drink and leaning against the wall, he heard his eldest two children arguing over which of them

7

would be eating out of the Transformers bowl this morning. Sipping on his coffee, he listened to their conversation.

'But I'M the eldest, so I should have it,' Harry heard Tyler say. Tyler had a slight Welsh twang in his voice that he had picked up from Harry, much to his English wife's amusement.

Harry wasn't surprised to hear his middle son, Arlo, retort with, 'Mummy said we are to take turns and it's my turn today, as you had it yesterday.'

Harry softly chuckled. *Arlo is wasted at primary school and should be in the United Nations as a diplomat instead.*

'Well you're NOT getting it, so there,' came Tyler's reply.

'I think you'll find that when mummy gets here, I will.'

'Not if I'm already eating my cereal from it, you won't.'

'Just you wait and see.'

Harry heard a small crash, followed by what sounded like dry breakfast cereal being scattered all over the kitchen table top and plink-plonking onto the floor, bizarrely reminding him of the popular Lemmings game from the 1990s.

'Now look what you've done,' Harry heard Arlo exclaim, in his squeaky six-year-old voice.

'I haven't done anything,' cried Tyler, as what sounded like a spoon fell onto the floor.

Harry stealthily poked his head around the door. He saw that Tyler was attempting to grab handfuls of the cereal and stuff it back into the box.

Harry took a few more quick gulps from his mug. *Time to intervene, before Tyler ends up tipping the cereal over Arlo's head and we have bowls being thrown against walls, like last time.*

'Now then, what's all this commotion about?' he said, stepping out from behind the door he had been hiding behind.

Good grief, it looks like that crime scene I attended the other week.

'He started it,' Tyler pointed at Arlo.

Harry looked at Arlo, who smiled back and shrugged his shoulders. *Yes, all he needs is a glass of whisky and perhaps a monocle to look the part of a diplomat.*

'It sounded to me like it was you, Tyler, not letting Arlo have his turn with the Transformers bowl,' Harry said.

'This is so unfair. I'm going to run away one of these days you know, then you'll be sorry,' said Tyler, his fists full of cereal.

'And where will you run to? Chris' house again? His parents will get fed up with you eventually,' Harry said.

'No. Somewhere *new* this time,' Tyler banged his fists on the table, cereal crunching as he did so.

'If it's somewhere nice, don't forget to send a postcard. But for now, you can get the dustpan and brush and start clearing up this mess you've made. Then it's time to get dressed. Ah, no arguments please,' Harry said, seeing Tyler open his mouth to object.

Hearing more footsteps on the staircase, he took a last quick mouthful of coffee, draining the mug.

'Harry? Harry, where are you?' he heard his wife, Polly, say from the living room.

'In here, darling.'

A few seconds later, she strode in holding two-year-old Finn, who was busy excavating his nose.

'Ah, there you are, I've been looking for you.'

'Well it's not as if I dug an escape tunnel and I'm currently hitchhiking on the M5, is it my darling?' he said.

'You think you're funny, but you're not. Look, can you get Finn dressed for me please, as I need to take my vitamins and have my morning tomato juice,' she said, handing Finn over to him. Having been married to her for over fifteen years now, Harry knew that Polly was overly conscious about germs and diseases and was convinced that she would catch every illness known to humankind if she didn't have her daily vitamins and fruit juice. Unknown to her, Harry had changed her vitamins for yellow Smarties two weeks ago.

'No problem, pass him over.'

Harry remembered a couple of years ago when Polly was convinced that she had contracted something similar to Bubonic Plague from an ill child whilst teaching at the local primary school. She had quarantined herself out in the garden in the children's playhouse for several days during the Easter break. During this period, she rewrote her will several times, favouring whomever hadn't run out of patience to still bring her paracetamol and fruit juice.

After all three children had eventually finished breakfast and gotten dressed, the Berwick family shuffled out of the backdoor into the sunshine that was gracing the South-West town of Taunton with its presence today.

Harry herded them all down the path that ran alongside the house and out into the street. They had a front door like every other of the eleven houses in Holdaway Close, but for some reason they never used it themselves - it was reserved only for important guests; such as the Queen, or, more importantly, Denzel Washington, who was a favourite of Polly's. The postman had become used to the two-minute wait after he rang the doorbell with a parcel tucked under his arm, whilst one of the Berwicks tore out of the backdoor and ran around the side of the house shrieking "Wait!", like someone might if they saw the last lifeboat being launched without them in it.

Once outside the front of the house, the family crossed over the little bridge that granted them safe passage over the trickle of a stream that ran along the bottom of Holdaway Close. As always, Harry saw Tyler cautiously glance over the side of the little bridge to see if there were any evil trolls or goblins hiding underneath. There was then the usual squabble between Tyler and Arlo, as to which of them would be pushing Finn's pushchair, which today doubled up as a racing car.

As the children shot off, Polly ran a hand through her hair and shouted, 'Don't go too far.' Tutting at him, as if somehow it was his fault, she went after them.

Harry adjusted his tweed Trilby style hat that he had bought after watching David Jason in some old crime programme and sighed. *The custody suite full of criminals at the nick is easier to control than this lot. Why, oh why did I ever leave the Welsh Valleys, get married and move here?* He thought. He set off briskly down the footpath after his wife and children, pondering what size rucksack he would need to fit all his essentials in, should he ever decide to take up tunnel digging as a hobby.

Two

Gerald

The music of Classic FM slipped elegantly through the gap in the door and glided gracefully out of the Laura Ashley wallpapered living room. It danced along the long hallway, past the Georgian telephone stand with a crystal cut vase full of freshly cut lilies on. Floating up the staircase, it twirled past the large bathroom with its heated towel rails, tip-toed along the landing and through the door of the master bedroom, finally resting in the ears of sixty-three-year-old civil service retiree, Gerald Makepeace.

He grimaced to himself as he sat at the end of the double bed, holding his tie, which proudly sported his civil service cricket team's crest.

'What a load of twaddle,' he whispered, before quickly glancing around to make sure that his wife, Valerie, hadn't crept up on him and heard his comments. She loved classical music and insisted on having it on all the time when they were home. What made it worse was when a piece came on and she tested him to see if he knew which composer it was.

He shuddered.

As he successfully finished his third attempt at tying the knot, he thought back fondly about his career. As a Grade Five, based at the secretive government listening department, GCHQ, Gerald had overseen ten Senior Executive Officers, fifteen Higher Executive Officers and countless Administrative Officers. He'd spent his career analysing intrinsically demanding situations, making tough decisions and having to answer to that back-stabbing bastard of a Home Secretary - which was all in a day's work. But when Valerie asked him which sodding composer had written what, he came out in a cold sweat and felt light-headed; it all sounded the same. He worked under the strategy that if he kept saying "Mozart" he'd be correct *some* of the time. However, *most* of the time, he got a glare and a disapproving tut from his wife of forty-two years.

He loved her dearly, but he had on occasion wondered if MI5 could help him arrange an "accident". Nothing *too* serious of course, just enough to stop her being able to turn on the radio for a week or seven. Like a freak incident involving the lid of a piano and a stray cat. Gerald had seen the intelligence about listening devices that were so miniscule they could fit on the back of a small insect, so surely they would be able to implant something in a cat to control it and make it jump around a little? Although, as a fully paid up member of the Cats Protection League, he did feel a little guilty about the idea.

Gerald stood up, brushed a few specks off his tie, sighed, and prepared to go downstairs.

Valerie sat upright in her wingback armchair, holding her cup of Earl Grey tea. Taking a delicate sip, she replaced the cup back in the saucer, the lemon bobbing up and down slightly. Valerie looked at her wristwatch and then up at the ceiling for the third time that minute. 'For goodness sake, where is that man?' she muttered, her patience exhausted. It was the same every Sunday, he would hide upstairs until the last possible second, then walk into the lounge in his overcoat looking at her, as if he were asking why she wasn't ready.

As the retired headmistress of the local primary school, St. Jude's, Valerie was used to getting her own way. When she had issued commands, she expected prompt and immediate action. She had run a tight ship, and was pleased that her school had achieved the prestigious Ofsted grade one status under her tenure. Now, it was a grade two, but she couldn't be held responsible for the actions that had been carried out since she retired two years ago. Probably something to do with the schoolchildren now calling the teachers by their first names. That, combined with girls being allowed to wear trousers nowadays, was most certainly the downfall of modern British society. No wonder the Wellington branch of Waitrose had to import its strawberries from Spain.

English language was Valerie Makepeace's passion and if she had overseen the National Curriculum, the country would be in a much better position that it currently was. She was an avid reader of *The Times* newspaper, which contained perfect syntax and flowed elegantly. She had made the mistake once of glancing at a news website and within seconds had identified spelling, punctuation and grammatical errors that had made her shudder and click on the little red square at the top right-hand corner of the screen. How could they be at such a low standard? It all started going downhill after they dismissed Moira Stuart from the Six O'clock News. She had such a beautiful voice and perfect diction.

Valerie checked her wristwatch once again and tutted to herself. She was fond of her husband, she just didn't understand the opposite sex or how their minds worked. They were like trying to understand the off-side rule in one of those noisy and pointless football matches that Gerald watched.

At that moment, the living room door opened and he finally entered, dressed in his suit and wearing his silly tie –

14

he'd never played cricket, so she didn't know why he wore that one.

'Are you ready, my dear?' he asked her, in the way you might ask a ticking time bomb to please not explode in your face as you decide which coloured wire to snip.

'I was ready *ten* minutes ago,' she replied, her steely eyes fixed on his menacingly, which over forty years of teaching experience had perfected.

'Sorry, my dear. I had to redo my tie several times. Mr Windsor wasn't playing ball this morning.'

'Funny how you wear a tie every day of the week, *my dear*, but it always misbehaves on Sundays.' She moved the handle of her teacup slightly.

'Perhaps it's God's way of telling me not to bother going to church?'

'Gerald Makepeace,' she said, darting her eyes back at him in a micro-second. 'You will be struck down by a bolt of lightning with an attitude like that.' She continued glaring at him until he looked out of the window at the cloudless late July sky. She could see him weighing up his response.

He looked back at her. 'Yes, my dear, sorry.'

'Yes. You should be. Now, fetch me my overcoat, the red one.'

She watched as he conducted a swift about-turn and beat a hasty retreat out to the corridor. She heard him open the door to the cupboard under the stairs - which she referred to as the cloakroom. She finished her tea, placing the cup and saucer down on the side table next to the armchair, ready for Gerald to collect and wash up later.

Standing up, she smoothed the creases out of her skirt and glanced at her watch again. Shaking her head, she headed out towards the hallway.

Three

Peter

A loud barking noise woke Peter up and it took him a good few seconds to realise it was coming from that blasted mobile phone contraption on his bedside table, rather than an *actual* dog in his bedroom – like the other morning.

One of these days he would have to get someone to show him how to change the blasted alarm setting to one that was a bit mellower. Like birds chirping, waves crashing against a sandy beach, or his favourite sound in the world; the *pop* noise a cork makes when you open a bottle of wine.

He thrashed his hand around on the top of the bedside cabinet until his fingers found the noisy device. Snatching it up, he contemplated throwing it against the wall to silence the ruddy thing. Only Satan himself would invent something so irritating and impossible to use. He only had it so he could phone the Indian takeaway down the road. They were good and normally didn't mind stopping off at an off licence for him on their way to delivering his food.

After he had pressed all the buttons and eventually managed to silence the alarm, he lay in bed for a few moments wondering if he was going to be lucky and escape the hangover today. In true form, he had stayed up late last night watching old episodes of a comedy starring an actress he couldn't remember the name of, as the vicar of some God-awful village town. The empty bottle by the bedside lamp told him that he was due a hangover.

He waited a few minutes and decided that he was in the clear.

No hangover. Lovely.

Not that that would stop him from filling up his hip flask with Glenfiddich before heading out of the door this morning.

Groaning and getting out of bed, Peter stumbled around his bedroom in the gloom, trying to find the clothes he had been wearing yesterday and quite possibly the day before. This reminded him, he really needed to get the washing machine fixed, after nearly two months without one, he was perilously close to running out of useable underpants.

After getting dressed, and nearly falling over twice trying to get his left leg into his trousers, he successfully exited his bedroom. His house had eight bedrooms in all and three spacious bathrooms. As it was just him living here, each year Peter slept in a different bedroom, as after a year in a bedroom, he couldn't move for the empty wine bottles and takeaway containers.

He looked in the mirror at the top of the stairs and the cobwebs hanging off it. 'I really must check the community newsletter for a cleaner,' he said for what he guessed was the 900th day in a row. 'Or perhaps an arsonist would be easier?' He added thoughtfully and wondered if he should check under *A* for arsonist, or *P* for pyromaniac first?

'Talking of pyromaniacs, I wonder if little Billy will be there today?' he grumbled. Billy was the local naughty kid, who had a passion for re-enacting stone age man's fire-starting days. At the grand age of just eleven, he had already claimed several roadside dustbins, the large refuse bin at the back of the Tesco's Express and recently, one of the sheds at the allotments. His mother insisted it was just "a phase."

Delusional woman.

Yawning, he gripped the banister rail firmly to go down the stairs to see if there was anything edible for breakfast, and at eighty-two, the vicar decided he was getting too old for this shit.

Four

The Two Cleaners

Morning had most certainly not broken when Jenny Webster had started work at five this morning, along with her best friend and fellow cleaner, Kelly Russell.

Normally she would start at around eight on a Sunday morning, do a little bit of sweeping and cleaning and a lot of gossiping with Kelly in their strong West Country accents, their cackling only stopping once Mrs Thorne arrived to warm up the church organ. However, both of them had had to start early today, as there had been a large wedding yesterday and there was confetti still scattered everywhere, making it look to Jenny as if a rainbow had been brutally murdered in front of the church door.

They were meant to have cleared it up last night, but the prospect of winning two hundred quid at the local bingo had been far more appealing. The local talent, Ben, was meant to have been there as well - according to the gossip they had heard from the cleaner at the bank Ben worked at. However, as she hadn't won a thing, and as Ben didn't show, Jenny had decided that getting drunk on cheap cider was the only way to lift their spirits. A decision that she was now regretting this morning, and judging by the look on her friend's face, she wasn't the only one.

'Why don't people buy proper confetti anymore? It's all this cheap Poundland stuff. It's so paper thin it floats around all over the place,' she said as she half-heartedly swept the path.

'It's confetti you gert numpty, it's meant to be thin,' replied Kelly.

Jenny watched her flick fag ash behind the gravestone of Arthur Brown, 1898-1942, take a swig from her can of cherry flavoured fizzy pop and then belch quietly under her breath.

'Me normal hangover cure doesn't seem to be having the desired effect this morning,' Kelly said.

'No, what I mean is, normal confetti, you throw it up, and it falls down in the same geographical area, like. This paper shite just floats around all over the place, going for bloody miles. It's a right bugger to sweep up,' Jenny said.

'Well, I think you're doing a proper job, my lover.'

Jenny stopped her sweeping and propped her arm on the broom, straightened her back and looked behind her, seeing Kelly grinning at her.

'Oi, lazy madam, pull your weight.'

'Well I don't wants to pull yours.'

'You cheeky cow. I'll have you know I lost two pounds this week.'

'Down the back of the sofa was it, my lover?' Kelly said, the cigarette in her mouth wobbling up and down as she spoke.

'No, lucky dip Lotto ticket. Not one number came up.'

'Aww, me heart bleeds for you.'

'I'll make yours bleed in a minute, if you don't help me clear this path before the Wing Commander arrives.'

The 'Wing Commander' was the less than affectionate nickname that was given to the church organist, Patricia Thorne. Patricia was retired Royal Air Force and liked everything to be done on time and in military fashion.

Rumour had it that Patricia had been flying a mission during the Iraq war and had been shot down behind enemy lines. Jenny had heard that she had evaded capture by surviving on rats and mice for a week. Although, as Patricia was quite a large lady, they would have been bloody big rats.

In an opinion that Jenny shared with most other people, the gun crew that shot her down should have been given a medal for bravery, or shot for stupidity. Patricia didn't suffer fools gladly and one of her famous disapproving glares would be enough for North Korea to abandon communism and welcome the rest of the capitalist world with open arms.

'Here, give us a fag will you, love?' Jenny asked.

Kelly lobbed the packet over to her, followed by the lighter; both of which Jenny dropped on the concrete floor instead of catching. Groaning, she bent down to retrieve them. After sparking up, she absentmindedly put the packet and lighter in her pocket, before looking around the floor and moaning to her friend.

'We're going to be here until flaming Christmas sweeping this lot up.'

'We are if you're just going to stand there and moan about it, yeah. Now give me back my fags, you cheeky pikey.'

'Oh, sorry, love, I wasn't thinking. Here, catch.' Jenny threw the packet and the lighter in Kelly's direction.

'Ta.'

'I mean, who wants to get married anyway. What is it now, one in three marriages ends in divorce?' Jenny said, scratching her head.

'God, you been taking your happy pills again my lover, you're on a right one today.'

'It's just an excuse to have a party and get pissed, isn't it really?'

'And that's one party you won't be having, unless you cheer up and stop scaring all the men away,' Kelly said.

Jenny pulled a face. 'Yadda, yadda, yadda. I don't see no wedding ring on your finger neither.'

'I'm just saving myself for Ben, once he ditches little Miss Field Mouse. I mean, seriously, what is he doing with her? I'd give him a night to remember.'

'Is that 'cos you'd give him one of your STIs?'

'You little witch, just you f-'

At that moment, they heard the distinctive crunch, crunch, crunch of the Wing Commander's precise footsteps on the gravel pathway around the corner. Jenny hissed at Kelly and they both stubbed out their cigarettes and scurried back to clearing up the scattered multi-coloured confetti that was still littered all over the church footpath.

Five

Peter

Having just put on all his robes, the vicar steadied himself against the oak table in the church vestry.

The hangover that he thought he had escaped was kicking in now.

'Why did I stay up so late watching television? And, why did I think it would be a clever idea to drink so much?' Peter mumbled to the crucifix on the wall. The one that was judging him and giving him evil looks.

He shakily took out his hip flask and took his fifth swig of whisky that morning.

Groaning, he remembered that there was a christening today, the ugly looking girl that belonged to those two hippies from Trull. *What is the baby's name again? Something modern and idiotic like Summer, or Rain?* He'd have to subtly find out from someone, perhaps Gerald. He seemed to know everything.

At that moment, the church organ started to bellow out, making his head hurt even more. It was like there was a tiny midget in there with a hammer, randomly bashing the brain cells he had left.

He had a nasty suspicion that today was going to be a very long day indeed. This really was an ungodly time to be awake on a Sunday morning.

After a final swig of whisky, he hauled himself to his feet and made for the vestry door, only swaying ever so slightly.

Six

The Two Cleaners.

'Did you actually see it happen?' asked Jenny, annoyed that she had been answering a call of nature at the time.

'Oh. My. Actual. God.' Kelly said, her bright brown eyes open wide. 'I most certainly did. I just wished I could have been quick enough to film it on me phone. I would have got hundreds of likes on Facebook, if not thousands.'

'Alright JJ Abrams, don't get carried away with yourself now, love.'

'But he *actually* dropped the baby into the font. Can you Adam and Eve it?' said Kelly, and she attempted to spark up a cigarette.

Jenny could see her friend's hands trembling with excitement, which meant it took a couple of attempts to light. 'Bugger it. I knew it was going to be a good one after he called the baby *"Autumn"* and *"she."*'

'I know,' cackled Kelly, almost choking with laughter, smoke escaping from her nostrils. '*"Brad"* sounds nothing like *"Autumn"*, so I don't know where Captain Crazy got that from,' she gasped. 'And I don't know what he was more concerned about, the kid going under, or that hip flask of his following the baby in.'

Jenny cursed herself, 'Blast my weak bladder, this is going to be the talk of the town for years to come, if not decades. It'll be like remembering where you were when TD4 split up.'

'And you missed it, you gert big numpty,' said Kelly happily.

'I can't believe it. Here, give us a fag, help cheer us up.'

Kelly offered up her packet of cigarettes, whilst at the same time rummaging around in her pockets for the lighter.

Accepting the packet, Jenny tapped out a cigarette. She studied the foreign writing on the side of the packet. 'Where are these from this week?' she asked, raising one eyebrow quizzically, whilst trying to pronounce the writing on the side, which read, *"fajčenie poškodzuje vaše zdravie".*

'Slovakia this week.' Kelly winked at her, taking back the packet and stuffing them back inside the front of her bright yellow fake designer handbag.

'Andrew get them for you again?'

'Yeah, wink, wink, nudge, nudge, you know how it goes.'

Andrew Farmer was the local undertaker, and in Jenny's opinion, one of the loveliest and funniest people in the town. He always had time for people and had a permanent gentle smile on his face. He was naturally funny, without having to make any effort. He also smuggled cigarettes back from other countries when returning from his regular holidays abroad, which he sold on for only a small profit, making him even more popular.

He had once had his suitcase randomly checked upon his return from Tenerife and the amused customs official had found 5000 Spanish cigarettes crammed inside his suitcase. Jenny had heard that Andrew managed to charm the customs bloke, and convince him that in his capacity as an undertaker, he was researching the effects that smoking had on the lungs. This was so that he could amend his embalming fluid accordingly when the time came for the deceased's final journey. As the local saying went, he would have been able to sell coal to the Welsh.

'Anyway,' Jenny said, 'I thought you was giving up the fags, love?'

Kelly looked at her, 'Yeah, I'm trying to, it's just hard, as I'm putting on weight again. It's my underactive thyroid.'

'Nothing to do with them Jaffa Cakes you're always eating then, my love?'

'Oh, shut your trap, or I'll shove this lit fag somewhere.'

'Easy, my love, easy,' she teased, taking a step back.

Whilst Jenny watched the last few people leave the hall there was a moment of silence between them as they puffed away. Finishing her cigarette, she flicked it behind a nearby hedge after a quick glance over her shoulder to make sure no one was looking.

'Come on then, my lover. Let's go and quickly clean up, then I think we deserve a quick pint at the Shepherd's Rest.'

'You're on, and if that Polish barman is working today, he can give me a quick one,' Kelly said.

Laughing with her and pulling up her sagging tights, Jenny followed her into the church hall, looking forward to the drink she was going to reward herself with later.

Seven

Helen

The Wednesday Night Book Club

As she hummed happily to herself, Helen arranged the chocolate biscuits on the plate. She brushed a few crumbs off the front of her knitted blue cardigan, from where she'd sampled one of the biscuits a few moments ago - for quality control purposes.

The Book Club met every other Wednesday evening, and each member took it in turn to host at their house. She found some of the homes more welcoming than others. Take Patricia's house for example. Patricia didn't believe in turning the central heating on, even when the temperature reached mind-numbing, fingers-falling-off minus figures outside. Instead, all she turned on was a very small one-bar electric heater in the front room, and whilst she was in the kitchen making the refreshments and plating up the broken rich-tea biscuits, fights would break out over who was going to sit the closest to the pitiful heater.

On the other hand, when she went to Chelsea's house, the heating was always on full blast and there was an extensive buffet spread of food available for the guests to nibble on during the evening. And she had napkins from M&S. Cloth ones.

Helen looked around her cosy living room, with its long comfy sofas with soft plumped up pillows and her black cat,

Mr Darcy, snoozing in the armchair nearest the window, which the setting evening sun was still just about warming. Helen enjoyed socialising with other people, but she loved animals more, especially cats. She was certain that her husband felt the same way about his train set as she did about cats. He would while away his time up in the attic, where he had placed floorboards over the beams and set up his impressive vintage Hornby set. The roof joists had been transformed into trees, hills and electricity pylons. Up there he blissfully ignored the world. And the world had pretty much decided to ignore him too.

In her capacity as a part-time school crossing patrol officer and midday supervisor, Helen knew most of the families and their children in the area, and she had been told that her bubbly and friendly nature made her a popular figure in the neighbourhood, although she always blushed and changed the subject whenever anyone made comments like this. She hoped that she was one of those people that no one had a bad word to say about. She had once heard a couple of hormonal teenage boys talking excitedly about the size of her ample cleavage, but she had chosen to ignore that, smiling shyly to herself instead.

The doorbell chimed, announcing the first of the Book Club members, which Helen knew that as sure as cats love cheese and tearing around the house at three in the morning for no good reason, would be Darren Cox. Darren was an out of work - or *"resting"* as he called it - actor. As far as Helen understood, Darren had not been in any big or famous stage productions, or anything major on telly, just bits and pieces of extra work. Someone had once said that he had been in a TV commercial advertising shampoo, but as Darren was as bald as an elephant's bottom, the shampoo must have had acid as one of its active ingredients.

Truth be told, she knew that he was a nice bloke at heart, although he did get some ribbing for still living with his mum at the age of forty-six. But as his mum had seven cats, Helen was not one of those who gently teased him, unlike Leo.

Darren was always early when Helen hosted, and she wasn't quite sure whether that was because he liked to bag the seat next to the biscuits, or if he was trying to steal a few minutes alone with her. If it was the latter, then his chat up lines were rubbish. In fact, they were dismal.

Helen placed the plate of biscuits on the small wooden table in the corner of the room and went to open the door. As she passed her cat, she gave him a gentle stroke and a quick tickle under the chin.

After they had all finally arrived, hellos and polite enquiries about health had been said and asked, the assembled mob of bookworms were all sat in Helen's front room. Helen looked around the group and took their drink requests. Tonight in her room were Harry and Polly, Valerie and Gerald, Patricia, Darren, Andrew, Chelsea and Leo.

After Helen had distributed mugs of tea and coffee, biscuits were dunked and teaspoons fetched to fish out the broken bits of chocolate digestive from the cups, the group were ready.

Every fortnight a new book was suggested and the group then dispersed to read said literature. They would then reconvene to praise, or more often than not in recent months, moan about the choice.

Helen thought back to the early days of the Book Club, when each of the group had taken it in turns to suggest the book. But as some people took criticism of their choice of book to be a personal attack on all their life choices, this was very quickly abolished. Instead, they would seek out suggestions and recommendations from the Internet, and have a vote on which one to choose. A really popular one a few months ago had been *Welcome To Wherever You Are,* which had been about different travellers and hitchhikers, who all stayed in the same hotel and shared their different stories, as well as some of their hidden secrets. There had also been some disastrous choices as well. *Mr Oak's Day Pass* had been particularly boring, about a maths teacher who took his class to a science fair, where nothing illuminating happened in any of the five hundred pages.

The choice this week was *The Winding River,* which according to the blurb on the back of the book had sounded quite exciting, about a journey of discovery, soul searching and adventure. In truth, it was as dull as Ed Miliband talking about politics.

'It was just so disjointed,' Valerie said, ending her five-minute monologue, which Helen thought had possibly had been even more tedious than the book itself.

'Well said, my dear,' said Gerald, probably more as a reflex than in actual agreement with his wife's views.

Most of the group nodded in unison, if only to prevent Valerie from feeling challenged and continuing her pompous spiel.

'Hmm, it defo wasn't the best we've had recently,' agreed Leo, scratching his designer stubble beard.

Valerie winced, 'Leo, it's *definitely,* not *defo.'*

'Sure thing, Mrs M.'

Valerie glared and looked like she was about to open her mouth to reply, when Andrew saved the day by changing the subject.

'Agreed,' he said. 'This certainly isn't going to be winning awards anytime soon is it? Well, I think we've all decided that that's one for the charity shop. Although, I think that's where I got mine from, so I'm not sure they'll want it back,' he mused. 'They were probably glad to be shot of it in the first place. Perhaps I'll have to chuck it in with the next cremation, send it up to its maker.'

This produced some grins around the living room, as well as a disapproving tut, which originated from Valerie's direction.

'Only joking, Valerie. I think this book is headed *down* to the fiery pits, rather than upwards,' he said with a cheeky grin.

'More tea anyone? Earl Grey for you, Valerie?' Helen quickly asked, before Valerie could fire back at Andrew.

There were nods all around the room and she started to collect the mugs.

Without being asked, Darren got up to lend a hand, shyly smiling at Helen when she looked over at him.

Perhaps he does fancy me? she thought, and made a mental note not to shut the door when they went into the kitchen. She could do without any awkward conversations this evening.

She took the mugs through to the kitchen, refilled the blue kettle and clicked it on. Turning around, she saw Darren hovering nearby blocking the doorway back into the living room. She smiled at him and asked, 'Oh, Darren, do me a favour please? Get the new packet of biscuits out of the cupboard, will you? The Hobnobs please. And can you then pop them on the plate for me? Thanks.' She pointed to the cupboard in question.

'More than happy to help. Anything you need, I'm your man, just ask. Anything at all, absolutely anything,' he replied enthusiastically, with an assortment of cat hairs detaching themselves from his clothes and spiralling down towards the kitchen floor. Judging by the colour of them, they must have come from his mother's vast array of cats.

It's not going to happen in a million years, sunshine. But at least he looked at her eyes when he spoke to her, rather than at her chest.

Darren moved away from the doorway and went over to the cupboard, standing on his tiptoes to look over the top of cans of cat food for the biscuits. Helen took this opportunity to escape from the kitchen and into the living room, where the others were still chatting about the latest disaster of a book. Helen leant against the wooden doorframe between the two rooms and mulled things over in her head. She was trying to remember some good books that she had read in the past, so that she could suggest them to the others. She'd enjoyed reading plays at school; not Shakespeare and stuff like that, but modern plays.

Then the idea hit her.

Eight

'Instead of reading other people's stuff, which we all generally hate, why don't we have a go at writing something ourselves?' Helen blurted out to the room before she could stop herself.

The chatter stopped and the room went quiet. Nine pairs of eyes looked over to her and she felt her cheeks flush.

'Well, we'd do better than some of these numpties' attempts. My cat could do a better job than some of the stuff we've read. And I'm sure his imagination is superior.'

There was more silence, and a few of the Book Club members looked from Helen to each other and then to Mr Darcy, who was busy washing his nether regions.

'Well, I think it's a great idea,' called Darren from the kitchen.

'Thanks, Darren,' said Helen.

Polly cleared her throat, 'I agree, I think that would be fun. Don't you think so too, Harry?'

'I do. If we did a crime drama, I could be a police consultant,' said Harry.

Polly just rolled her eyes in response. 'Honestly, you watch one series of *Line of Duty* and you think you're Sherlock Holmes,' Polly said, putting a hand on Harry's knee.

'Yeah, I'd defo be up for that, too. Writing something sounds exciting,' piped up Leo, looking at Helen, his blue eyes glinting with excitement.

Andrew and Chelsea both nodded their agreement to the idea. Everyone else turned to Valerie and Gerald. Gerald raised his eyebrows in a 'For the love of God, please don't ask me' motion. The sets of eyes all moved slightly to the left, to where Valerie was sitting, her legs crossed at the knee and her hands lying delicately in her lap, one hand resting on top of the other.

Helen bit her lip.

There was a dramatic pause that Ant and Dec would have been proud of, before Valerie finally spoke up.

'I don't know why I didn't think of this myself, what a marvellous idea,' came the verdict. There was a nearly audible sigh of relief throughout the room.

'I mean,' Valerie continued, 'English *is* my subject, I was a headmistress for seventeen years.'

Helen saw Polly's eyes roll once again, this time with raised eyebrows as well.

'Excellent, that's settled then,' beamed Helen as Darren gently brushed past her carrying the tray of drinks that she had completely forgotten about. 'Now, what shall we write about? Any ideas?'

Silence once again filled the air, whilst all assembled seemed to ponder the question.

'Hey, I know, how about a singing undertaker?' Andrew said.

'Ooooh, yes,' joined in Leo, tucking a few stray blonde hairs behind an ear. 'We could turn the book into a musical and put it on stage. We could have dance routines! I can do the choreography.'

'I'm not sure you would want to see me dance,' said Chelsea, taking her mug from Darren.

'Hmm,' Valerie started, 'I hardly think that's appropriate for a church book club, do you? We cannot be dancing around the aisles, can we? What on earth would the vicar say?'

'It's a bit wild, but I do like the idea of doing a play though,' Helen said, coming to Leo's defence.

'Yes, that would be fun. I've always fancied giving acting another go since doing a bit at school,' Andrew said.

'We've gone off on a complete tangent, but I think we could be onto something here,' said Harry. There were other supportive murmurings around the room.

'A play would be a splendid idea,' said Valerie. 'How about something traditional, like Shakespeare or Ibson? Or one of Oscar Wilde's many plays? I could be Lady Bracknell.'

'I thought the idea was that we wrote something ourselves?' Polly said.

'Ah, but of course. My mistake,' Valerie pursed her lips.

Silence descended upon the room and whilst the group were taking sips of tea and looking deep in thought, Helen moved from the doorway and sat back down in her seat. Mr Darcy was keeping her chair warm, but when she sat down next to him he stretched, yawned and then jumped down onto the floor and looked about the room, as if wondering who all these people were invading his wooden beamed cottage.

She watched as he prowled around the limited space in the room, winding his way around the different sets of legs that were occupying his territory. He looked like he was plotting which of the legs to launch his attack on, when his attention seemed to be drawn to his stuffed rat that she had picked up from one of the pound shops that occupied the town centre's High Street. She watched as he crouched down, eyes alert. He wiggled his bum a few times, before pouncing on his scarred foe.

An idea started to develop in her head.

She scratched her chin and turned to the others.

'Call me crazy, but how about we write and then put on a pantomime? That would appeal to families in the community, and everyone finds them fun.'

The others glanced her way.

No one spoke for a few moments.

'What a fab idea, sweetie. I can see that really working. As you say, something for all the family and the old biddies too,' Leo nodded subtly towards Valerie.

Helen saw Andrew hide a smirk behind the *Game of Thrones* mug he was holding. Leo was lucky that Valerie didn't see his gesture, otherwise winter would have arrived pretty sharpish.

Valerie cleared her throat before asking, 'What pantomime did you have in mind, Helen?'

'Well, just as a suggestion, how about Dick Whittington and his Cat?'

'I can't remember how that one goes, is that the one with the flying car?' said Andrew, now munching on a biscuit as he sat forward to hear more.

'No, you tit, that's Chitty-Chitty-Bang-Bang, with Dick Van Dyke,' chortled Leo.

'Language, Leo,' came the stern authoritarian voice of Valerie.

'We could always do Matilda instead,' Leo said. 'That's about a wicked headmistress, I wonder who we could get to play that part?'

'Dick Whittington,' said Helen quickly, 'is about a chap who leaves his home town as it's dead boring and goes off to London, where he thinks the streets are paved with gold.'

'He didn't live in Taunton by any chance, did he?'

'No, Andrew, I don't think he did,' Helen grinned at him. 'In fact, I'm not sure where he lived – up North somewhere, possibly? He did have a cat though, which is where I got the idea from, when I saw Mr Darcy attacking his toy rat.'

'I don't think it's a wise idea to have cats on stage, they would be awfully hard to control. One can only imagine the mess they would make, fur and whatnot everywhere,' said Valerie.

'I wasn't meaning to have *actual* cats on stage, Valerie. It was just where I got the idea from.'

'We could get some of the schoolchildren to play the part of the rats?' Andrew said. 'Here, Leo, you're a florist so you must be good with your hands? You could help make the costumes.'

'I am good with my hands, who did you hear that from?' winked Leo.

Andrew grinned and returned the wink. 'Common knowledge, old boy.'

'Less of the *old*, thank you very much.'

'What I meant was, you could help make some of the rat costumes. Ears and tails, that sort of thing.'

'Yep, that shouldn't be a problem,' Leo nodded, and reached for a biscuit. 'I got a C in GCSE textiles.'

'Out of interest, what did you get for PE?'

'Detentions for skiving, mostly.'

'Gentlemen, gentlemen, more focus please. And you are getting ahead of yourselves. We haven't written it yet,' said Valerie.

'Nothing wrong with ambitious thinking, Valerie,' Andrew said with a smile.

'I think it's only right that I oversee the writing,' said Valerie, sitting up menacingly.

'Perhaps I could lend a hand as well,' said Polly, staring Valerie straight in the eyes. 'I mean, I did specialise in English literature as a part of my teaching degree.'

'Hmm, yes,' came the terse reply. 'I suppose two heads are better than one.'

'Indeed, so that's settled then. Anyone else want to join the writing team?' asked Polly.

Helen saw there were lots of shaking heads around the room, the prospect of working with Valerie perhaps a little intimidating.

'So, Valerie, shall we meet up one evening and start planning the synopsis?' said Polly, obviously not sure if she was permitted to take the lead in this conversation with her former boss.

'Yes,' Valerie said. 'I'll telephone you tomorrow evening with some dates, once I have had the opportunity to consult my diary.'

Polly nodded and leant back in her chair.

'There's one more thing we should discuss,' said Harry. 'If we're going to put on this pantomime, we're going to need some space to rehearse in, and a director.'

Patricia, who Helen thought had been unusually quiet this evening, coughed slightly before speaking. 'I'm sure we'll be able use the church hall, so long as we tidy up after ourselves. I'm not sure the domestic budget will stretch to getting the cleaning girls to do it afterwards. And we'll have to supply our own tea and biscuits of course, as we have to ration out the church's supply as it is.'

Helen nodded along and agreed with the others that they would all muck in with the housekeeping.

'Harry,' Leo said, 'I think you'd make an excellent director. I mean, you're used to bossing people about....rather, you're good at organising things, what with being a copper and all.'

Harry uncrossed his legs. 'I'd be delighted to help out.'

'It's settled then, unless anyone has any objections?' queried Leo. He looked around the room.

As there were no protests, the conversation then moved onto the best material for rats' tails, and more importantly, the schedule for buying the chocolate biscuits.

Nine

Harry

Saturday evening at the Berwick's house was either vegetable lasagne with home-made sweet potato chips, if Harry was chef, or tinned spaghetti hoops on toast, if Polly was cooking.

Tonight was Polly's night, and Harry looked over at her fondly from where he stood at the sink. She had many, many outstanding qualities, but cooking was not one of them. Unless you counted mashing up a banana and spreading it on toast as being a culinary masterpiece that was ahead of its time.

Harry did the majority of the cooking for the family, unless he was either on shift or Polly insisted that he have a night off and relax, whilst she attended to the family meal. In reality, when Polly did 'cook', it wasn't a particularly relaxing time for Harry, as he ended up doing the washing up, because Polly used every single pot, pan, dish, spatula and wooden spoon in the house to create 'something' on toast. He would spend more time in the kitchen than he did when it was his turn to cook.

As he stood at the sink, trying to scrape off welded-on burnt tinned spaghetti from the bottom of a saucepan, he continued the conversation he had started with his wife a few minutes ago, whilst she fed Finn who was sitting in his highchair.

'You really think you can work with her then? Without wanting to rip her arm off and hit her with the soggy end?'

'Hmm, well I think so. Although it will take all of my patience and reserve not to. Open wide, Finn, there's a good boy.'

'Just don't expect me to bail you out of jail if you do. The inspector is P-I-S-S-E-D off with me as it is, without having my wife locked up for murder as well. Not sure that would help my chances of promotion really,' said Harry, employing the well-known parenting technique of spelling out certain words in front of children, as Finn sat there and put spaghetti in his ears.

'I did manage to work with her when she was Head. Although, admittedly, our paths didn't cross too much, thankfully. She did give Tina James a really tough time though.'

'Wasn't she the one that was caught in a compromising position with the school's caretaker? Whatever his name was. The one you said had a really bad B.O. problem?'

'Yeah, that's the one. Interesting and alternate use of the school gymnasium's horse bench.'

'How lovely. And these people are responsible for our children's education and upbringing.'

'There are some amazing teachers there as well, yours truly included in that statement.'

'Of course, my darling,' Harry agreed quickly, getting a new scouring brush out from under the sink cupboard. 'When are you going to meet the Ice Queen and start the ball rolling with this project of ours?'

'She's popping over at some point in the next few days.'

'What? You've invited her here? Are you insane?' He stopped chipping away at the burnt-on food and turned to face Polly. 'She'll only B-L-O-O-D-Y comment on

42

everything, and you know how much she wound you up the last time we had the Book Club here.'

'I know, I know. I just couldn't face going to her place by myself. Knowing my luck I'd knock over some expensive lamp from John Lewis and have to sell a kidney to pay for it. It's just safer for all concerned if she comes here,' she said, taking a bite out of Finn's toast.

'If that did happen, we could always sell one of the children on the black market instead? Tyler's being a little S-H-I-T again, so we could trade him?'

'Marvellous idea, get rid of him before he reaches his teens. Goodness only knows what horror that'll turn him into. With any luck, he'll pick up a serious drug habit and get carted off to borstal for all his teenage years and return when he's a normal human being.'

'I wouldn't count on it, darling,' Harry said, unconvinced.

He continued to do the washing up, as Polly made train noises, trying to get Finn to open his mouth and eat some of his mother's carefully prepared culinary masterpiece - most of which was currently spread all around his face, down the front of his top, and over all of the floor that was within a two-foot radius of his chair. A single piece of hooped spaghetti had even made its way as far as the cat's bed in the corner. It had landed on top of the cat, who could only be pretending to sleep; surely wishing to herself that she had gone to rest in the cardboard box that was in the conservatory instead.

'I'm rather excited about being the director actually,' Harry started up again, as he chiselled away at the pan with a dinner knife. 'Perhaps I should give up on policing and trying to pass the sergeant's exam, and go to night school to study performing arts instead?'

Polly looked at him as one might a small child who had just declared that they wanted to be an astronaut when they grew up. 'Let's not get carried away now, darling, we've still got to write the panto, find actors to perform that can walk and talk at the same time, sell a load of tickets and put on a good show first. Maybe, after that, you can think about being a student again, growing your hair and getting something pierced.'

Harry tutted in mock disappointment. 'Ok, ok, you're right. I had better go and cancel that hippy jumper and clapper board that I ordered online, I guess. But seriously, it will be good fun I'm sure.' Giving up on the saucepan and deciding to let it soak overnight – or just buy a new one, he picked up a dirty plate and started to rinse it under the hot tap.

'Time will tell. You never know, Valerie might be the one that ends up in jail for killing someone from the Book Club. She's got psychotic eyes I keep telling you. Anyway,' she said, picking Finn up from his highchair, 'okay if I leave you to finish up in here? I'm going to go and hose Finn down now that he's finished his dinner.'

'Yep,' said Harry, surveying the bombsite of a kitchen, and the mound of dishes next to him. 'No problem, leave it with me, I'll have this sorted out in a jiffy.' *Perhaps it is the right time to run away and join a travelling theatre company? One that is heading far, far away from here.*

Ten

Harry

As the freshly appointed director, it had been decided by Valerie in a phone call to him last night, that Harry should speak to the vicar. He had been instructed to tell Peter about the project and to confirm that he was agreeable for the show to go ahead in the church hall, and that they could also use it for rehearsal space.

Harry was sure that Peter wouldn't have an issue with it in the slightest. But if the vicar wasn't happy about it, then he would not so subtly remind him about the occasion when Peter had reversed into a bright yellow bollard in his car, to be discovered by Harry, smelling of whisky that no amount of Werther's Originals could cover up. Harry had walked Peter home and not made the matter official, so the vicar owed him one.

Humming the tune to a children's programme he couldn't remember the name of, Harry turned the corner into the road with the vicarage at the end of it. It was only early August, but there was already a slight coldness to the air. 'So much for the scorching summer everyone keeps promising,' he said to himself, as he confidently strolled down the road, his arms swinging gently by his sides.

He continued down the small windy road, which didn't have a footpath, small stones being knocked here and there by his size nine black police boots.

Reaching the gated house, he opened the latch and strode down the footpath to the oak front door. It was certainly an impressively large house, although a bit of TLC was needed here and there, and the garden needed some serious weeding.

He reached out and rang the doorbell, which produced a cacophony of musical noises somewhere in the depths of the house. After thirty seconds or so of waiting, Harry rang the doorbell again and checked his watch. It was just after twelve thirty, so the vicar should be awake. He hoped the old bugger hadn't carked it inside, that would involve a barrage of paperwork. He raised his hand to try knocking instead, when the door slowly opened inwards, revealing the vicar wearing some Star Trek pyjama bottoms and rubbing his eyes.

A waft of whisky fumes laced with spices assaulted Harry's nose. If he wasn't mistaken, there were bits of prawn cracker stuck in the vicar's chest hair.

'Peter, err, is everything alright?'

The vicar looked at him blankly, until a sign of recognition spread across his face. 'Yes, yes dear boy. I was just, um...getting changed so that I could do something. Yes… I was going to do some painting here and there.' He started to have a coughing episode, which made him bend over double.

'Why don't we get you a glass of water and have a sit down,' Harry said, stepping inside the hallway. Taking hold of Peter's elbow, he started to steer the vicar in what he hoped was the direction of the kitchen.

'Yes, thank you. If you see my cigs lying about anywhere let me know.'

Piloting him down the corridor, Harry glanced into one of the rooms they were walking past, and spied boxes and boxes of cheap imported cigarettes, alongside a crate of what looked like whisky. 'Will do,' he replied, whilst still heading towards the kitchen.

The state of the kitchen reminded him of a cross between Primark during sale season, and a ransacked house following a burglary by a team of teenagers on speed. There were heaps of unwashed plates, takeaway containers and empty wine and whisky bottles. *Kim and Aggie would just have splashed around a can of petrol, followed by a lit book of matches, before calmly walking away and downing several G&Ts to get over the shock,* he thought. The vicar, however, seemed completely at home and not in the least bit embarrassed about the state of his kitchen. One of the advantages of being eighty-two and not really caring what the world thinks of you anymore, Harry presumed.

Looking around him, Harry asked, 'Vicar, where do you keep your glasses?'

'Don't tell me I've lost the damn things again? I last had them when I was watching some TV earlier this evening.'

'Eh? No, I meant drinking glasses. And I think you mean last night, not earlier.'

'Oh. Buggered if I know. There's a stack of plastic picnic cups somewhere. Try underneath the IKEA bag. No, not that IKEA bag, the red one over there.' he said, waving his hand in the general direction of a collection of Sainsbury's bags.

Harry left the swaying vicar and went to investigate the bags for plastic cups. Finding a stash of them, he took one out, before negotiating his way to the sink and turning on the cold tap. The pipes clanged and then spluttered out brown coloured water for a few seconds, before eventually turning clear. Tentatively filling the plastic cup, Harry took it over and gave it to the vicar, who was leaning against the kitchen table, which was stacked high with pizza boxes and Indian

47

takeaway containers, remnants of the food still stuck to the sides.

After taking a couple of mouthfuls, Peter turned to him. 'Thank you, dear boy. Now, what can I do for you on this fine day?'

'Well, I was wondering if I might ask you a favour? The Book Club have decided to write and put on a play, well, pantomime. We were hoping if we might use the church hall for rehearsals and then put on the play there as well? We should be able to raise a few quid towards something for the church? Maybe some new toys for the Sunday School kids?'

'What's the play going to be about? Will it have sex and bad language in?' Peter asked him, as he wiped his mouth with the back of his hand.

'We're thinking of doing Dick Whittington and his rat, or cat, or whatever it is. Valerie and Polly are writing it, so I can assure you it won't have anything untoward in.'

'That's a shame,' grinned the vicar. 'Oh and if you do raise any cash, it can go towards the OAPs' spring day out next year. Depending on which of them survives the winter of course. I've got a five-quid bet on with the verger that old Susan will croak it before Christmas.'

'Not the Sunday School lot then?' said Harry, trying to change the subject away from profiting from the loss of one of the church's flock.

'Na. Kids get everything nowadays; spend some money on the old wrinklies for a change.'

And the deal was done.

Eleven

Polly

As she hadn't seen the pile of Lego until the last minute, Polly had just fallen down the last three steps of the staircase. She had tried to do a mid-air ballet style move to avoid it, but instead, she had gone down like a Donald Trump speech at a Mexican employment conference.

'Who left this here?' she yelped, whilst hopping up and down on one foot.

'You've just destroyed my mountain base,' said Arlo, his little brown eyes filling with tears, his bottom lip quivering.

'Stairs aren't really the best place for mountain bases. Now pick it all up and take it to your room. It's bedtime anyway, so you should be getting ready for bed, not building evil lairs.'

'But mummy, it's too early for bed,' cried Arlo, lying face down on the floor sobbing.

Just to rub salt into the wound, Tyler said, 'It's only bedtime for you Arlo, as you're a kid. I get to stay up later. I'm older. I'm ten.'

As Polly opened her mouth to tell Tyler not to wind his brother up, Arlo picked up a book and hurled it at Tyler, catching him squarely on the chin - a shot that would have made any marksman proud - producing a small nuclear explosion from Tyler.

'Will you two just pack it in and listen to your mother,' bellowed Harry who had rushed into the room, his Welsh accent reverberating in Polly's ears. 'Now go up to your bedrooms straight away.'

Polly saw Harry pause and after a heartbeat of non-movement from the two boys, he began again. 'One, two...' and she watched both boys achieve warp speed scampering up the stairs to the safety of their rooms. Doors slamming and picture frames rattling on the wall next to her.

'Honestly, I give up with those two,' Harry said, helping her balance by holding her elbow, whilst she continued to wobble about on one foot, whilst massaging the other.

'I know. They need to start acting their ages. Or sending down the mines. Where's Finn?'

'He's busy in the kitchen throwing pasta at his own reflection from the glass in the back door. For a two-year-old, he's not a bad shot.'

'Marvellous. Just marvellous. Valerie is due any minute and I have to convince her that I'm a respectable English teacher, even though we have a pack of wild animals for children.'

'It'll be fine, darling. She was a teacher herself, she knows what young children are like.'

Polly looked at him. 'I'm not so sure. I think they were still using the cane when she used to teach. Can you imagine any child misbehaving in front of her?'

'No. You have a point there, sweetheart.'

Polly jumped slightly and looked at the door as the bell shrilly sounded out its seemingly premature summons.

'Oh, flippity floppity flapjack, she's here already.' She turned and faced Harry. 'You nip out and get her, whilst I quickly tidy up.'

'We can't bring her around the back, she'll only make some sarcastic comment.'

'Do it,' she hissed at him. 'Buy me some time to tidy up this mess!'

'Ok, ok, I'm going.'

As Harry set off grumbling loudly, Polly feverishly tidied up all the toys and action figures that were scattered far and wide in the main living room. She plumped up the cushions and turned the TV over from the Disney channel to something more sombre, pressing random buttons until the channel changed. Dashing into the kitchen, she had just about finished picking up bits of pasta from the kitchen floor when the back door reopened.

Trying to calm her rapid breathing she ran a hand through her hair which she knew would be a mess. 'Ah, good evening, Valerie. How are you? Do come in.'

Valerie looked at her, her eyes burning a hole in Polly's soul. 'Thank you, Polly. Other than being made to use the tradesman's entrance like a common greengrocer, I'm very well, thank you.'

Standing behind Valerie, Harry pulled a face and mimed blowing his brains out with his fingers.

Quickly looking away, she addressed Valerie. 'Oh, yes, sorry about that. Still haven't found the key to the front door yet. It's got to be around here somewhere, I'm sure it will turn up eventually. Can I get you some tea? Harry, take Valerie's coat, will you?'

'Yes please, that will be lovely. Earl Grey, with a thin slice of lemon,' Valerie said, and without looking at Harry she held out her coat for him to take.

Out of the corner of her eye, Polly saw that this time Harry's method of suicide was by hanging.

Twelve

Polly

Hoping that she had cleared up everything, Polly ushered Valerie through the kitchen into the living room. The smell of Marmite and bananas caught Polly's nose, and she prayed she hadn't left an old sandwich lying around. It would be just her luck for Valerie to sit on it.

'Do take a seat, anywhere,' she said, taking a quick glance around, checking there wasn't a festering sandwich lodged somewhere.

'Thank you,' said Valerie, stepping over the body of Superman to get to the armchair by the bookcase.

'Harry will bring your tea through shortly, but in the meantime, shall we have a chat about the panto and bounce some ideas around?' Polly said, as she took a seat on the sofa opposite.

Valerie looked up at her, and without blinking said, 'Polly, can we refer to it as a *play* please? *Panto* sounds so very vulgar and working class.'

'Err...of course. Play it is then.'

'And one does not *bounce ideas around*,' Valerie said, opening her tartan handbag and taking out a plain black notebook, a silver fountain pen and her glasses. 'One must cultivate and nurture the embryos of imagination,' she continued as she looped the glasses' chain over her head.

'Err, yes, of course,' Polly said, wondering if Valerie practiced being irritating or whether it came naturally.

'You keep saying that, I do hope you have a wider vocabulary, otherwise I can see that the input for this play will be very one sided.'

'Hmm, I mean, absolutely, unquestionably and unequivocally,' stumbled Polly.

'Jolly good, then let's begin. So, first, I presume you're familiar with the story of Dick Whittington?'

Polly scratched her head and wished she'd found time to Google it earlier. 'I think I can vaguely remember. He gets fed up at home and then goes off to London to find his riches?'

Valerie sighed. 'It's a little more complex than that, but in essence, yes. Would you care to know the full details of the escapade?'

'Yes. Please enlighten me,' said Polly, hoping that her sarcasm wasn't too apparent.

'Certainly, listen carefully, as I don't like to repeat myself. Now, Richard Whittington was a real-life character, not make believe, as is often the case with other such tales. Richard, or Dick as he is now referred, was an orphan boy, who lived up in the county of Lancashire. So one imagines he had one of those strange Northern accents. But perhaps in our version he can be from Bridgwater, Wellington or North Petherton.'

Valerie looked pointedly at her, and Polly looked back wondering if she was meant to agree. Valerie continued looking at her, until eventually saying, 'Well, are you going to make some notes? I did say I don't like repeating myself.'

'Yes, of course,' Polly said, looking for a pen and her notebook.

'Now, Dick hears that the streets are paved with gold in London. Being a naive boy, he decides to seek out a new life for himself and travels down to London. He's also an uneducated mite, and he underestimates how long it will take him to walk there. He soon finds himself cold, tired and hungry and decides to rest for the night in the gatehouse of a grand manor on the outskirts of London. This house belongs to a wealthy merchant by the name of Fitzgerald. Write that down, Polly.'

Harry, sci-fi addict that he was, had once joked to her that if the Death Star had fired death stares instead of a big laser, then as a comparison, the stare Polly had would put the Death Star firmly into second place on the list of deadliest weapons in the galaxy.

Oblivious that in an alternate universe Polly had just blown her into a million pieces, Valerie continued with her saga. 'Mr Fitzgerald comes out and finds the boy asleep, takes pity on him and gives him a bed and a job working in the kitchen washing dishes. Now, it's whilst working in the kitchen he meets -'

'Cinderella?'

'- the grumpy and bad-tempered cook, whom we'll have to make up a name for. Now, this cook used to spank Dick and blame him for the mess all over the kitchen worktops.'

Polly bit her lip and looked around the room for something to concentrate on.

'Dick's only saving grace was that he adopted a cat on his travels, and this cat would catch all of the rats that were plaguing the house and the kitchen. Until that is, one day the owner of the house sold Dick's Cat to a ship's captain. This put Dick back in the bad books with the cook. She continued to make his life a misery. One day it became so intolerable for Dick, that he decided to run away. He got as far as the next large town, when he heard the London Bells chiming, which seemed to be telling him to: "*Turn again Whittington, Lord Mayor of London.*" So, he promptly went home.

Whilst all of this was going on, the cat was being put to good use on the ship, catching all the rats and vermin that were on board. One evening the ship ran into a fierce storm, was blown off course and ended up having to put to port on an island. This so happened to be where an Island King lived with his subjects. Being a jolly good chap, he bought all the ship's cargo in exchange for gold and then put on a fine spread of food and wine for his seafaring guests. Sadly, this happy event was ruined by the arrival of hundreds of ghastly rats. This is where Dick's cat was once again put to effective use, and resolved the rat problem for the Island King. The King was delighted with this result, and paid a huge amount of gold for the cat.'

Polly started to doodle a picture of a cat attacking Valerie on her notepad.

'The ship set sail and returned back to London, where the captain handed over the gold to Fitzgerald, by way of thanks and gratitude. Fitzgerald, in turn, then presented Dick with the gold, as he was a fair and honest gentleman. Dick then ended up marrying the merchant's daughter, Alice, I believe her name was, and he eventually went on to become the Lord Mayor of London.'

There was a pause, while Polly waited to make sure Valerie had finished.

'Excellent, definitely lots of potential there I feel,' Polly said, hoping she sounded at least half intelligent.

Valerie took her glasses off. 'I agree, Polly. We just need to dramatize it a bit, introduce some other characters and give names to the ones that don't have one yet.'

Polly swallowed hard and said, 'How do we want to do this? Should we divide the story up into scenes or acts, and then write individually, or shall we both write as we go?'

'I feel that the most effective solution would be for us to divide up the story into scenes and write individually. I can then review your work and make any necessary amendments.'

Polly crossed her arms. 'Yes. And I can do the same with the scenes that you write.'

Valerie smiled over at her and said, 'I hardly think that my work will need any additional scrutiny or amendments.'

'And mine will?'

'Well, dear, I was headmistress for a considerable number of years. I only meant that I have vastly more experience than you, and I am keen to share my wisdom with you.'

'You're *too* kind.'

'Not at all,' replied Valerie to her. 'Now, shall we get started and divide these scenes up and decide which of us is going to write what? Oh, and where *is* my tea?'

Polly pondered what it would be like to kill someone with a biro.

Thirteen

Peter

In the vestry, the vicar was sitting down and had just popped some tablets out from a couple of blister packs. Wincing as he looked upwards at the bare bulb of the ceiling light, he necked two paracetamol and two ibuprofen; which he hoped was part prevention, part cure and the whisky he'd knocked it back with was part hair of the dog.

Rubbing his head and closing his eyes, he thought, *Thank goodness that there are no blasted christenings to do today. I certainly couldn't cope with any of them feeling like this. It must have been a bad batch of whisky last night.*

Peter picked up the notes for this morning's sermon, which was one that he'd used before, a couple of months ago, but he hadn't been in a fit state last night to come up with anything new.

I mean, what is the point anyway, it's not like I'm going to be nominated for a Nobel Prize. There was something that I had to mention though, what on earth was it? Something to do with the Sunday School? The planned coach trip to Exeter?

He took a swig from his hip flask and tapped a finger on top of the lid and scrunched up his face trying to remember. *Oh yes, that's it. The panto that the copper and the Book Club lot are doing. Daft sods.*

Standing up cautiously, he straightened out his cassock and checked his watch. *Just enough time for a quick fag out of the window.* With that he had a brief swig of the communion wine, before disobeying his doctor's advice and sparking up, inhaling the smoke deep into his old and tired lungs.

Peter held onto the lectern for support as the congregation took their seats, having just muddled their way through hymn number 617. His sermon had been before the hymn, and if he was honest, he was impressed that anyone was still left awake to sing. Thankfully Patricia's enthusiastic organ playing had reminded everyone that they had to stand up and participate. It hadn't escaped his notice that a few of the older members of his flock had taken the opportunity to slyly check the time on their watches.

Time for a reading, which means I get to sit down by the choir for a few minutes, he thought as he shuffled over and sat down next to them. *If five old-age, tone deaf coffin-dodgers can be categorised as a choir.*

As he repositioned himself on the wooden chair in a bid to get comfortable for a few minutes, he was suddenly aware that a silence had fallen upon the church. A silence that grew from a dramatic pause, to a pregnant one, and then finally to an awkward one.

It's not me again already, is it?

He saw one of the altar boys nudge the other, and point over towards him. The boy eventually got up, vaguely bowed towards the wooden cross at the very front of the church, and then sauntered over towards him.

The young lad bent over and whispered into his ear. 'It's, like, time for the church notices, vicar.'

Sighing and using the arms of the chair to help him, he wearily got back up again and searched about his cassock for the pieces of paper he had stuffed in there earlier.

He walked slowly to the centre of the chancel area and gave what he hoped was an apologetic smile.

'And now for some notices,' he began, replacing his glasses back on the end of his nose. 'Firstly, the flower arranging committee will be meeting on Friday this week, rather than Thursday. If anyone has any bric-a-brac or homemade crafts for next Saturday's coffee morning event, can they please see Greg after today's service.' He squinted at his own handwriting. 'And lastly, a rather exciting notice now. The Wednesday night Book Club have decided to take matters into their own hands, and to write and then put on a panto. This is to be held in the church hall at the beginning of next year.'

Hearing a loud tut, he looked in the direction that it had come from and he saw Valerie, looking like she'd just had a nose full of wet dog smell.

Ignoring her but wondering what he'd said wrong, he continued. 'The Club is in the process of writing a modern-day version of the panto Dick Whittington and his Cat, and will be looking for budding actors and actresses who wish to audition. There will also be people needed behind the scenes to help build sets and props. If anyone is interested in helping out, either on stage or backstage, then please see Harry, Polly or Valerie afterwards. And I think there's a poster somewhere at the back with more information on as well.'

He cleared his throat. 'Now, let us sing hymn number forty-five, *Lord of the Dance*, which is quite appropriate, don't you think?'

As the congregation rose to its feet, one of the older members of the congregation turned to her friend Jane and asked, 'What did he say?'

Jane turned to her, looking slightly bewildered and said, 'The Book Club are putting on a porno and they want to know if anyone's interested in taking part.'

Her spluttering was drowned out by the thunderous sound of organ music.

Fourteen

The Two Cleaners

Jenny rubbed the sleep from her eyes as she slowly made her way down the stairs towards the ground floor of her house, holding onto the bannister rail for support as she plodded down the carpeted steps. Pushing the door at the bottom of the stairs, it swung open slowly, and she wondered if it too needed a strong coffee before facing the rest of the day, and lumbering into life as a fully functioning door.

She walked over to the window and took a peek behind the curtain at the weather outside. Grey as normal, but she shielded her eyes as even the dull light was too bright for her eyes this morning.

Letting go of the curtain quickly, she berated at herself for going to the pub last night with Kelly. *Why on earth was I drinking some cloudy cider shit? What was the name of it?* *"Just go out for one drink", Kelly says, so why did I end up having five pints, followed by shots of Sambuca, rounded off with a couple of Jagerbombs. Which I can still taste.* She shuddered as she padded towards the kitchen, cursing the day that she had ever worked at the supermarket which had meant meeting Kelly, who had also worked there at the time.

Opening the cupboard nearest the kitchen door, she picked up the packet of half used painkillers. Popping two into the palm of her hand and then into her mouth, she picked up a clean glass from the draining board, filled it with water, letting the tap run for a few seconds to give the water a chance to go cold. She swallowed the tablets, screwing up her face at the chalky taste left behind on her tongue.

A vague recollection of trying to impress the Polish barman by counting to ten in Polish entered her head. Which was puzzling to her, as she didn't know any foreign words other than "bonjour" and "un oeuf".

Shaking her head, she filled the kettle with water and then flicked it on. Whilst it started to grumble into life, she opened the bread bag. After checking there was no evidence of any blue mould, she popped a couple of pieces into the toaster and pushed the button down. Groaning to herself, she went to another cupboard and fished out the jar of raspberry jam from the top shelf, grabbed a side plate and a teabag and stepped back towards the kitchen worktop.

She gazed out of the window while she waited and looked up at the sky, wondered if it was going to rain, which would mean taking her unflattering green-spotted umbrella to the pub later. She put the teabag into her favourite mug and the toast popped up and the smell of food quickly reached her nose, causing her mouth to water slightly. She hungrily spread margarine followed by the jam onto the toast and took a big bite. Chewing, she filled her mug with hot water from the kettle and added a big dollop of milk.

Retrieving her battered phone from her 'Little Miss Chatterbox' dressing gown pocket, she entered her pin number and pressed the Facebook app. Scrolling down the news feed, she snorted as she scanned her way through the recent posts.

Soon bored by the usual pictures of either food or cats, and messages from mothers asking when the summer holidays would be over, so they could rid themselves of their little monsters, she pondered what to do with her day. *Some more online shopping perhaps? I do need a new top. Or maybe waste an hour or two on Tinder checking out the talent of Taunton?*

Looking at a cat related post that her friend Roscoe had tagged her in, suddenly her phone started vibrating and she wasn't surprised to see Kelly's face fill the screen. Swiping the green icon, she answered.

'Morning, my lover.'

'Oh hello, you picked up then, you living proof that evolution can get it wrong.'

'Hey! That's not very nice. And looking at you, I can see why some animals eat their young.'

'Well, it's thanks to you that I'm currently hungover to hell.'

'Oh yeah, forcing the drinks down your neck, was I?'

'At one point, yeah, you were. God knows why I never learn my lesson and don't touch Sambuca. You've got a lot to answer for, Jenny bloody Webster.'

She grinned. 'Oh dear, my lover, sounds like you're getting old. Shall I pop you up to the nursing home?'

'Shut your face. God, I think I'm actually dying,' came the reply from the phone.

Jenny tutted. 'Oh, shut your noise and die quietly will you, some of us are trying to enjoy our breakfast you know. Hang on, just going to put you on speakerphone, love,' she jabbed at her phone with a sticky finger, leaving a fine smear of raspberry jam across the screen. Wiping her fingers on her dressing gown, she took a large gulp of tea.

'Anyways,' she continued, waving a piece of toast around like it was her forte on *Britain's Got Talent*. 'Why are you calling me up at this time of the morning?'

Jenny's kitchen was filled with the sound of Kelly having a coughing fit down the phone. Waiting for the noise to die down she took another big slug of her milky tea.

'Sodding fags,' came the eventual curse down the phone.

Jenny rolled her eyes. 'As much fun as this is, my lover, did you actually call for a reason, or just to put me off me breakfast?' She considered putting some more bread in the toaster.

'You couldn't run me into town, could you? I need to get a birthday present for my sister's little one. She turns one next week, so I needs to get a card and a present of some description. And I could also do with seeing if they sell new lungs in Boots, as don't think these ones are going to last much longer.'

Jenny had been half expecting this request. 'What am I, your personal taxi service, or what?'

'Go on, please, I'm dying on my arse here, don't make me catch the bus.'

Can I be bothered to get dressed? 'Hmm.'

'I'll buy you a jam doughnut and we can go and ogle at Ben in the bank if you like?'

Perhaps I can after all. 'Sold. I'll go and put my face on and pick you up in an hour.'

'Takes you that long to get ready, does it?'

'Do you want this lift or not? You cheeky mare.'

'Alright, calm yourself. Don't go bursting a blood vessel. See you in an hour then, if I'm still alive.'

'Later, love.'

She hung up the phone and stared at the toaster, again contemplating having some more toast and jam. *No, I better not. If I'm off to see hunky Ben, I need to watch my figure.* With that thought, she drained the last of her tea and headed back towards the stairs and her bedroom, trying to decide what outfit to wear and if it was still warm enough for a short skirt.

Fifteen

Polly

A swarm of blood-thirsty native American Indians were busy racing around the whole of number twelve Holdaway Close, surrounding the injured and dying cowboy, who had run out of ammunition – like in one of the dull Western films that Harry insisted on watching when he did the ironing. Or at least that's how Polly felt; but rather than ammunition, she was just about out of patience with her boisterous children. She had been trying to write these new scenes for at least an hour and a half now, but she just wasn't getting any peace to do it. As soon as she'd placated one of her children, another would be grief stricken about not being able to find their latest Disney Blu-ray.

As the children's volume increased to an ear shattering crescendo, Polly's tolerance decreased in equal measure, and she longed for the dreary August weather to warm up again, so she could chuck the children outside to play in the garden. Or the little stream that ran alongside the side of the house. Or with some of the neighbour's kids - so long as they were away from her so she could get five minutes to herself, she really didn't care.

Looking down at her laptop once again, she desperately thought of something to type, but her brain just wasn't working and felt like it was full of vast empty space.

Hearing the back-door open and then shut again, she felt an enormous surge of relief flood through her veins. *The cavalry has finally arrived to help.*

'Hello, anyone home?' Came Harry's voice, which to her sounded far too cheery.

'Yeah, daddy's home, yeah, yeah,' screamed the Indians running past Polly. She was glad that they were launching a pre-emptive strike on the cavalry, it would mean they weren't bothering her for a short while.

Whilst she heard Harry chatting with the kids for a few moments, asking them about their days at summer school and nursery - getting the standard "dunno" replies - Polly stared at the ceiling. She was looking for inspiration, motivation, and ideally, several pre-written scripts taped up there in amongst the cobwebs.

She could feel her stress levels rising again, as the kids started howling and running about, charging through the front room once more, and crashing up the stairs. She watched little Finn wobbling a few steps behind his older brothers.

Polly looked over as Harry stuck his head into the room and smiled at her.

'Hello, darling, everything alright?' he asked.

She looked up at him and could feel the pressure building up inside her head. 'No, I'm about to have a nervous sodding breakdown!'

'Oh dear. What's up?' he said, walking towards her.

'What's up? *Your* children not giving me five seconds of peace so far this evening is *what's up*. And I've got to write these two scenes before I next meet the Ice Queen.'

'Ah, I see. Being their normal selves, are they? And I see they've become just my children once again.'

'I think they're actually worse than normal, if that were possible. It's as if they have some sort of sixth sense, and know that I need to get this finished, so they decide to test my endurance. And they're doing a *really* good job of it too, I can tell you.'

'Shall I call the children's home and see if they have any spaces? We could drop them off this evening, and then pick up chips on the way home. Oh, I can convert one of their bedrooms into my man cave.'

She glared at him, fighting the urge to find something heavy to throw. 'It's not a joke, Harry. I'm at my wit's end here.'

'Okay, I'm sorry, why don't you go into our bedroom and hide away up there for a bit? I'll keep the monsters down here until it's bedtime for them.'

'That would be perfect, thank you.' she sighed and saved the blank Word document on the laptop.

'No worries. Boys? Boys, can you come down here please?' Harry called up the stairs.

Above them there was an almighty crash, which sounded to Polly like an elephant had jumped from a diving board into a swimming pool devoid of water, causing the ceiling lamp in the front room to sway gently from side to side.

'Honestly,' Harry said to her. 'One of these days they're going to come through the ceiling. Then we'll have to go and live with your parents. And when that day happens, just to warn you, I'll be leaving you.'

Polly shot a glare at him, she wasn't in the mood for his abstract sense of humour this evening.

The children raced down the stairs, each of them jumping the last few steps onto the floor. Finn fell flat on his face, causing a torrent of tears and high pitched crying that could have woken the dead, if they hadn't already moved years ago, due to the noise pollution.

As Harry went over, picked Finn up and comforted him, Polly decided that enough was enough.

'Right, that's it,' she said, picking up her laptop, notepad and pen. 'I'm going where I can get some peace and quiet.'

'Siberia?'

'Nope. I'm going outside and I may be some time!'

'In this weather? Are you crazy?'

'Getting there, believe me, I'm getting there,' said she to him, with what she hoped was the ferocity of a poisonous snake who's just been stood on by a plump lady wearing high heels.

With that, she marched out of the front room, through the bombsite of a kitchen, and out of the back door, into the darkness of the night.

Sixteen

Harry

He had to bribe the kids with promises of smiley faced potato waffles, Quorn sausages and beans to get them to sit at the table and eat something. But eventually he managed to get all three boys fed and watered, and after the normal battles, tears and arguments, finally to bed.

Once he was back downstairs in the kitchen, he popped the top off a bottle of real ale and took a mouthful from it. Leaning back against the kitchen worktop, he let out a deep sigh and looked around at the half-eaten food and spilled drinks on the table top.

As he was looking around, it was only at that point that he noticed Polly's car keys were still hanging up on one of the hooks by the back door. He had assumed that she had piled the car up with her laptop and books and headed off to some quiet café that was still open at this hour.

Strange, he thought. *She can't have walked very far with all of her stuff.* He took another long swig from the bottle, before placing it down on the worktop and headed towards the dining room next door, flicking the redundant beer bottle top into the bin as he walked by.

The lights were off in the dining room, as it wasn't a room that the family used that often, apart from at Christmas time or when the kid's grandparents came over to judge Polly and Harry on their parenting skills. Out of habit, Harry didn't turn the lights on, and went over to the French windows that looked out onto the long garden. Scouring the garden - which was punctuated with a swing, footballs, water pistols and a sandpit - Harry noticed that coming from the playhouse at the bottom of the garden was a soft glow from one of the plastic windows.

So that's where you're hiding.

He returned to the kitchen and reached first for the vodka bottle and then for the tomato juice from the fridge. After pouring a healthy amount of vodka into a tumbler, he then filled the glass up with the juice, before setting off out the door and into the garden.

As he drew closer to the playhouse, the face of his wife became clearer, as the reflection from her laptop illuminated her like a ghostly entity, comprising of just a floating head with a fixed scowl on her face.

Reaching the hobbit-sized door, he crouched down and knocked against it with the bottom of his ale bottle. The top of the stable-style door opened, and revealed Polly hunched over her laptop taking up most of the space inside the pretend house. She had found a disused ceramic flowerpot from somewhere in the garden, and had turned it upside down and fashioned a makeshift stool from it, the laptop balanced on her knees.

'Thought you might need one of these,' he said, passing her the glass. 'It's a Welsh Bloody Mary, which is a Bloody Mary with no Worcestershire sauce or celery stick, because we've run out. And it's Welsh, because I made it.'

Despite having heard this line used on her before, on more than one occasion over the years, Polly accepted the drink with a smile, and took a sip.

'Not bad, boyo, not bad. If you ever jack in the police work, you should go into bartending.'

He pulled a face. 'And miss all the fun of ordering people around? You must be joking. Anyway, how's it going, Miss Potter?' he asked her, taking a swig of his own drink.

'Yeah, alright actually. I've got most of it done now, just having a read through and making some tweaks.'

'Why don't you come inside? The coast is clear, all the little trolls are tucked up in their caves for the night. Besides, it's nippy out here now, you'll catch a cold. I thought it was meant to be summer time?'

'Give me a few minutes more, I'm on a flow and I don't want to interrupt the thought process,' Polly said to him, taking another sip of her drink and then another straight after.

'Ok, well don't stay out here too long, it really is getting chilly.'

'Won't be long. My laptop battery is at twenty percent anyway, so I'll be there in a sec.'

'I'll leave you to it then, see you in a bit,' and with that he retreated towards the house and the warmth, careful to not trip over the sandpit that had lost its sand last summer after the boys had built a beach down by the stream.

Seventeen

Harry

The Church Hall

A key rattled loudly in the lock and the door was given a hard shove before swinging inwards, and Harry stumbled into the room.

'It's like Fort Knox this place,' he said to the empty room as he sucked on the knuckle he had just bashed opening the door.

Finding the row of light switches, he flicked them on, and most of the fluorescent strip lights that ran up and down the cold church hall flickered into life. Some were not as prompt as others, taking a little longer to come out of hibernation and spring to life. There were a couple, that sadly, had lost the fight and remained unlit, just waiting there in situ for someone to replace them and take them off to the big lighting shop in the sky; or the recycling centre - whichever was closer.

He looked about the church hall, hands on his hips. The room was a substantial space - the vicar had told him that it had been built as an add-on when the church had been rebuilt ten or so years ago and doubled up as a community centre, due to its capacity.

'Decent size,' he said to the cobwebs.

He estimated it was a good fifteen metres wide and about double that in length, giving a generous amount of space to entertain the variety of different uses it was put to. He knew this included yoga on Mondays, Morris dancing practice on Tuesdays, flowering arranging club on Thursdays and the Cubs and Girl Guides on Friday evenings.

Once upon a time, the Book Club had met here on Wednesday evenings, but as most of the members needed thawing out after being sat sedentary in the hall for a few hours, it was decided that they should meet in the warmth and comfort of the club members' homes instead.

On the left side of the hall, just down from the entrance door were the male and female toilets, pegs for hanging coats and jackets, as well as a store room for tables and chairs. To the right of the entrance, at the far end was the kitchen, which was separated from the hall by a door at the side, and a metal shutter at the front, which when opened produced a good-sized serving hatch.

After a quick cursory glance around, he strode off towards the boxed off kitchen area at the end of the hall. Producing another key from the deep recesses of his pocket, he gained access to the kitchen. Shivering, he turned the heating on and dialled the thermostat up to twenty-four degrees, to try and get the place warmed up before the others arrived.

He ran through his checklist, using the switches located in the kitchen to turn on the lights in the toilets and the storage area at the other end, before activating the wall mounted hot water system ready for the teas and coffees.

He noticed that the Morris dancers from last night hadn't cleaned up the kitchen properly when they had left, and made a mental note to give it a quick clean before he locked up – he didn't want Patricia blaming *him* for the mess.

Turning, he heard the outside door open, and then close a few seconds later.

'Hellooo? Is there anybody there?' came Polly's distinctive voice, which echoed around the hall.

To Harry, it sounded as if his wife was trying to summon a ghost from the spirit world, like in those shows where the medium gets taken over by the spirit of great aunty Yvonne, who wants to tell you how long to cook Brussel sprouts for at Christmas.

He stuck his head around the corner of the kitchen door to reply.

'Hi, darling. Babysitter eventually turned up then?'

'Yep. I did consider hiring a lion tamer, but when I called around, they're all at a health and safety conference in Prague.'

'Just as well, next door would only complain about the noise.'

'Need a hand?'

'Please. Do you want to get a couple of chairs from out of the back room?'

'Okey-dokey.'

'Ta. I'll get the tables out in a second. Just making sure the heating is working.'

'Not warm in here, is it,' she said, heading for the store room.

The outside door creaked open for a third time, and Harry watched as Valerie paraded into the hall, followed by Gerald and Patricia. Valerie stood there for a moment, looking around, a bit like Darth Vader when he boards a captured rebel ship. In fact, he wouldn't be surprising if Valerie could do the death grip thing as well.

'Ah, Harry, Polly, good evening. Apologies for our slight delay,' Valerie said, with a sideways glance of disapproval at Gerald, who straightened his tie.

'Certainly not a problem, Valerie. We only got here a few moments before, and we're running ahead of schedule anyway,' Harry said. 'It's only just a few minutes after seven, so we have just under half an hour before they start turning up.'

'That's if anyone does turn up,' Polly said, as she placed a couple of chairs in the middle of the room.

'Of course they will, positive thinking, that's what we need,' said Valerie.

'I know, I was only joking.'

'Umm, right, shall I go and get some tea sorted out for us all?' said Gerald, rubbing his hands together and smiling at everyone.

'Thank you, Gerald, that would be lovely,' said Polly.

'Yes, cheers, Gerald,' Harry agreed.

The plan for this evening was that the five of them would sit behind the table, and the performers would act out a monologue of their own choice. Then they would be asked to sing a song, for which Patricia would accompany them on her keyboard.

As well as the notice in the church foyer, Harry had also placed a small advert in the local community newsletter. This reached a good proportion of the population within a reasonable distance from the church, so he was hopeful that they would get a good array of talent. Or at the very least, not just having the WI turn up with their gossip about the soaps and what the Kardashians were up to.

While Gerald was off busying himself making tea in the kitchen, Patricia headed back out to her car. She returned with her piano keyboard, which she set up next to the table that Harry had just put down. After fiddling about with wires and switches, she started to run through a couple of scales to get herself warmed up.

Harry unpacked a small box he had brought with him, putting out paper and pens for any notetaking.

Seeing that Patricia was watching him, he said, 'I was going to pinch some clipboards from the police station earlier, but since the community sergeant's crime prevention stickers went walkabouts, the stationery cupboard has been kept locked at all times. You can't trust anyone these days.'

The kitchen door half opened, and then closed again. It then reopened, with Gerald carrying a tray of steaming mugs and a packet of Jaffa Cakes held between his teeth.

'Teees uwp,' came the noise from his mouth.

Immediately Valerie spoke up, 'Gerald. What have I told you about speaking with your mouth full? Honestly man.'

'Sowwy dwaer,' he said, followed by a sheepish look, as he set the tray down on the table and removed the packet from his mouth. 'I couldn't remember who has sugar, so I just brought the pot out for you to help yourselves.'

There was a chorus of '*thank-yous*' from Harry and Polly, and Patricia gave him a quick nod and stopped playing the keyboard. Harry smiled as he saw Gerald give Valerie a chipped 'kiss me quick!' mug, and watched as Valerie just turned her nose up at the proffered mug of tea and pulled out her flowery notebook and silver fountain pen.

'Do we know how many we have coming this evening?' Valerie asked, unscrewing the top of her pen menacingly, as if she were preparing to go into battle.

'I had a couple of people come up to me after the service the other day, including Ben, who seemed keen,' Harry said. 'Oh, and Darren from the Book Club said that he wanted to be on the stage, as opposed to working behind it doing scenery or whatever.'

'We also had a few phone calls following on from that advert you put in the newsletter, didn't we, Harry?' Polly said as she sipped at her tea.

'Yep, one bloke called and wanted to know if there were going to be any nude scenes, as apparently, he's a life model at one of the colleges and was offering his services as a body double.'

'Good heavens above,' said Valerie. 'What on earth did you tell him? I do hope he's not going to turn up this evening and take off his clothes in front of me?'

'No Valerie,' Harry said, trying to hide a smile but failing. 'I told him what we were doing and that it was unlikely we would have any nude scenes. Unless you decide to write one in?'

'I most certainly will not be doing anything of the kind,' she shuddered, pulling her knitted woollen scarf a bit tighter around her neck.

'Jolly good, couldn't have any of that, what would the vicar say to you if you did?' said Harry.

Gerald looked dramatically at his watch, perhaps wanting to divert the conversation onto another topic. 'Look at the time, we'd better get ready before the hordes show up.'

'Yes, great idea, Gerald,' Polly said.

Patricia muttered her agreement and took her place behind the large table. Each of them holding, apart from Valerie, piping hot mugs of tea in both hands to get the circulation going. Gerald passed the Jaffa cakes around and winked at Polly when she took two.

At seven thirty-six there was a polite knock at the door, and the auditions for Dick Whittington began.

Eighteen

Gerald

Classical music once again filled the entire house. Gerald was hiding up in the spare room that he had commandeered for his own use, feeling every stroke of the screechy violins, or cellos, or whatever the hell it was that was causing that infernal racket downstairs.

In his head, he referred to the spare bedroom as the 'library'. As a collector of old, but not necessarily valuable books, he had managed to fill the five floor to ceiling bookcases that were in there. He had often tried joking with Valerie, that if there were ever a fire in the house, it would be seen for miles and miles; indeed, if not from the International Space Station. The one the public didn't know about. The secret one.

An old colleague had tried to persuade him to get one of those Kindle devices, but he just didn't like the idea of that. It wasn't him being old fashioned, he just liked the smell of books and loved turning the pages and marking his progress with a makeshift bookmark; it was all part of the love and the fun of reading and relaxing. Plus, his old team had bugged loads of Kindles belonging to suspected enemy agents, so he just didn't trust them.

He was currently reading a book called *The One* by John Marrs, and he was really enjoying it so far. He was already halfway through, having only started it the day before. Well, he was trying to read it anyway, but he couldn't concentrate with the last night of the Proms taking place in his living room.

He considered going down and passive aggressively ripping out the appropriate fuse from the fuse box and smashing it into a thousand pieces using the M&S vase that was in the hallway. *Perhaps some Dutch courage will help?* he thought.

As a history buff, he knew that in the First World War, before deserters were shot, they would be encouraged to drink an entire bottle of whisky first. Gerald considered following the same approach, but knowing his luck he would drunkenly fall down the stairs and break his neck before being able to speak to his wife and then being marched up to face the firing squad.

He carefully placed an old envelope he was using as a bookmark into the novel, before delicately placing it down on the side table that was next to his red leather arm chair. He stood up and considered putting his tie back on before going down. Deciding against it, he made his way downstairs, the music getting louder. He took a deep breath before opening the living room door onto no-man's land.

Valerie was sat hunched over the dining room table, her reading glasses resting on the end of her nose, and holding her silver fountain pen in her hand, which was hovering over a big pile of printed paper. Hearing the door open, she glanced up at him and took off her glasses.

'Unbelievable,' she said.

He cleared his throat. 'Everything all right, my dear?'

'No, Gerald. Everything is not all right, as you so delicately put it.'

'What is it, my dear?'

'I've never seen anything like it.'

'Would you be able to enlighten me, darling?' *As my powers of telepathy are obviously failing me today.*

'She's supposed to be a teacher. Didn't she say that her specialism is in English? I'm just reading through what she's been writing for some of her allocated scenes for Dick Whittington, and I think she's been enlisting the help of some of her year fives to do it instead.'

'Oh dear.'

'Yes, Gerald, very much "oh dear".'

'Do you think that perhaps she's just writing in a modernist style?'

'Dick Whittington is a timeless tale, Gerald, you can't just suddenly force it into the modern day.'

'Of course, you're right.'

'I should think so, I was headmistress for seventeen years, *in case you've forgotten*, so I do have some level of knowledge of the English language,' she snapped.

How could I ever, ever forget? You remind me every five minutes. 'Sorry dear, what was that? I can't quite hear you over the music, can you say that again, please?'

'Well turn it off then.'

He went over and turned the volume right down.

'I said, I was headmistress, so I think that outweighs a mere year five class teacher, don't you?'

With her last comment, Gerald was half expecting a plume of fire to extend from his wife's nostrils, like a mythical dragon. He certainly was no Saint George.

'Yes, my dear. I can see you're busy, so I will leave you to it, as I don't want to disturb you any further. Just let me know when you would like some dinner and I'll put the oven on. I thought lamb for this evening?'

Valerie looked at him as if he'd just suggested robbing the grave of the last Archbishop of Canterbury.

'I honestly worry about you sometimes. I think you're on a different planet to the rest of us. *This* must be my priority this evening, Gerald.'

'Of course, my dear, my apologies,' he said, walking slowly backwards.

Valerie sent him one final scowl of disapproval, before replacing her glasses onto the end of her nose and turned back to face the pile of papers once again. She immediately tutted and scribbling down a note on her lined pad.

Reaching the door, Gerald quietly opened it, glided through with the stealth of a fox sneaking into a chicken shed, before gently closing it once again.

He stopped outside the door and paused, listening to the blissful peace and quiet. With a smug grin, he ascended the stairs back to his library. He decided that he deserved a reward of whisky. With any luck she would be occupied all evening, so a four-fingered measure would be a suitable recompense for his outstanding bravery and cunning in the face of the enemy.

Reaching his sanctuary, he poured himself the promised amount of smoky amber coloured liquid from his crystal cut glass decanter that had been a retirement gift to him from the head of Section D.

He retook his place in his favourite chair and once again picked up his book, and opened it where he had left off and was transported away. Far, far away; one of the characters was currently in Australia, which would do him quite nicely.

Nineteen

Ben

Ben entered his six-digit security code into the heavy steel door that separated the bank that he worked at from the rest of the outside world. He considered himself a reasonably confident guy, but he always got a little nervous entering this number into the doors at the bank. You were only allowed to enter the number incorrectly a set number of times, before alarms went off, followed eventually by armed police, dogs, helicopters and Batman. Or in truth, his grumpy, target obsessed bully of a boss, Stacey. Stacey, who had stupid corny business phrases like "a starter for ten", "we are where we are" and "pick the low hanging fruit". She also had this annoying habit of saying "interesting" when asked a question, instead of giving a helpful response or any useful advice.

He, along with most of the other general banking staff, couldn't stand her and some clever sod had christened her with the nickname "The Wicked Witch of the West Country". Despite many of her own team loathing her, for some unknown reason, the area manager for the Somerset region absolutely loved her and thought she was the best thing since washable paper money.

He walked through the foyer area of the bank, heading for the main entrance as he was off on his lunchbreak to grab a sandwich, and have a quick fag before his afternoon appointments.

He spotted the two loony church cleaners by the information stand. They were intently studying a leaflet on something or other.

Pretending not to notice them, he pulled out his mobile phone and looked through the messages and started to type out a mock message. He did have five texts from his girlfriend, Jessica, but he wouldn't reply just yet. She would only reply straight away and want to have a text chat, which he didn't have the time or the energy for now. He also had several messages from that scary Scottish nutcase about the late payment of the unofficial loan that he'd taken out, which he also decided to ignore for the time being.

Having reached the safety of the outside, he removed his name badge, and started digging around in his jacket pocket – remembering too late that he'd given up smoking in an attempt to save money; and keep Jessica from moaning on about having to kiss an ashtray. 'What is it about control freaks wanting to be in my life?' he muttered, still checking his pockets, but this time looking for some chewing gum instead, and not finding any, which didn't improve his mood.

Well that's just great, no cigs and no gum either, he thought, as he turned and started walking up to the takeaway sandwich shop, Ed's Edibles, that he liked going to. They were cheap, and you got a proper doorstep sandwich, not one of those crappy thin sarnies like from some other places. The ones that used the cheap cardboard tasting bread from one of those supermarkets that scan your shopping at one hundred miles an hour, effectively chucking it at you and then shouting for immediate payment.

As he walked up the High Street, he noticed that there were council workmen putting up the Christmas lights already, even though it wasn't even the end of August yet. *Good old commercialism in action*, he scoffed. But goodness only knows how he was going to be able to afford Christmas this year, what with being up to his eyeballs in debt, thanks to his little gambling issue. Jessica had been not so subtly hinting at getting engaged; well she could forget that, unless she was happy with getting a ring from an Asda Smart Price Christmas cracker.

Reaching the shop and after waiting for a few minutes to be served, he ordered his favourite; a cheese and coleslaw sandwich on white bread, with salt and pepper, and a packet of cheese and onion crisps. Proper gert lush.

He would normally wait until he got back to the bank's staff room before tucking into his lunch, but today he was ravenous. He unwrapped his sandwich as he walked back and took a hungry bite into the soft white breaded goodness. If he ever found himself in America and on death row, this is what he would have as his last meal. Sod having steak and all the usual requests, this would be way better.

He was so caught up with his food, that he didn't see the lady walk out of the door just in front of him until too late, bumping into her shoulder and jolting him back to the real world.

'Woh God, I'm sowwy,' he apologised, his mouth still full of cheese and coleslaw.

'That's fine, no harm done,' came the reply from the lady. She turned to face him and then grinned at him. 'Benjamin, you clumsy oaf, I might have known it would have been you.'

Now also grinning, Ben swallowed his mouthful and replied. 'Hello, Chelsea. Sorry about that, I was miles away. You okay?'

'I'm good thanks, oh, and you've got some, uhh, something just there,' she said, pointing at his chin.

Slightly embarrassed and wiping his hand across his mouth he said, 'Better now?'

'Much. So how are you then? Apart from nearly killing women in the street.'

'Yeah, I'm good, just having a quick lunchbreak, before heading back,' he said, checking his watch and pleased to see that he still had a bit of time left yet. 'You?'

'Yes, fine thanks, just going off on lunch myself, later than usual, as the pharmacy is inundated with people that have got this late summer bug thing that's going around, so it's been manic all day. Thankfully it's quietened down for a few minutes, so I can nip over to M&S and grab something,' she said.

'Yeah, I've had customers coughing and sneezing all over me this morning at the bank. I expect I'll be coming down with it next.'

'Aww, well you know which pharmacy to come to if you do get ill,' she said.

'I certainly will. That reminds me of something I was going to ask you actually.'

'Oh yes?'

'Yeah. But it's a bit, umm, err, sensitive,' he said, looking around him.

'Man's problems? We have some very good desensitising gels that can help you with that.'

'What? Err, no, no, nothing like that. That's all fine, no problems there.' He looked at her again and saw that she was smiling. *Oh, that smile.*

'I'm teasing you, you wally. Now, what's up?'

'Well, you know that you, like, work in a pharmacy.'

'Yes Ben, I'm aware of where I work, you oaf. Come on, what is it?'

'Well, I was thinking of starting my own business, as a side line type thing, to try and earn a few quid, for, you know, Christmas.'

'Sounds like a worthwhile idea, go on.'

'I was, err, thinking of selling, umm, certain pharmaceutical enhancers for men on the Internet, and I was wondering if you, being a pharmacist, would know where I could get a batch from?'

'Oh sure, if you pop round the back at six, I'll let you have a few boxes from our store room.'

'Really? Excellent.' *That was easy.*

'No, you doughnut, of course not really. After eight intensive years of studying and exams, I'm a licensed pharmacist, not some drug dealer. Do you think I'd be willing to throw all that away?' she said, gently swatting his shoulder.

'No, ummm, I suppose not. Stupid idea, pretend I didn't ask you.' *Ben, you idiot.*

'Look, selling something to make a few quid for Christmas is a great idea, why don't you consider T-shirts, or socks, or something sensible. Something that won't land you, or me, in prison; as I don't think the food's any good there, and we're both too pretty for jail,' she winked at him.

'Yeah, you're right. God knows what I was thinking. Perhaps I am ill after all, eh?'

'I think so.'

Ben decided that a quick change of direction was needed. 'Did you audition for Dick Whittington?' he asked, shuffling his feet and feeling like a teenager.

'Trying to change the subject, Benjamin? And yes, but I wasn't able to get down there until later in the evening for the audition, as I had to drop off some prescriptions, since the work van was out of action. Did you?'

'You're a modern-day Florence Nightingale! Yeah me too, but not sure they were overly impressed with my singing.'

'Not going to be entering X Factor anytime soon then?'

He couldn't help but laugh. 'No fear. I can sing, it's just in a key that no one has ever heard of,' he said, as he folded over the top of the paper bag his half-eaten sandwich was in, and made a cursory glance down the front of his jacket to make sure there were no crumbs or bits of coleslaw.

'I'm not sure mine was any better to be honest. Still it's worth a try, isn't it? And it should be a bit of fun.'

'Yeah, it'll be good. Jessica auditioned as well, but I think she only did so that she could keep an eye on me,' he said, checking his watch again. 'Damn, look at the time, Stacey will have my kneecaps if I'm late again. Sorry, Chelsea, got to dash. See you soon, yeah?'

'Abandon me then, see if I care,' she grinned. 'No problem, get back before your boss sends out the hit squad. See you soon, Ben.' She leant in and gave him a kiss on the cheek.

'See ya,' Ben said, as he scurried off back towards the bank, hastily taking bites out of his sandwich as he went.

What on earth were you thinking, you pleb? he thought as he went back to the bank. *Of all the dumb ideas you've had, that's probably the winner. But where am I going to get the cash from now?* He had heard rumours about that Scottish loan shark. Rumours that involved kneecaps and hammers. He briefly considered how he could get money from the bank, but decided to knock that idea firmly on the head as well. Even he knew that that wouldn't end well, for anyone.

Turning into the bank, with just a few minutes to spare, he scuttled through the main reception area and let himself back into the secure area at the back, legged it up the stairs two at a time and made it back to his desk with seconds to spare, which was lucky, as he could see The Wicked Witch of the West Country headed his way. He quickly logged into his computer and stared intently at a spreadsheet, putting what he hoped was his best thoughtful look on his face.

Stacey strode past the row of desks like the captain of a slave ship, and without stopping said, 'Ben, you've got your lunch all over your tie. I do hope that you won't be greeting our valued clients like that? First impressions count for everything you know.'

Ben glanced down at his tie. *Damn.* 'Yes of course, I'll clean that up now, Stacey. Sorry.'

'Interesting,' was all the reply he got from her, as she marched off to make someone else's life hell.

He turned around in his swivel chair, and gave her a two-fingered salute, before dashing off to the gents. *Yep, this day was going really, really well.*

Twenty

Harry

It was their turn to host the Book Club meeting this Wednesday evening, so earlier after work, Harry had popped into town when his shift had finished to pick up some posh biscuits.

He was partial to a slice of shortbread or two himself, so he made sure he picked some up to nibble on later - providing Darren didn't get to them all first that is. Nice bloke, but he wasn't shy at demolishing an entire pile of biscuits. But he was in his forties and still living at home, so perhaps he should cut him a little slack. If he had been still living at home with his parents in Wales, then he would have been getting through a bottle of Hendricks gin a night, never mind the sodding biscuits.

When he had finally arrived home after doing battle with rubbish Taunton home-time traffic, he'd thoroughly run the hoover around the living room and the hallway whilst Polly walked the kids over to the babysitter. He had offered, but Polly had wanted some fresh air after being in the house all day watching Peppa Pig.

He went around picking up the toys that were once again strewn around the living room. Harry wasn't really house proud as such – you can't when you have kids - but he did believe in cleanliness. Especially when visitors were expected. Especially when *Valerie* was expected.

After the cleaning was all done and dusted, he brought in a couple of extra chairs from the dining room, as their two large sofas and armchair wouldn't be enough seating space for everyone coming this evening.

After a quick couple of slices of cheese on toast, followed by a piping hot shower that helped wash away some of the stress of the day, Harry waited patiently for them all to arrive. he flicked through the TV channels and wondering where Polly had got to – probably still apologising to the babysitter for what happened last time.

There was a rat-a-tat-tat from the back door, so he switched off the television and went to let in whoever it was in out of the cooling evening air.

Once the group were assembled, and after Harry had ignored a few glares that had been exchanged between people who'd been made to sit on the dining room chairs, they were all ready to commence the meeting.

Polly handed round the biscuits and apologised again for being slightly late.

'Right everyone, let's begin, shall we?' Valerie said.

'Take the floor, Valerie,' Harry said.

'Thank you. Now, if we're going to do this properly, we will need someone to record the minutes of the meeting.'

There was a pause, and the group looked anywhere, except at Valerie.

'Come on. Someone needs to do this.'

Andrew coughed. 'I can, if no one else wants to?'

'Well volunteered,' Harry quickly said.

Andrew frowned at him, before turning and smiling at Valerie.

'There's a spare pad of paper behind you, on top of the bookcase.'

'Yes. Thank you, Harry,' Andrew said.

As Andrew looked daggers at Harry, Valerie proceeded to drone on about the rota for buying teabags and digestive biscuits, and whether they should be chocolate ones or not.

Finally, they arrived at the main agenda item for this evening's meeting; deciding what tasks had to be completed for the production, and to whom they would be assigned.

'So then,' Valerie began. 'Let's note down all the different jobs and responsibilities that we need, and we can decide between us who shall do what, and by when. Are you ready, Andrew?'

'Yes, ma'am,' said Andrew, as he tapped his pen against the notebook in front of him. 'We'll need some flyers and posters designing and then printing out pretty sharpish, if we want to ensure packed houses,' he continued.

'Good point, Andrew,' said Harry. 'Anyone want to take that job on?' He looked around the room.

'I can do that if you like?' said Leo. 'Well, the designing and the printing part that is. I don't really fancy trudging the streets in this chilly weather putting flyers through letterboxes.'

'I think we should all help, as it wouldn't be fair on only one person doing it,' said Harry.

Helen put her mug down and said, 'I'd actually given that some thought and perhaps I could give out some flyers to the mums and dads as they take their kids to school in the mornings. Make my lollipopping duties a little more interesting.'

'Nice idea, but let's check with the school first and make sure they're ok with you doing that. We don't want someone finding out and saying that you were too busy handing out flyers for the local panto, rather than watching their little darlings safely across the road,' Harry said.

'Will do, officer,' Helen smiled.

Harry grinned at her.

'Perhaps we could put an advert in the community newsletter again?' said Leo. 'That would save us trudging about.'

'Yep, another good suggestion to consider,' said Andrew, making notes.

'It might be nice if we handed out some flyers during late night Christmas shopping in December as well,' said Helen.

'Great idea,' said Harry.

'Right, a good start to proceedings,' said Valerie. 'Now what other tasks are there? I believe I'm not mistaken when I say that Leo is responsible for the costume department?'

'Spot on, Mrs M,' Leo confirmed. 'Polly and Harry have kindly ordered some rolls of fabric for the rats' costumes for me, and I'll be designing and then creating all the other characters' costumes as well. Polly has given me a list of all of the different characters and what sort of outfit they might wear.'

'Has she now,' said Valerie. The icy tone of her voice evident to all.

'Err, yes, I thought that might be helpful,' said Polly.

'I see. Perhaps, Leo, you could allow me to glance over the *helpful* instructions that Polly has provided you with? That way I can offer any constructive opinions on the matter.'

'Defo, I'll send it your way.'

'Hmm. Now, what else do we need to organise?'

'There's the set designing and building that needs doing,' said Harry.

Valerie looked over at her husband. 'Gerald, perhaps you could lend a hand in that department? You're always saying that you enjoyed doing woodwork when you were younger.'

Gerald was mid bite through a piece of delicious Scottish shortbread and evidently not really paying attention to his wife. Upon hearing his name, he looked up at her, like a slightly bewildered shrew.

Valerie, who was sitting upright like a barn owl on sentry duty gave no clue as to her question and merely raised an eyebrow.

Gerald looked at Andrew for help.

Andrew said, 'Shall I give you a hand with the set design and building, Gerald? I mean, I am an undertaker, so I do know a bit about working with wood. Although there probably won't be much need for coffins in our production.'

But we may need one here before the end of the night, Harry thought.

'I'm good with wood, too,' said Leo cheekily.

'Thanks, Andrew, that would be most kind of you,' said Gerald, ignoring Leo.

'You're most welcome. We'll catch up at the pu… coffee shop for a planning meeting one evening.'

Gerald eagerly nodded.

'I can give you guys a hand if you like? I did woodwork at school and didn't do too badly,' said Ben.

'Thanks Ben, that would be great. You can do the complicated bits whilst Gerald and I drink tea,' said Andrew.

'Typical management.'

'Splendid, thank you gentlemen. That's another item crossed off the list,' said Valerie, who was looking at Andrew, checking he was recording the minutes accurately.

'I guess we will need someone to oversee the ticket sales and the general finances for the show,' Chelsea said, balancing her mug of tea on her knee. 'If no one else fancies it, I don't mind taking responsibility for this. I'm used to dealing with numbers and accuracy at work, and I'm keen to help out and do something, as I don't really fancy set building.'

'Helpful suggestion, Chelsea. We need to keep a track of what money we've already paid out, so that we can claim it back from the ticket sales as well. I've got a couple of receipts from stuff already that I can let you have.' said Polly, taking a carrot stick out of a packet and taking a small bite, before delicately placing the half-eaten carrot back into the bag.

'Are we in agreement that Chelsea can be our official accountant and book-keeper?' Valerie asked.

Everyone nodded in agreement, except Darren, who was leaning across to the biscuit plate that was on the coffee table with the stealth of a middle-aged panther that still lived with its panther parents.

'Excellent. Thank you, Chelsea,' said Valerie. 'Although I think we do need to have an agreement that before purchasing any items over a certain amount we need to discuss it as a committee first. To see if the cost is justifiable. Shall we say anything over ten pounds?'

'Erm, Valerie, there's not much nowadays that will cost less than a tenner,' said Harry. 'Especially if we will be buying wood for the set building. Even cardboard boxes cost a bomb nowadays. When our next-door neighbour moved, he told us that he spent over fifty quid on boxes alone.'

'You raise a valid point, Harry, but we can't go spending money willy-nilly can we. I still think we need to keep a rein on the spending so that we don't go overboard. On that note, what does everyone think is a suitable price for selling the tickets? Twenty-five pounds?'

Harry just about stopped himself from choking on a mouthful of tea.

'I think that's a bit steep,' Helen said. 'I know that almost all of the families that take their kids to school wouldn't be able to afford over a hundred pounds, just to see a panto in a dusty church hall.'

'I agree, that would be totally unrealistic, especially just after Christmas as well. Most people are skint until the end of January and pay day,' said Polly.

'Fine. What do we think is a suitable amount to charge then?' said Valerie, tapping her pen against the side of her leg.

'Well, if we're trying to appeal to the family market, especially after Christmas time, then I think we should really look to keep the cost for a family below about thirty quid,' Helen replied.

'Thirty pounds? That's far too little,' came the outraged reply, bits of her spittle shooting across the room like fireworks, in the direction of the biscuit plate.

'If you think about it, if you charge ten pounds per adult and a fiver for children, that seems fair and realistic to me. With perhaps children under five going for free?' Helen said.

'For *free*?' Valerie nearly imploded.

'We're not the West End you know, Valerie. We're a bunch of amateurs putting on a pantomime, not Andrew Lloyd-Webber putting on a performance of Cats at the Apollo Theatre,' Helen said.

'I agree with Helen,' said Andrew.

He was very quickly joined by Harry and Polly, Chelsea too nodded in agreement.

After a few moments silence, which somehow didn't end in the eruption of a fiery volcano and the immediate disintegration of everyone in the living room, Valerie spoke. 'I suppose that this is a joint venture and it appears that I have been outvoted on this occasion. Shall we move on?' she said, pursing her lips tighter than a duck's backside in monsoon season.

'I've just recorded in the minutes the prices we have just mentioned,' said Andrew. 'What's left to organise and delegate out?'

'I'm finding that as I'm writing, the characters are using everyday items in the scenes, such as mixing bowls and pots and pans for the cook, and other such items. So I guess we'll need to get these props and things for our actors to use,' Polly said.

'I expect we should be able to get most of this stuff ourselves, from our own kitchens and the like,' said Harry. 'So it shouldn't cost us anything at all really.'

'Jolly good, that's the kind of thinking we need,' said Valerie.

'But,' began Harry, and Valerie's eyes darted straight over to him, almost taking on a red glow in the soft lamplight, 'we will need someone to take responsibility for the props. Make sure they're in the right place at the right time, and keep them stored somewhere when they're not being used.'

'That's something I would be happy to take on,' said Polly. 'I mean, if I'm one of the writers, I'm going to know better than most when and where the props will be needed. And after Valerie and I have finished writing, there won't be much else for u... for me to do.' Polly then reached inside her handbag for another carrot stick.

Valerie slowly closed her eyes for a couple of seconds, before opening them again. 'Thank you for volunteering, Polly, what a splendid idea. I of course will be preoccupied with the important task of making sure that the script doesn't need any adjustments as we start rehearsing. On that note, I believe that one of the jobs at a real theatre is for a prompt; someone who sits at the side of the stage, following the script and prompting the actors if they lose their way at all.' Valerie spelt out, as if conducting a school assembly to a bunch of infants. 'If we're to put on a good, professional show, we really should have one of these as well. Patricia, you don't appear to have been allocated a task yet, would you be happy to oversee this aspect?'

Clearing her throat, Patricia said, 'Of course. Happy to help where needed.'

'Excellent, that's settled then. Now, Andrew, did you document all of that in the minutes?'

'I did indeed, M'Lady.'

'Good. Can you ensure that I get a copy by the weekend, Andrew?'

'Certainly, Valerie, it would be my pleasure,' the hint of sarcasm in Andrew's voice was apparently completely lost on Valerie, but not the others.

'Splendid. Now, I think a spot more tea would be in order. Harry, kindly do the honours.'

Harry stood up dutifully and started collecting the mugs from the others and placing them on the wooden tray that he had placed by the side of her chair after the first round of drinks. As he did, he saw both Gerald and Darren reach for the last piece of shortbread. Greedy sods.

Twenty-One

Harry

He glanced over and saw Polly pull the collar of her coat up around her neck and shudder slightly as they walked along the footpath by the stream. They were heading towards Valerie and Gerald's house, where they had been summoned this evening. The casting session a week or so ago had attracted a good amount of interest, as well as some people that were clearly delusional about their acting and singing abilities. Harry, Polly and Valerie had decided to give it some thought before casting the actors into the various roles.

Polly shoved her hands deeper into the pockets of her coat and then looked his way. 'Harry, you must remember to dig out the winter scarves and gloves from the attic this weekend. It's definitely getting cooler, and I don't want the boys getting cold.'

'Is that's because you don't want them catching a cold and passing it onto you?'

Polly glared over at him as they continued their march. 'Do you really want me to give you an answer to that question? And just where would you like to sleep this evening?'

'What I meant to say was, yes, darling. I'll fetch them down next Saturday afternoon, whilst you take the boys swimming.'

The Berwick children attended a Saturday afternoon swimming club at one of the local pools. Ten-year-old Tyler had taken to swimming like a fish to water, and so had Arlo, eventually. Harry remembered that at first Arlo had seen swimming as a complete waste of his time and energy and refused to get in the swimming pool. This had resulted in him being chased around the side of the pool, the swimming instructor circling in from the left, and Harry from the right. To escape capture, Arlo had jumped into the pool and Harry was sure the irony was not lost on his six-year-old son. But once he had learnt that he could swim faster than his brother, which annoyed the hell out of Tyler, Arlo finally started to enjoy swimming.

What irritated Harry was that all the parents would sit at the side of the pool in the viewing area, stating loudly to anyone who would listen how good their child was at swimming and that they were obviously advanced for their years, and would be the next Olympic swimming champion. Harry couldn't stand this inter-parent rivalry rubbish, so always did whatever he could to get out of taking the children. Thankfully, his police shift pattern often dictated that he was working during the swimming club hours. Fetching the winter clothes down from the attic was a perfect excuse to get out of going.

'Great, thanks,' said Polly, dabbing her nose with a tissue.

Valerie and Gerald lived about a fifteen-minute walk from Harry and Polly, and Polly had decided that they should walk over there this evening rather than take the car. Harry suspected that her main reason behind wanting to walk, was that she'd be able to stomp her way home later, taking out her aggression after the foreseeable disagreements that they would have with Valerie over the casting. As they turned the corner into Prospect Road where the Makepeace's house was, he heard her sigh melodramatically.

'Come on, darling, it won't be *that* bad,' he said, putting his arm around his wife's shoulders and giving her a gentle squeeze. 'And if it is going to be that bad, let's have some fighting spirit. Imagine how the hundred soldiers of the Welsh regiment at Rorke's Drift felt when they were surrounded by thousands of Zulu warriors. Did they sigh and give up? No, they kicked arse, didn't they?'

Yes,' said Polly looking over at him again. 'But they had rifles with great big bayonets at the end of them. I've got a cat notebook and a chewed biro.'

'What is it they say? "The pen is mightier than the sword".'

'Ha-ha.'

'We'll just stand our ground. And if she annoys us too much, I know an excellent place to hide a body,' he said, grinning.

'You big oaf,' she said, affectionately swatting his arm. 'Right, let's get this over and done with shall we?'

Harry started to hum the tune to 'Men of Harlech'.

Twenty-Two

Valerie

With her hands resting on either side of the chair, Valerie sat upright in her armchair with her eyes closed. She was conducting the London Symphony Orchestra as they played Tchaikovsky's 1812 overture. The orchestra was building up to her favourite part - with the cannon fire - when the beautiful classical music was rudely interrupted by the doorbell ringing out shrilly.

Valerie opened her eyes and took a deep calming breath. She waited for Gerald to attend to the visitors and show them through to the living room. She heard the front door open and mumbled greetings in the hallway. The distinctive sound of the cloakroom door being opened, and then after a slight pause, being shut again.

The quiet footsteps then padded towards the living room door, which after Gerald's polite rat-a-tat-tat knock, gently arched open.

'Polly and Harry are here, my dear,' he said.

'Yes, I can see that. Show them in, Gerald, don't loiter like a butler,' she said, as she rose from her chair, like an empress from her throne, taking off her reading glasses and letting them swing gently around her neck on the metal chain. 'Good evening, Polly, Harry. You did wipe your feet, didn't you?'

'Yes,' Harry said, stepping out from behind Gerald. 'We remembered to take our shoes off this time.'

Valerie still hadn't forgiven them for traipsing mud all through her house on a previous visit. Gerald had had to spend a good couple of hours with his marigolds on, clearing up the mess afterwards.

'Hello, Valerie,' smiled Polly at her. 'How are you?'

'I'm well, thank you. Do come in, take a seat. Gerald will fetch you some refreshments. Won't you, Gerald?'

With a nod, Gerald dutifully tottered to put the kettle on and open the new packet of digestives.

There was an awkward silence in the room. Valerie hoped that Polly and Harry would be feeling like they had been naughty schoolchildren who had been summoned to the headmistresses' office. Them not knowing if they could speak first, or whether that would seal their doomed fate - if headmistresses had Laura Ashley sofas situated in their offices that is. Valerie loved having this small bit of power over people; how she missed running the school. She let the moment continue for a short while longer, while she carefully repositioned her glasses on the end of her nose. She finally spoke, 'Polly, did you bring your notes from the auditions?'

'I did indeed, I've got them here somewhere,' Polly said, whilst rummaging around in her bag, 'Harry, hold these bananas for me, would you? Ah, found them,' Polly waved her crumpled cat notebook in the air triumphantly.

'Good. Now, whilst we're waiting for our drinks, shall we make a start?' Valerie said, picking a bit of fluff from her skirt.

'Certainly,' said Harry.

'Now,' Valerie began, 'we have the following main characters to cast. Dick Whittington, his Cat, Mr Fitzgerald, his daughter, Alice, and their Cook. We then have the Ship's Captain and lastly, the Island King. And then an assortment of minor characters, such as Dick's family, passers-by and so on and so forth. let's start with the main characters, shall we?'

'Uh-huh,' said Polly, chewing the top of her biro, which was one of Valerie's pet hates.

'So, most importantly, Dick Whittington.' Valerie said. 'May I remind you, that traditionally the lead male part in a production of this sort is played by a lady.'

Harry cleared his throat and said, 'Polly and I both liked that young actress; what was her name, Polly? Kate something or other?'

'Yes, we did. Kate, umm,' Polly checked her notes. 'Taylor. Kate Taylor. We thought she came across really well, lots of depth and passion.'

'Was that the young lady with the dark hair?'

'Yep, that's the one.'

'The one that kept mentioning she was a marathon runner, yet had a whiff of stale wine about her?'

'Well, I don't remember picking up on that,' said Harry, looking over at Polly, who shrugged.

'Hmm, well as it happens, I quite liked her for the part also. I did briefly consider Chelsea for the role, but I'm not sure she's got enough *umph* about her.'

Polly nodded. 'We were of a similar opinion and thought that perhaps Chelsea might be best suited to the role of Alice Fitzgerald? The daughter of the rich merchant who gives Dick a home,' said Polly.

'Yes, Chelsea is a pretty girl isn't she. I think she would fit the part of Alice well,' Valerie said, nodding her head once in approval.

'Good, so we're agreed so far,' beamed Harry.

Just then, the living room door reopened and Gerald rattled in with a tray laden with cups and saucers. The teapot was complete with a tea cosy and there was a sugar bowl with little silver tongs. This was accompanied by a plate of biscuits that had been artistically arranged with the chocolate side alternated with the non-chocolate side.

'Sorry for the delay everyone, I couldn't find the tea cosy anywhere,' Gerald said and put the tray down on the oak coffee table that was in the centre of the living room. 'Shall I be mum and pour?'

'Oh, yes please. Thanks,' said Harry.

Valerie cleared her throat, ignoring her husband altogether and continued where she had left off prior to the interruption. 'Now for the part of the Cat. I think this should be played by a male role, so that we have the right dynamic on stage.'

'Valerie, we didn't really feel that there was any male actor suitable for playing the part,' Harry said.

She peered over the top of her glasses. 'What about Ben? He probably shares the same level of IQ as a cat.'

'Well, that might be true, but he's six foot six, or near enough. We can't really have a cat that's taller than their owner, it would look a little odd, don't you think?'

'That might add to the comedy of it?' suggested Gerald, before handing Valerie a cup and saucer.

Polly screwed up her face. 'Hmm, possibly, I suppose. But we thought that Ben might be better as the part of the Island King. I mean, he's a good-looking boy, so I'm sure there will be some women, and men for that matter, that might appreciate seeing him as a scantily clad native warrior.'

Valerie couldn't believe her ears. 'Scantily clad? I *do* hope you are joking, Polly? Don't forget we are putting on a performance in a *church*.'

Polly took a deep breath and continued, 'We're actually putting it on in the church *hall*. And there's not going to be any real nudity or anything. Perhaps just a ripped top.'

'I should hope so too. What would the flower arranging ladies say about half naked men running around the place?'

'That would put them off their pansies for sure,' said Harry. 'But it might encourage them to abandon flower arranging and make banana cake instead.'

Valerie just looked at him in bewilderment for a few moments, as if he belonged in a secure unit at a hospital that was in the middle of a cold and windy moor.

Gerald, poised with a pair of small silver tongs in his hand spoke, 'I think you two are right, let's have Ben play the part of the Island King. But,' he added, as Valerie glared at him, 'we really must ensure that he is in suitable attire.'

'Agreed,' said Polly quickly. 'So, what about the Cat? The only other half decent male actors are Darren or Andrew, and we still have the two other male roles to fill.'

'Hmm, we are in a bit of a predicament,' Valerie said. 'Perhaps we do need to cast a female in the role after all. As we've lined up that halfwit Ben for another role, how about we cast his female companion, Jessica, as the Cat?'

Polly scratched her head, 'Jessica Benterman? The quiet girl with red hair, freckles and a lovely smile?'

'Yep, they've been dating for about six months, apparently,' Harry said.

'Well, well. I would never had put those two together.'

Valerie tutted. 'Enough of the schoolyard gossip. What about casting her as the Cat?'

'Yeah, that could work you know,' said Harry, scratching his beard thoughtfully. 'We had thought about placing someone else in that role; do you remember that feisty girl, Jo something. Waters, or Walters? But now that you mention it, I do think Jessica would be a good choice. What do you think, Polly?' he said, turning and facing his wife.

Polly was looking at him already, her eyes slightly closed with an expression on her face that suggested that he'd asked her to strip naked, cover herself in mud, and sing kumbaya whilst skipping up and down the street outside.

'I thought we'd agreed that Jo would be good as the Cat?' she said coldly.

'Uh, well. I do think Jessica would play the part well,' Harry said.

'Fine.'

'Marvellous,' said Valerie. 'It's settled then. Jessica will play the part of the Cat.

There was a deep sigh from Polly, which Valerie chose to ignore.

The conversation continued for another hour and forty-five minutes, before it was finally agreed who should be cast in which role.

Twenty-Three

The Two Cleaners

Swigging from a can of supermarket branded diet cola, Jenny glided her car to a stop outside the house of Kelly Russell. She looked over to her friend's front room window and saw that the lights were on. This was good, as it meant the silly farmyard goat hadn't overslept, like she often had the habit of doing.

They hadn't gone out last night, as there had been some film on that Kelly had wanted to stay at home to see, so they had both had a rare Saturday night in. Normally, come rain or shine, heatwave or Arctic blizzard, the two of them would be parading around town from pub to pub, before ending up in a bar with a late licence and a questionable selection of men.

Jenny drank from the can again, and thought back to a few years ago, when one of the pubs had had a promotion on, where you paid fifteen pounds on entry, but then the rest of your drinks were free all evening. That was the night she had ended up being arrested, wearing nothing at all, except her bra over the top of her head covering her ears, as apparently, her ears were cold – so Kelly had told her the next day after collecting her from the police station.

'Come on, you chocolate teapot, where are you?' she said and considered tooting the horn. Letting out a long belch instead, she watched as the front door opened and Kelly finally stepped outside. Locking the front door, she dropped her keys twice, before eventually joining her in the car -

107

muttering under her breath as she pulled the car door shut and fastened her seatbelt.

'It's amazing that you even manage to dress yourself in the morning, love,' said Jenny, as she drove off again, slowly caressing her way through the car's gears until she reached the main road once more.

'I had a couple of voddies last night, and me head's a little fuzzy this morning.'

'Good film?' she said, putting the car into fourth gear.

'God knows. I was pissed by eight. I woke up at half three this morning, halfway up the stairs with a finger of KitKat up my nose, which had melted. Don't have Polish vodka on an empty stomach, my love, mark my words,' Kelly said, rubbing her forehead gingerly, like she was stroking a sleeping lion.

'I've warned you about drinking that stuff, it's like cheap cider mixed with nail polish remover.'

'Well, I didn't have any other booze in the house, did I. Trying to be good at the moment. But I found a bottle behind the tins of beans when I was making me tea, and thought why the hell not just have one. The rest of the evening is kind of blurry,' Kelly opened the car window an inch and pressed her face against the glass.

Jenny shook her head. 'It's a medical wonder you're still alive, my love.'

'I know. I keep telling you that Channel Four should do a documentary about me. Give us a fag, will you?'

'They're in me handbag, down by your feet. Spark me up one too.'

Jenny slowed down for a traffic light, and looked over at Kelly, who was hunting in the depths of the bag.

'Christ almighty, what have you got in here? Hundreds of rubber jonnies, and what's this packet of blue pills? Viagra?'

Kelly turned to look at her, her eyes wide open. 'Are you on the game again, my love?'

'No, you muddy cattle grid. I just like to be prepared. That's me going out handbag, I picked up the wrong one by accident this morning, didn't I. And here, what do you mean *again*? Cheeky mare.'

'Alright, alright, don't let your head explode. Why have you got this Viagra in here, and where did you get it from? That light's gone green by the way.'

Putting the car quickly into first gear, Jenny pulled away from the traffic light. '*Sorry* my love, I didn't realise you were the frigging handbag police. Well, it's just *helpful* if you have some in your bag, you never know when a gentleman may have had one or two too many, and need a helping hand.'

'You nick them from somewhere?'

'Na, you can get them from an online pharmacist. You just pretend you're a bloke. Fill in a few questions, saying you're too stressed with work to get it up, pay fifty odd quid and the next day you get a little packet of blue pills through the post. Easy.'

'Well I never.'

'Yep.'

'WhatsApp me the link, will you?'

'Uh huh.'

They carried on chatting for the few remaining minutes it took for them to reach the church. As she drove there, Jenny looked about at the early Sunday morning streets that were deserted; bar the odd drunken teenager with messy hair, zig-zagging their way somewhere on the pavement.

Soon, she was pulling up outside the darkened building and switching off the ignition. With both of them yawning and stretching, they got out of the car, slamming the doors shut and not caring that they might wake someone up.

'The one thing I likes about the approaching autumn and winter, is that there's very few blasted weddings,' said Kelly.

'Amen to that,' Jenny said, and they shuffled up the stone-laden church path. As they approached the doors, she got out the big set of keys that Patricia had given her.

'Urgh, key's stuck again,' Jenny said.

'Give it a good push. Put your back into it girl. You should be used to that.'

Once inside in the relative warm, they both headed for the cleaning cupboard, which was just inside the ladies' toilet. Getting out the mops, buckets and hoover they put all their cleaning equipment in the main foyer, ready and accessible for when they needed them.

As Jenny was propping the hoover up against the wall, she noticed that there was a new notice pinned up on the board. Scanning through it, she called her friend over. 'Oi. Come and see this.'

'Mmm, what is it?' said Kelly, as she tried to tie her tabard strings behind her back.

'This notice up here. They've put up a list of who's playing what part in that panto thing they're putting on.'

'Oh right,' Kelly said. 'I thought it was going to be something interesting for a moment.'

'Ben's name is on it.'

'Let me see,' said Kelly, as she abandoned her untied apron strings and joined her by the noticeboard.

'Yeah, thought that might grab your attention. You're as predictable as a pair of young rabbits in mating season.'

'Where's his name? Oh yeah, I see it. Island King? What kind of a part is that?'

'Don't know. I can sort of remember what Dick Whittington is about, but can't remember anything about an Island King.'

'He is a king though, isn't he? The king of my heart.'

'Pass me that bucket so I can vomit, will you?'

'I was being romantic.'

'No wonder you're still single then. Christ alive.'

'Google the story and see what part the king is. OMG, where's my phone gone now?' Kelly patted her pockets hastily.

'Will you stop swearing, you're in a church, for Christ's sake woman. We'll be vaporised.'

'I think you've got more chance of being chatted up by David Beckham, my love.'

There was some more frantic patting of pockets before Kelly finally found her battered mobile phone and typed her question into the search engine. Kelly had told Jenny that she bought the phone as she'd liked the idea of speaking into and having replies from it – like the adverts on TV. Sadly, it didn't recognise her West Country dialect and garbled vocabulary.

Kelly was now muttering, as she read through the various websites and skimmed the plot, missing out the words she didn't understand. 'It says here, that the Island King is only in one scene, where they're having a meal and loads of big rats come along.'

'Only one scene? That's rubbish that is. Our Ben should be the star of the show.'

Kelly looked at her, 'I know my love, these people clearly need their heads looking at, don't they.'

Jenny grinned and said, 'Well, let's do something about that shall we, my love.'

Kelly raised her eyebrows. 'Err, like what?'

Jenny nodded towards a door. 'Nip into that church office and see if they've got any Tippex, or something similar.'

'Ah, I see what you have in mind there. Good thinking, cocker.'

'Ta. Now hurry up will you, we don't have a lot of time.'

A minute later, she returned with a small bottle of crusty Tippex and a black pen with "Jesus loves a sinner" printed down the side of it. 'There we go,' Kelly said, passing it to her.

And a moment later, the handwritten notice was amended.

Standing back to admire her handiwork, she turned and said to her accomplice, 'I've just had another thought. These actor types all prance around wearing tights, don't they? We'll be able to see the bulge of his huge coc-'

At that moment, they heard the approaching footsteps outside, signalling the arrival of the Wing Commander. With hushed swearing and giggling, the two of them set about looking busy, something they did with practised ease.

Twenty-Four

The Church

David, the greasy twelve-year-old altar boy, eagerly pushed opened the heavy wooden door to the vestry, so that he could see if it was his turn for ringing the church bell on this blustery Sunday morning. He loved coming into this part of the church, as it reminded him of the headmaster's office from the *Harry Potter* films, with all the wooden panels, old furniture and dusty books; all it needed was that cool bird and it would be complete. The room had a funny smell to it, a bit like the one that came from his dad after he'd been to the pub with his mates to watch whatever sport was on the big screen.

As the door gradually opened inwards, David's nose could tell the vicar was in the room before he saw him, a mix of cigarette smoke and pub aromas. When he was finally revealed by the opening door, the vicar was leaning back in a worn leather chair with his eyes closed, blowing smoke rings far out into the room.

The vicar suddenly opened his eyes and then attempted to quickly sit upright, fanning the dissipating cigarette smoke away with his non-cigarette holding hand.

'I was just, err, it's a bit cold outside today, so I was just, err, having a quick smoke before the service.'

David continued to stand in the doorway, uncertain of the etiquette in this type of situation. This was a new one to him; his twelve years on this planet had mainly involved playing video games and making fart noises with his hand in his armpit.

The vicar continued, 'Shut the door dear boy, we don't want the smoke going down the corridor, do we?'

David stepped into the room and let go of the wooden door, and it started to silently close again.

'What are you looking for? Candles?' The vicar spoke once again. David knew his name was Peter, but his mum had told him to never call him by his first name. He wasn't sure why. Perhaps it upset God. A bit like when he didn't tidy his room and eat all his cauliflower – so his mum said anyway.

'I was just gonna see if it's my turn to ring the bell today,' he replied, brushing a lock of his black hair across his forehead as he spoke.

'Right, right, well the rota's up there,' the vicar pointed to the wall. 'Take a look then be on your way, eh. Oh, and best not mention to anyone that you saw me smoking; Patricia would only nag me,' he said jokingly, as he took one last quick drag, before dropping the cigarette butt into a half-drunk mug of something brown.

David scuttled quickly over to where the rota was, scanned it, grinned to himself and then hurried back to the door again, opened it, and was off.

Peter shook his head despairingly and thought, *Stone the crows, do these youngsters today just not speak at all?* Checking his wrist watch that his father had given him over half a century ago, he saw that there was still about half an hour to kill before the start of the service, which was just enough time to top up his hip flask and have another crafty cigarette. 'This time I had better have it out of the window,' he muttered.

Just then, there was a knock on the door, and Harry stuck his head around the side of the door. 'Morning Peter, not interrupting, am I?'

Peter smiled, trying to hide his mild frustration. 'Not in the slightest, Harry, I was just reminding myself of the story of when Jesus turned water into wine.'

'Lovely. I was going to ask a favour please?'

'Fire away, dear boy. What can I do for you?'

'You might have seen that we've put a notice up on the board, saying who's got what part in our pantomime. However, Polly had the idea of you announcing it instead? What do you think?' Harry raised one eyebrow at him.

Trying to remember if he had placed his online home-delivery order or not, Peter replied. 'I'd be delighted to, might liven things up a little, eh?'

'Ah Peter, your services never need lightening up. But if you're sure you don't mind, that would be great, thanks.'

'Don't mention it, dear boy,' Peter said, holding out his hand for the notice, all too aware that this conversation was eating into his hip flask replenishment time.

Harry handed over the notice to him, thanking him once again before departing. He folded up the paper and put it with his other notes and Bible that were sitting patiently on the desk. He was reaching for his flask, which was secreted amongst his robes, when there was yet another knock at the door.

For the love of Saint Jude himself, I'm going to have to get a lock on this door, he thought, as it opened once again. He put on his best smile, whilst holding the hip flask behind his back. His hand trembling only slightly.

The last few notes of the electronic church organ came to a dramatic finale, and the scattered congregation sat down as a collective once again. Peter closed his hymn book and set it down on the lectern in front of him and still quietly cursing the secretary of the Morris Dancers for wittering on at him for twenty minutes, so that he wasn't able to top up his whisky flask. He picked up the piece of paper that Harry had given to him earlier in the vestry, and unfolded it carefully.

'And now for the church notices,' Peter said, clearing his throat before carrying on and taking off his glasses. 'As you are all hopefully aware,' he addressed the church, 'our beloved Wednesday night Book Club have decided to write their own pantomime between them, which they are then going to entertain us all with in the New Year,' he looked around. 'The auditions were recently conducted and this morning I was presented with the list of the actors and actresses that have been successful, and I have been asked to read this out this morning to you all.'

With this, some eager faces looked up at him expectantly and started to pay more attention to the proceedings.

'So here goes,' he began, placing his glasses carefully back on the end of his Rudolph-red nose.

As he read out the list of the different characters and announced who would be playing them, he noticed that there were some smiles and grins around the room, as well as a few people catching the eyes of others and giving a congratulatory nod or a wink. There were also some confused looks being exchanged between several members of the casting committee - and he wasn't certain, but he was sure he heard sniggers coming from the two cleaners sitting at the back of the congregation.

Twenty-Five

Polly

The Church Kitchen

Pacing. There was a lot of pacing up and down happening in the church hall's kitchen. And considering there were four of them in the kitchen and it wasn't exactly spacious, to Polly it looked like there was a strange, middle-aged-people version of bumper cars going on. She corrected herself, as perhaps a more accurate description would be three bumper cars and one armoured tank.

'And you are quite certain that one of you didn't amend this by accident?' Valerie asked for the fifth time, like one might ask a blatantly guilty schoolchild who is adamantly protesting their innocence at the fire alarm being set off.

'No, of course we didn't,' said Polly, almost at the point of snapping and telling Valerie to shove the script up her *culus*; as the Romans used to call it - in between feeding the odd Christian to a bored lion.

'I'm only asking, as someone had to have changed it,' Valerie hissed. 'It didn't change all by itself now, did it?'

'Well it certainly wasn't either of us. We wanted that Kate Taylor girl to play the part, remember?' Polly reminded her.

'Hmm,' was the only response from Valerie, although her eyes spoke a thousand words, and the pacing continued once again.

'So, how are we going to move forward with this?' said Harry looking around the room.

'One of us is just going to have to tell him,' Valerie said.

'We can't do that. Did you hear him excitedly talking about it with everyone after the service?' said Polly.

'Quite. This does put us in rather an awkward spot,' said Valerie, with Gerald stood behind her looking like he didn't want to speak, in case he said the wrong thing and set off the self-destruct mode on his wife.

'I'm just not sure I can see Ben carrying the part off well enough,' Harry spoke up.

'Thank you for pointing out the obvious, but I think we all share that concern, Harry,' Valerie snapped.

Polly tapped her foot, 'So what are we going to do then?'

The four of them looked around at each other, each hoping that one of them might have some clever idea as to how to get them out of this current predicament. But no one spoke. The glancing around became almost frantic, but still nothing. The silence continued and a gloom descended over Polly.

'There's no going back now, not since the vicar has announced it to the entire world half an hour ago. I think we'll just have to live with this decision, come what may.'

Valerie glared at her.

'Tea anyone?' asked Gerald.

Twenty-Six

Polly

Polly sat there impatiently, tapping both her index fingers on the front of her laptop, as if warming them up before the start of an Olympic typing race. Or before reaching out and strangling the last living breath out of the other person in the room, and then dissolving the body in a bath of bleach. And while waiting for the body to break down, she would smash up all the silly China knick-knacks in the room.

For the last ten minutes, Valerie had been busy intently reading through the latest scenes that Polly had written over the last couple of evenings after the boys had eventually stopped arguing and gone to sleep. Valerie appeared to be scrutinising every sentence as if it were a binding legal contract, for which the prospect of world peace was at stake. Judging by the amount of tuts and hmms that were coming from Valerie, Polly had a nasty feeling that she was going to be trapped here for all eternity. Unless she just reached out and put her hands around Valerie's throat. *Could I plead insanity?* she thought. *Or what was that other one that was used a lot? Diminished responsibility? Yes, I've definitely got some of that.*

She was dying to break into her comfort bag of carrot sticks, but previously her crunching had drawn a look from Valerie so savage, it was safer to just go without. *How Gerald puts up with this is a mystery, perhaps he's got that Stockholm Syndrome condition*, she pondered.

It wouldn't have been so bad if she could have checked some of Valerie's work in return, even up the odds a little bit. But Valerie hadn't given Polly any of her own writing, simply quoting her usual blurb of having been a headmistress for seventeen years, yada, yada, yada. Polly was dying to see the finished script, so that she could scour over Valerie's scenes with a magnifying glass, hoping with baited breath that there was a grammatical error submerged somewhere. *There has to be, no one is that perfect*, she plotted.

Finally, Valerie put down the papers that Polly had had to print off to give her to read, took off her glasses and turned to face her.

'Your syntax is a little weak in places, but generally acceptable.'

As marvellous as that is to hear, I don't think little children and old ladies will be too concerned with my syntax, Polly thought, clenching her fists. 'Okay, thanks Valerie.'

'I think your character dialogue is robust, and the pace is acceptable,' Valerie continued. 'After all, we don't want any of our audience members falling asleep on us now, do we?'

'Of course, most certainly not,' she nodded.

'Good. There was just one element that I feel needs some rework.'

Polly tightened her fists again. 'Oh yes?'

Valerie looked at her over the top of her glasses again, which was really starting to get on her nerves. 'Yes, the island scene with the rats. I think that the king of the island isn't particularly vocal enough.'

'He's a native of some description, I'm sure he would only have a basic understanding of English.'

'And therein lies your problem.'

Who the hell uses words like "therein"? 'Um, I'm not sure I follow?'

'You said just now that he's a native of some description. You clearly haven't thought this through and developed the character properly, or thought about a backstory for him, have you?'

For God's sake. 'Um, he's the Island King of a far off distant land, and he only makes a brief appearance in the pantomime, I'm not sure how much character development he needs really, to be honest with you, Valerie.'

'That's beside the point. To successfully write for a character, you must become one with that character.'

Give me strength. I wonder how much time I'd get off for good behaviour? 'Fine, I'll spend some more time developing the five lines that the character has got and get back to you,' Polly said instead of slapping Valerie.

'Excellent, I'll look forward to it.'

She glared over at the bespectacled dragon. 'So how are you getting on with your scenes? Do you want me to have a quick read through?' She just couldn't stop herself.

'I really don't think that my writing needs proof reading, Polly. I was a headmistress; specialising in teaching English prior to that.'

'Oh, really? You've never mentioned it before.' Harry had once told her, that if she were a wine, her description would be *"full bodied but bitter, with subtle hints of sarcasm and an undertone of rebellion."*

'Polly, you really should listen more.'

'Yes,' Polly muttered. 'I should have listened to Harry and moved to Wales to teach.'

'What was that, dear?'

'I said, I should do, you've got a lot to teach me.'

'Quite.'

'So, I guess we're pretty much there then, with the script?'

'Indeed, just a few minor tweaks to do, and once you've done those we should hopefully be ready to go.'

'Thank goodness.'

'I agree,' Valerie said, clearly misunderstanding her meaning. 'It will be exciting to step up a gear or two and start to see my - our creation come to life.'

Polly crossed her arms. 'I just hope that Ben will be up to the challenge.'

'I concur. Thankfully we have some strong supporting actors and actresses, to try and divert some of the focus.'

Strong supporting actors and actresses? She clearly wasn't at the same auditions as I was, thought Polly. There was silence for a few moments, and Polly swallowed, wondering what they had let themselves in for.

Twenty-Seven

Andrew

Bowing his head, Andrew solemnly drew back the small curtain gently, but promptly, revealing to the tearful grieving family the mortal remains of their recently departed loved one on the other side of the glass. The body looked peaceful, with a tastefully embroidered blanket covering the body from the shoulders down, with the hands lying on the deceased's stomach, the fingers interlocked.

His firm had been successfully running for over fifteen years now, with just one other full time colleague working with him. Andrew had always had a strange curiosity about death and the processes that followed a person dying, and after leaving school with an above average set of qualifications, he had gone straight to work at one of the undertaker firms in the centre of town. There, he had started out by washing and polishing the limousines and the hearse ready for the funerals. He was soon promoted to washing and dressing the bodies, taking great care and respect to do a thorough, presentable and professional job.

Over time, he had worked his way up the ladder, gaining valuable experience of all the various aspects of the job, which is why when he had eventually set up his own business, he had very little need to advertise his services, as his gentle and expert manner guaranteed a steady word-of-mouth trade.

Andrew preferred giving his clients a more personal experience, which is the reason he kept his staff and business small rather than expanding and potentially losing the personal touch that he and his clients benefited from so much. He did everything from taking the call, to collecting the body, measuring it for the coffin, preparing it for the funeral, completing all of the necessary paperwork and liaising with the appropriate church or crematorium; and all the while having all the time people needed to ask him questions and explain the process.

When the need arose to hire pallbearers, Andrew knew of a few retired firefighters, paramedics and police officers that were happy to volunteer their services for a few hours free of charge; Andrew had that way about him.

He also had a sense of humour, and he was not above playing practical jokes on his colleague, or the hired help - his young apprentice had only just started talking to him again.

A few minutes passed by and when he sensed that the family had viewed the body for the necessary amount of time, he sensitively drew the curtain closed again. He silently ushered the family back into the main office, where he confirmed the final outstanding arrangements for this Thursday's funeral, and bid them goodbye. He again made sure that they had his mobile telephone number, as well as the main office number in case they remembered any questions they wanted to ask him later on.

Sitting back down at his modest desk, he started to go through the paperwork to ensure that all the *Is* had been dotted and the *Ts* crossed. Screw-ups didn't go down well in his line of work; something he remembered from his earlier days as a young apprentice, when a body had been delivered to the wrong church. By bizarre coincidence, the church had been full of people waiting for another coffin for a funeral. It wasn't until the service had started and the name of the deceased had been read out that the mistake had come to light. He had told the young apprentice that if you looked up 'awkward' in a dictionary, there should be this example.

The entrance door opened and he set down his pen and looked up, preparing to give his full and undivided attention to his new guest. Instead, once he saw who it was, he picked up a nearby scrap piece of paper, quickly screwed it into a paper ball, and hurled it at the visitor.

'Be gone, evil man, be gone, you're not welcome around these parts.' He grinned at his good friend.

Harry ducked the paper ball, and smiled back at him. 'Do you want to be arrested for the attempted murder of one of her Majesty's finest police officers?'

'Finest? Pah. Don't make me laugh. You're only a copper as all the decent professions rejected you. Even the traffic wardens didn't want you in their ranks.'

'Adding insults to your list of services now, are we? Is that part of the Gold service, or just a free added extra?'

'Insults and sarcasm are always free, especially for the local fuzz. Now, what do you want? I do hope you haven't had another prisoner accidentally fall down several flights of stairs? The public will eventually catch on you know, they're not as daft as they look.'

'Not yet. But when we catch the little sod who's been throwing dog shit off the multi-storey car park at old dears, we might. Then you'd be organising a closed casket funeral for that joker. Seriously, what is it with you English, you're all balmy.'

'You're just pissed off because it's not sheep shit.'

'Hilarious. Not heard a sheep based joke before,' Harry said as he rested against the wall by the door.

Andrew tilted back in his chair. 'Alright toad face, why have you darkened my door? Shouldn't you be hounding criminals, rather than harassing poor local business owners trying to make an honest living.'

'It's about the panto,' Harry said, inspecting his nails, picking out a bit of dirt.

Hearing this, he sat up straight again. 'Ah, you've come to apologise, and tell me that I'm playing the leading role after all?'

'No, your acting skills barely got you the part of the Ship's Captain, so don't push your luck.'

'Are you saying that Ben's acting skills are superior to my own?' Andrew joked, and put on a mock expression of astonishment.

'You heard about that then?'

'Oh yes, that's provided me with hours of amusement.'

'Don't. If I find out who changed the casting notice before I gave it to the vicar, their behind will be having a serious conversation with my boot.'

'Just make sure you're not wearing your uniform at the time, don't give the local rag a story to write about. However, it would make a pleasant change from their usual "pigeon stole my lotto ticket" stories.'

'Hmm. Anyway, I've come to talk to you about set building.'

Andrew picked up a pen, ready to take notes if needed. 'Fire away, Spielberg.'

'Have you spoken with Gerald about any of the set designs yet?' Harry asked.

'No, not yet. We're meeting up this week for a pint and a chat. Get the poor chap out of the house for a bit. I wouldn't be half surprised if the crafty so-and-so is plotting his escape as we speak.'

126

'Excellent. Glad the ball is rolling.'

'The ball will be rolling so fast, it will be on fire, my friend.' Andrew said, clicking the top of his pen a couple of times.

'Ok, let's not get carried away with ourselves.'

'Spoil sport.'

Harry smiled. 'Don't suppose there's any chance of a cuppa, is there?' he asked, scratching the side of his mouth.

Andrew pushed his chair back slightly, 'Good grief, don't you lot do any work at all?'

'I'm not on duty yet, I'll have you know.'

'Some of us *are* trying to work, however.'

'Milk and half a sugar please.'

'Half?'

'Polly keeps telling me I'm getting fat.'

'You are.'

'Sod off. Got any biscuits?'

'Your brain is going to be fascinating for a doctor to dissect one day.'

'I'll take that as a compliment.'

'Hmm.'

Andrew got up from behind his desk and motioned for Harry to follow him through to one of the back rooms, where there was a worktop with a kettle, microwave and a toaster, as well as a battered red sofa bed which had small white flowers on, which Harry plonked himself down onto and stretched out his legs.

The two of them had been friends for a number of years now, first meeting through their respective employment when Harry had been a new police officer attending his first post mortem. It was a particularly nasty road traffic collision involving an articulated lorry, a sharp bend in the road, and a cyclist. Andrew, as the attending undertaker collecting the body from the pathologist, had seen a queasy looking young constable outside, and had taken time out to make sure that he was ok, and showed Harry compassion that had bonded them first as colleagues that watched out for each other, and very soon as friends. As they both had serious jobs, they regularly caught up for a moment or two of absurd silliness and banter, which they both found so important in their lines of work.

'You got some ideas for the set designs then?' Harry asked as he absentmindedly picked up a crumpled brochure on cremation that had been lying on the sofa.

Andrew wiped a tea towel around two mugs. 'Yeah, I've jotted a few ideas down, and I think we're going to need four main sets. A travelling set for all the walking bits, the house belonging to what's-his-face, the merchant chap?'

'Fitzgerald.'

'That's the one. Anyway, him. Then the boat and lastly the island.'

'Makes sense,' said Harry.

'Thanks, I do occasionally, when I'm not sniffing the embalming chemicals.' He opened a cupboard looking for the coffee jar.

'No wonder you have a glowing complexion.'

'I think the island and the travelling sets will be dead easy to do. A few palm trees for the island and a few lampposts and the odd bench or whatever for the other one.'

'How about the other two?'

He turned and looked at Harry, waving a teaspoon about. 'They're going to be a little more complex. We can't really get away with a couple of cardboard boxes for my ship. I was thinking of basing the design on Lord Nelson's flagship, *HMS Victory*.'

'Shouldn't that be *HMS Disappointment*?'

'*HMS Illustrious?*'

'*HMS Muppet?*'

'Ok, enough,' said Andrew turning back to the small worktop. 'The point is, it will take some designing. Also, for the house too, although that will be easier than the ship. Just a few painted boards at the back with a door cut into one of them maybe.'

'Any idea where you're going to get the wood from?'

'Just some DIY place I expect, we only need to get some cheap chipboard, nothing overly expensive.'

'Cheap and nasty, just like your coffins.'

Andrew turned and glared at his friend, and waving a teaspoon again at him said, 'When you finally do us all a favour and pop your clogs, I'm going to stuff you inside a couple of bin bags and chuck you in the incinerator, along with all the other useless rubbish.'

Twenty-Eight

Harry

The marked police patrol car moved slowly down the road, its occupant looking for the right house number, which was easier said than done in the gloom. Finally spying the right house, the patrol car came to a controlled halt. The handbrake was applied calmly and the engine switched off. When Harry had been at the police training college, during part of the police driving course the instructor would place a glass of water on the dashboard and if the young constable-to-be sent the water flying during one of the manoeuvres, the test would be over, and the offender sent back to re-examine his or her life choices. That element of control and measured approach had stayed with this police officer, especially when he had to deliver bad news such as this.

Harry got out of the car, locked it and looked around, surveying the urban landscape and then crunched his way down the short gravel stoned driveway to the front door. Before knocking on the bright yellow door, he removed his police issue helmet and sighed. This was not what he had signed up for, he thought, as he absentmindedly ran his thumb over the metal shield at the front of the helmet. The shield was dented at one side from when, as a new PC, he'd been on foot patrol one evening down East Street in the early hours of one Saturday morning, and someone had decided to take a pot shot at him with an air rifle from an open skylight on the opposite side of the street. He'd dived over the nearest wall and crash landed into the side of a greenhouse, sending glass and green tomatoes in all directions and denting his helmet in the process. Still, at least it wasn't his head, although he did twist his ankle in the process. Not that he'd had any sympathy from his colleagues back at the station, most of whom still laughed about it to this very day. Rotten bastards.

He tucked his helmet under one arm, as it was less imposing there than wearing it; took a deep breath and knocked confidently on the front door.

Twenty-Nine

Harry

Hearing what sounded like the slamming shut of an oven door, Harry straightened up. A few seconds later a shadow fell across the light behind the front door and the jingle of keys followed shortly after.

Leo opened the door slightly, peering out cautiously into the darkness outside. Seeing it was Harry, he grinned and then opened the door fully. 'Hi, Harry. I didn't expect to see you. You gave me quite a shock at first, seeing a copper standing there. I thought I was in trouble for a second.'

'Hello, Leo. Sorry, didn't mean to frighten you.'

'That's alright. Do you want a cuppa, or a glass of wine? Come in.'

'No, I'm fine thank you. And I'm on duty, so better not have a drink, got the patrol car parked up outside,' Harry said as he stepped inside.

Leo closed the door behind him and went to the window to peek behind the curtain. 'God, it's not outside next door's house, is it? She'll give me hell if you've parked in her husband's space, copper or not.'

'Fear not, it's parked a few houses down, next to the post box.'

Leo stepped away from the window, letting the curtain gently fall back into position. 'Phew. She's a right old battle axe, I think she just needs a good sha- never mind.' Leo said, his cheeks reddening. 'Anyway Harry, what can I do for you?'

Harry shuffled his feet awkwardly a little. 'I think it is best that you sit down, Leo. I have some bad news that I need to tell you.'

'Oh, right, ok. You're starting to worry me now.' Leo sat down on the sofa, which was piled far too high with an assortment of fluffy scatter cushions. Harry took a seat in the armchair that was placed next to the sofa in the spacious living room. The carpet looked new, and he wondered if he should have taken his shoes off.

Harry cleared his throat and looked up. 'So, Leo. As I said, we've got some unfortunate news. You know we ordered a roll of that fabric to make all the rats' costumes? Well, we've just had an email from the supplier. To cut a long story short, they haven't placed our order yet, and there's some sort of backlog they need to clear. This means that it won't be delivered until two days before the show is due to start.'

There was a pause.

'You are kidding me? How the hell am I meant to create twenty rat costumes in just two days? I do have a full-time job as well you know. Well, let me tell you, that is not going to happen,' Leo ranted.

'Leo, I -,' Harry started.

'And another thing,' Leo continued, 'I can't go off work, as we're dead busy and Adam will have a fit if I call in sick. And believe me, you do not want to cross that man.'

'Leo, it's -'

Leo crossed his arms, 'Well that's it, you'll have to cancel the show, because there is no way that I'll have time to do all that.'

'Leo, it's ok -'

'Don't you tell me it's *okay*, you're not the one that's got to cut out and stitch together hundreds of rat outfits. *Why* did I ever say I'd get involved with this? I should have kept my mouth shut and kept out of it, but oh no, me and my big gob.' He got up and stared to pace around the room.

'We've sorted it,' Harry snapped. *Grief, my three kids are easier to deal with, and Tyler could test the patience of a saint. A saint whose sainthood was due to having lots of patience.*

'Oh. Great.' Leo sat back down on the sofa. 'How?'

'We had a think about it, and looked around at other suppliers, but in the end to make things easier, we've just ordered the costumes readymade online. It's costing quite a bit more, but it will just be the easiest thing to do. The ticket sales should hopefully cover it anyway.'

Leo crossed his arms again. 'Ah, I see. So, you don't need my expert skills then. Fine.'

Harry just looked at him for a good ten seconds before answering him. 'Leo, of course we need your expert tailoring skills. We still have all the other costumes to make, and the material for that is definitely arriving in the next few days, as we checked with the suppliers. Do you still want Polly to give you a hand?'

'Ah ok, I see,' Leo brushed his blonde fringe away from his eyes. 'That should be fine. I'll be able to sort out the other ones, no problem.'

'Good, good. Ok, well, I can smell you have dinner cooking, so I'll leave you in peace to get your food sorted out.' Harry said, standing up and smoothing down the front of his uniform issue trousers.

'Sorry about my outburst, Harry, long day at work. Umm, you sure you don't want a drink before you get on?'

'Leo, it's no problem at all. With having three kids and being in my line of work, I'm certainly used to it. It's fine, really,' he reached out and gave Leo's shoulder a friendly squeeze.

'Thanks, Mr B. Thanks for coming around and letting me know. I'll see you out, make sure you don't pinch anything,' Leo grinned awkwardly.

'You caught me, I was eyeing up some of these cushions.'

'Tell you what, I'll make you one for Christmas.'

'Ha, thanks.' *Please don't.*

They stood up and Leo ushered Harry towards the door. 'Give my best to Polly and the kids won't you.'

'Of course, and when the material arrives for the other costumes, either Polly or I will drop it round and leave it in your safe hands.'

'Excellent. Take care and see you soon,' Leo said, opening the door, and Harry stepped past him and out into the evening air.

'Take care, Leo,' Harry said, smiling.

'See ya.'

As soon as the door was closed, Harry dropped the smile from his face. He noticed that the curtain of the nosey next-door neighbour was twitching, so he made a show of walking around the car that was parked outside of her house, checking the tyres, before pulling out his notebook and pretending to document something. Hopefully some of the other neighbours would notice, and she'd be the subject of the street gossip for a change.

Getting back into the car, the radio sprang into life and Harry caught the tail end of the transmission, which was something about a herd of cows on the loose. Ah, small town life. Some might call it dull, but give him a rogue herd of animals over some nutter in one of the bigger inner cities any day of the week. Just a shame he wasn't in Wales, these English were off their rockers.

Thirty

Andrew

There had been an overly complicated discussion about where the set building was going to take place. Trying to be helpful, Ben had suggested that they meet at his town centre second-floor apartment and construct the set there. It had been pointed out to Ben, nicely, that that idea would probably not be the best, as he lived in an apartment. A small apartment. A small apartment on the second floor. A small apartment on the second floor with no nearby parking.

After Ben had grasped the gravity of this, Gerald had then suggested they meet at his place to do the work. That had quickly been vetoed by Andrew as he couldn't face the thought of Valerie looming over them. She would be like an ancient pharaoh with a whip, watching the construction of her pyramid take place and handing out lashes with pleasure at every available opportunity.

After several more pints at their planning meeting, they had decided to just do the construction in the church hall and leave it there.

Shortly after that, the first planning meeting had been adjourned, as Ben wanted to get some dry roasted peanuts, before attacking the karaoke. While Ben was up singing, Andrew and Gerald put the world to rights, deciding that they themselves should be running the country. Well, Andrew and Gerald that is, Ben would only be allowed to make the tea, if his leadership skills were anything like his singing.

The second planning meeting had taken place in a coffee shop that didn't serve alcohol.

After the initial sketches of the different sets had been drawn, and the cardboard replicas of the scenery had been put together, they felt that they were ready to start the official building work. Andrew had sourced the wood from a contact of his in the DIY trade who owed him a favour. Ben, under Gerald's close supervision had been allowed to buy the paint, using some money from the petty cash that Chelsea had given him; with very strict instructions to let her have the receipt *and* the change.

This was how Andrew, along with Gerald and Ben found himself to be in the church hall at nine on a Saturday morning. The floor was covered in several dust sheets, pots of paint piled up against the wall ready to be used at a later date and ten sheets of plywood stacked in the middle of the hall.

The three of them were currently hard at work drinking tea and working their way through a bag of jam doughnuts that Ben had picked up from the supermarket on his way there this morning.

Jenny had let them into the hall, and was loitering around somewhere, occasionally popping her head around the door and asking if they needed anything, like more tea. Or if Ben needed a hand with his big tool.

'So,' munched Ben, jam dribbling down his chin and sugar all around his lips, 'how are we going to do this then?'

Gerald took a big bite out of his jam doughnut and looked at Andrew, clearly handing responsibility for all decisions over to him.

Licking the sugar off his lips, Andrew said, 'I thought we could start off by first marking out on the wood the various sets and scenery we need, before then cutting out the various parts we've drawn. A bit like an Airfix model for grownups really,' he chuckled. 'We can then start fixing them together, like we've done with the cardboard models.'

'Ok, great. You got some tape measures and stuff?' Ben asked eagerly, like a schoolboy who has been let loose in his dad's workshop for the first time.

'Yep, the tape measures and marker pens are in the red box, the one with the spirit level next to it,' Andrew said, nodding towards the small pile of boxes that he had brought in from the car with him, and dumped down next to the stack of plywood sheets.

'Ta,' said Ben as he walked over and started searching about.

'Have you got the plans there, Andrew?' Gerald asked.

'They should be here somewhere.' Andrew patted his pockets. 'Nope, not here, they must still be in the car, give me two seconds.'

Andrew made his way over to the church hall's door and pulled it open, stepping outside and making his way to the small car park where he'd parked up this morning to unload all of the tools. He pulled out his car keys and zapped the car unlocked as he approached it. Seeing the scribbled drawings on the passenger seat, he opened the driver's door and leaned in to retrieve them, glad that he hadn't mistakenly left them at home as he feared he might have done. Locking the car with the remote, he headed back to the hall, clutching the papers in his hand.

'Got them. We're good to go, chaps.'

There were mutterings of approval from both the other two, who looked like they'd run out of conversation with each other in the thirty seconds that he was gone.

They set about laying out each sheet of the wood all over floor, before attempting to measure out the required set pieces and drawing the necessary shapes over the wood; some easier than others, with lampposts baffling Ben for quite a while. Gerald made little work of sketching out the various components of the ship on the big pieces. Andrew took charge of the set that was for the indoor house scenes, and all three of the men worked in near silent concentration. This was only punctuated by the odd swear word or two from Ben, who kept muttering that manual labour was not for him, and perhaps working in an office and putting up with his evil witch of a boss was not that bad after all.

After a good hour or so of preparing the wood from the sketches, ready to be cut out, and Ben turning over several bits of wood so that he could start again, they completed their initial work. When Andrew suggested they stop for lunch, Ben and Gerald didn't need asking twice.

Three cheese and pickle sandwiches, several mugs of tea and a half-hearted conversation about football later - which was mainly Ben talking about betting on different football fixtures and the other two pretending to listen - lunch was complete and now it was time for the fun stuff. The sawing.

Amongst the vast assortment of tools that he had brought along, Andrew had included his two handheld saws, as well as an electric one. Knowing what a complete numpty Ben was, he was in two minds about whether to give him the power saw or not. In the end he decided that it might be easier to trust Ben with it, as the handheld ones could be quite tiring to use after a while and angles could be a little tricky to a novice.

Picking up the saw, he went over to where Ben was wiping something from his mouth. 'Here you go, Ben, you can have this one. Gerald and I will use these,' Andrew said. 'Have you used one of these before?'

'Not recently, but it can't be that difficult to pick it up again, I mean, how hard can it be eh?'

'Well, yes,' Andrew said scratching his head and already starting to regret his decision. 'But do please be careful. I'm fully booked for funerals for the next few weeks, so I wouldn't be able to fit you in for ages if anything did happen to you, so just bear that in mind, eh.'

'Don't you worry, I'm sure it's like riding a bike.'

'Just be careful.'

'Ok, ok. You two are like Jessica, always wittering on at me about something.'

Andrew looked over at him. 'Smart girl that one, best you pay attention to her.'

Ben rolled his eyes dramatically. 'Yeah, yeah, yeah,' and he started to use the electric saw. Andrew observed him slyly for a few minutes, just to make sure the numpty was getting on ok. When it became apparent that Ben wasn't going to hack his own arm off and ruin the scenery with jets of blood spurting out everywhere, Andrew got on with his own carpentry, after quickly checking with Gerald that he was fine with what he had to do.

Andrew was glad that he had brought along the dust sheets, as the sawdust was going everywhere. They had probably been too ambitious in thinking that they could construct and paint the set pieces all in one day – even with the three of them doing the work. Well, two and a bit men anyway. They'd have to arrange to come back a couple of evenings during the week if they could; or next weekend if they couldn't come in during the week because of the hall being hired out. It had been agreed that they would be able to store the set in the reasonably sized store room where the tables and chairs were kept and that in the interim period the tables and chairs could be stacked up at one end of the hall, to make the necessary space in the store room.

Andrew sensed the door open, and without looking he knew it would be Jenny, back yet again to see if they needed any more teas or coffees. He suspected that she had a soft spot for Ben, as she always seemed to linger around him for quite a while, asking him several times if he wanted another drink or some biscuits. She was a nice enough girl, but he couldn't see her being Ben's cup of tea – not whilst there was a planet full of other women anyway. He looked up and saw that it was indeed Jenny, and put down his saw. Ben was either trying to ignore her or totally engrossed in his work, as he carried on sawing away.

Jenny, seeing that Ben was still working, walked over to where Andrew was standing.

'Alright Andy, me cocker? How are you handsome boys getting on?' she said, having to shout a little over the noise of the electric saw that Ben was using.

Andrew wiped the sawdust from his hands on the back of his tatty jeans and wiggled his fingers. 'Getting there I think, Jenny. But we're not going to get all this done today, we'll have to arrange to come back another time to get finished off,' he checked his watch, blowing some sawdust from its face, 'I don't think we're even going to attempt to start the painting today.'

'That's fine, my love. You boys are welcome back here anytime you like. Just make sure Ben's with you, eh.'

'Sure thing,' Andrew said, with a knowing wink to Jenny, his suspicions confirmed.

'Good lad, Andy Pandy,' she returned the wink, before glancing about the room, her eyes resting on Ben's backside as he bent over, still sawing away.

Suddenly remembering, Andrew said to her, 'Oh, Jenny, I know what I was going to ask you.'

'What? Nothing to do with that clip that's on YouTube is it? Only I was pissed as a newt at the time, and really don't remember it happening, to be honest with you.'

'What? No. Nothing to do with, err, that,' he said, clueless to what she was gibbering on about. 'I've got some more cheap cigarettes if you're interested?'

'Same price as normal for two hundred?' She raised an eyebrow at him quizzically.

'Yep, special deal for you as you're one of my most loyal customers.'

'Go on then. I don't get paid until Tuesday mind.'

'That's fine. I've got some sleeves in the boot of my car,' he gestured over his shoulder. 'Remind me and I'll dig them out later after we have finished up here.'

'Spot on, my lover. Will do, and thanks.'

'Not a problem,' he grinned. He genuinely liked Jenny, as she really didn't care what people thought of her, she was just happy being her. *Shame there weren't more people like that really*, he mused.

She looked at his empty mug. 'Do you want another brew?'

'Yes, please. That would go down a treat. And if there's any more of those chocolate biscuits lying about, I wouldn't say no.'

By this point, Gerald was looking over at the pair of them, and she mimed the internationally recognised sign for "do you want a cup of tea?" To which he nodded and gave a left-handed thumb up, his saw still in his other hand.

Ben was still hard at work with the noisy electric saw with his back to them. Andrew watched as Jenny shook her hair about a bit. She then strode over to Ben. Reaching him, she tapped him gently on the shoulder.

Judging by how much Jenny jumped, she was as surprised as he was when Ben screamed out loud, like she had used a cattle prod, rather than one of her chipped and battered French manicured fingers.

Thirty-One

A blood curdling scream filled the large room and Ben spun around wildly, one hand clutching the other.

Andrew could see that blood was seeping through Ben's fingers and dropping onto the dust sheet below, his face a picture of both pain and astonishment.

Jenny stood there looking like she had just sat on a cactus.

'What have you done?' Andrew asked calmly, reaching Ben first; gently but firmly manoeuvring Jenny out of the way in the process.

'Bloody hell!' Ben said, turning white.

Andrew covered Ben's hands with his own. 'Ok, let me see.'

Ben looked him straight in the eye. 'Bloody hell!'

'Yes, you said that already. Now let me have a look.'

'I've cut my finger off!' Ben said, staring at his clasped hand and the bright red oxygenated blood that was dripping everywhere.

Andrew glanced inquisitively behind Ben and saw that there was indeed about an inch of bloodied serrated finger lying on the wood in the middle of the sketch of a park bench, not too far from where the discarded saw was now lying on its side. He chewed the inside of his mouth for a brief second. 'Jenny, fetch me a chair would you. Gerald, I can't remember seeing a first aid kit anywhere, so can you get a couple of clean tea towels from the kitchen please. And can you see if there's any ice in the freezer while you're there.'

As they scuttled off to get the required items, Andrew continued to talk to Ben, adopting his famous calm bedside manner.

'Now, Ben, I want you to look at me. Look at me Ben. That's it, good lad. You're going to be fine, you're just in shock. We'll get you up to the hospital and they will be able to sew it back on for you, ok?' *Possibly, if you're lucky,* he thought.

Ben's brow was full of sweat. 'Right, right. You think so?'

'Most definitely, they do this sort of thing all the time. Look, here's Jenny with the chair, so let's just sit you down for a few moments, eh. Thank you, Jenny.' Andrew gently helped Ben sit down on the plastic chair which Jenny had brought over from the stack at the back of the hall. Gerald too had returned at that point, with clean tea towels and a grim expression on his face.

'There wasn't any ice, but there were some frozen fish fingers, so I've brought those,' Gerald said, holding the half empty packet by a corner like he might hold a pamphlet on preventing unwanted teenage pregnancy.

Andrew waved him over. 'That will be fine, I'm sure. Ben, I'm going to ask you to let go of your hand, so that I can wrap this tea towel around your fingers, ok?'

Dread filled Ben's face, but he answered with a quiet, 'Okay.'

As Ben let go of his injured hand, Andrew saw that it was Ben's little finger that was missing its other half and deftly wound the cloth around all four of Ben's fingers, in a makeshift splint for the injured digit. 'There we go, now let's get you to hospital, shall we.'

'Ok,' Ben said, his voice still quiet.

'Right, I'll just grab my car keys and clear the stuff off the passenger's seat, so I'll be back in a moment. In the meantime, Jenny and Gerald will look after you, ok? Jenny can you sit with Ben, please and look after him for a few moments?'

Jenny tore her eyes away from Ben for a few seconds to look at Andrew as she replied to him. 'No problem, I'd be happy to.'

'Good, right, I'll be back shortly,' Andrew went to go and sort his car out, only to return seconds later. 'Slight problem, I've got a flat tyre. Gerald, did you walk here this morning or have you got your car?'

Gerald, who had backed off out of the way like an obedient puppy, suddenly came to life again. 'I walked up here this morning, wanted to get some fresh air and stretch my legs for a change. Plus, Valerie wanted the car so that she could go into town shopping.'

Andrew looked about the room. 'No problem. We'll just have to call him a paramedic. Have you seen where I put my mobile?'

'I've got me car here,' piped up Jenny, 'I could take him up to Musgrove Hospital?'

Ben, hearing this, looked like a startled rabbit caught in the headlights of an oncoming seven and a half tonne lorry that contained tins of rabbit-flavoured cat food. 'Umm...' he said, looking at Andrew for help.

Seeing no other option, and not wanting to tie up an emergency ambulance for a non-life-threatening injury, Andrew replied, 'Good idea, Jenny. Do you want to bring your car around to the front door here?'

'Umm.....' said Ben again uncertainly.

'Will do, my love. I'll go and get the car now,' Jenny said, already heading towards the door with her car keys in her hand.

Ben continued to look at Gerald for help, but sadly none was forthcoming.

A minute or so later, Jenny reappeared, slightly out of breath and excitedly let them know that her car was out the front and she was ready to transport the patient to the local Accident and Emergency – Musgrove Park Hospital.

Ben was walked out like a condemned man to the car by Andrew, with Gerald hovering a few paces behind, like a prison officer, in case Ben decided to make a run for it. And before he knew it, Ben was being whisked off to hospital by a grinning maniac in a blue cleaner's tabard.

Thirty-Two

Polly

Polly came back into the room and looked down at the family tabby cat, Clover. She seemed to be really enjoying sitting on Leo's lap. She watched as Leo played with Clover's ears, as well as stroking her head gently.

'She seems to like you,' said Polly, putting Leo's mug of tea down on top of the bookcase next to where he was sitting. 'She's normally fussy about whose lap she sits on, so you should be honoured.'

Leo continued to stroke her head and glanced up at Polly. 'She's a gorgeous cat. How old is she now?'

Polly looked up at the ceiling as she worked it out. 'She'll be getting on for seventeen years this year. A good old age for a cat.'

'She doesn't look that old, but I suppose it's harder with animals to age them.'

Polly nodded, 'She can still the give the boys a run for their money, when they're after her.'

'I bet. If I lived with three young kids, I'd just hide away all the time. Umm, no offence like.'

'Ha, none taken,' Polly smiled. 'I quite often wonder why on earth we decided to have children. They're enough to send you insane, they really are. And I've hidden outside in the kids' playhouse on more than one occasion now.'

Leo remained quiet and just sipped from his mug of tea.

'Have you told him how we got her?' said Harry from the kitchen, doing the mound of washing up after Polly had cooked beans on toast earlier that evening.

'Got who?' Polly asked. 'The cat?'

'Of course, the cat, who did you think I meant? The slave we've got locked up in the cellar?' Harry said teasingly.

'Alright you cheeky monkey, less of that thank you.' Polly retaliated. 'Leo, have I told you before how we came to have Clover?'

'I don't think you have Mrs B, no. Enlighten me.'

'It's not a particularly long, or even interesting story to be honest, so I don't know why Harry brought it up. Anyway, my mother was a teacher too, and she came out of work one evening to find a cat curled up on the passenger seat of her car, as she'd left the window down by mistake. She tried to get the cat to leave, but she wouldn't, so she took her home with her.'

'A catnap,' Leo said.

'Yes, you could say that,' Polly said, trying very hard to make it sound like she had never heard that joke before. 'Anyway, this was in the days before Facebook and the Internet. I'm not even sure they had mobiles back then either. So, over the next few days, she knocked on all of the doors to the houses that were near the school, but no one claimed the missing cat. So in the end she decided to keep her, but as she already had a, a…. what's the collective noun for cats? Harry?'

'A pride?' Harry called out.

'No, that's lions, you wazzok. I think it's a herd? No, wait, that's not right either.'

'A cunning of cats? A weave in and out of your feet trying to kill you of cats?' Harry suggested again.

'A clowder? Actually, it doesn't matter, she had a shed load of cats, so she palmed Clover off onto me. We called her Clover, as her favourite place to sit in the garden was on a small patch of clover, down by the greenhouse of my student accommodation.'

'Aww, and you've had her since she was a kitten then?' Leo asked putting his drink back down on top of the bookshelf.

'Yep, she's stuck with us in the madhouse ever since. Poor old girl.'

Leo played fondly with the cat's ears, and her purring increased in volume.

'But I'm sure you didn't come here to talk to the crazy cat lady about her elderly cat,' said Polly sitting down on the sofa opposite Leo. 'Shall we get down to panto business?'

'Sure thing. I've drawn up a couple of draft flyer designs that I wanted to go through with you before I email it to the printers.'

'Oh good, let's see them then,' she said, feeling excited.

'They're on my iPad, which is in my bag. Umm, it's over there by the door. I don't suppose you mind? I don't want to disturb Clover.'

'Not at all,' said Polly, getting up and retrieving Leo's rainbow coloured shoulder bag and passing it to him.

'Thanks Polly. Ok, here we go.' Retrieving it from his bag, Leo fiddled about with his tablet for a few moments, until he brought up the three different designs he had put together. 'I put these together last night with the aid of a nice bottle of red wine, to help my creative imagination get to work.' He leant over, careful not to disturb Clover and passed the tablet to Polly.

'Ha,' she laughed, 'I do the same thing when I'm marking the children's homework. How do I see the next one?'

'Just swipe the pictures to the left to see them all. There's three of them altogether.'

'Ah, ok, I see,' Polly said, stopping herself from saying anything when she swiped past the designs and came across a photo of a semi-naked man, with what looked like a maths textbook covering his private parts. Quickly going back to the three designs and hoping that her face wasn't going too red, she spent a good few minutes studying the designs, zooming in on particular sections, and mentally correcting a couple of spelling mistakes. 'These are good Leo, well done. As the designer, do you have a preference on which one we use?'

Pausing mid cat stroke, he replied, 'I do. I like all of them, but I wasn't sure about the one with the church on it. I don't want to turn away the non-religious types, by making them think we'll be trying to convert them, or throwing holy water over them or some such thing.'

'Hmm, yeah. That's a good point really. We don't want to put anyone off coming by thinking they're going to be bible-bashed. Ok, so let's maybe put that one to one side for the time being.'

'Have you seen the one with the cat on? I think that's probably my favourite one to be honest,' he said, as he carried on stroking Clover, who appeared to be fast asleep.

'Mmm, I like that one too. Quite a simple design, but really effective, just a cat sat on the stage with the spotlight beaming down,' said Polly thoughtfully.

'I think I over complicated the last one, there's too much going on in the picture, with the bells, mice and the boat,' Leo said. 'Probably because I was quite pissed by that point.'

Polly selected the image they were talking about and looked at it again. 'Oh, I don't know, I quite like it. It has a lot of character to it and has a lot of good visual references. Harry?'

'Yep?' came the reply from the kitchen.

'Come here for a second and have a look at these designs that Leo's done.'

Harry, still drying his hands on a West Somerset Railway tea towel as he came into the living room, bent over the top of Polly, so that he could get a look at the designs on the tablet.

'They look good, Leo. Well done,' Harry said, in the Welsh sing-song tone that Polly loved so much.

'Thanks, Mr B.' Leo grinned and picked up his mug of tea.

'Which one do you prefer, Harry?' asked Polly.

'The cat one is a winner for me,' he tucked the top of the tea towel into his trouser belt.

'Yeah, we liked that one the best too,' agreed Polly. 'It's settled then, let's go with that design.'

'We're not going to run it by She Who Must Be Obeyed first?'

'You mean Valerie? No, stuff her, let's just go with it shall we,' Polly said, hoping she sounded braver than she felt.

'You're daring. If she goes mental and starts sacrificing virgins, then I'm blaming you entirely,' said Leo, and Polly knew that he wasn't joking in the slightest.

'I can live with that,' Polly said, wondering if there was any wine in the kitchen to help her feel as defiant as her statement.

'It's decided then, excellent. Shall I email this over to the printer's tomorrow morning? How many copies shall I get done?'

'I think Chelsea said there was enough money in the budget for about five hundred or so initially. We might be able to get more done at a later date, once we have some money in the kitty from the ticket sales. If we have any ticket sales that is.'

'Of course we will,' Leo said optimistically. 'It's going to be a smash hit and taken to the West End of London. We're going to be rich, rich, rich baby.'

'I love your enthusiasm, but let's take one thing at a time.'

'You're sounding more and more like Valerie every day you know,' Leo said. And he didn't see the cushion that was thrown at him until the last second, making him cry out in surprise, causing Clover to dig her old, but still razor-sharp claws deep into his leg and catapult herself off to safety, like a fighter jet from an aircraft carrier.

Thirty-Three

Polly

Polly had just arrived at the church hall, and she was feeling excited; tonight was the first rehearsal with the whole cast, and she was eager to hear what people thought of the script. Harry was feeding the kids at home and waiting for the latest babysitter to arrive.

It was a good job she had arrived before time, as the Flower Arranging Club had left the hall in a right state; bits of leaves, twigs and ribbon everywhere.

'What a mess. Still, if it keeps middle-aged women from garrotting their husbands with a pair of laddered tights, then it can't be too bad,' she said to herself as she fetched a broom and got to work.

The floor swept, she then arranged the red plastic chairs in a circle in the middle of the hall, as she had been asked to do by Harry. The cast would just be doing a read through this evening, to familiarise themselves with the script and the other cast members.

'Hiya, darling,' Harry said, as he stepped in through the door and joined her in the hall.

'Hello, boyo. Babysitter turned up then?

'Eventually. Looks nice and organised in here, thanks.'

'Don't mention it. I turned the hot water urn on just now, so I'll go and make a big pot of tea, ready for when the others arrive in a bit.'

'Great idea. Get their voices warmed up,' Harry said.

'Did you remember to bring the scrips?' Polly said, brushing dust from her hands.

'No, I thought I'd leave them at home, and we'd get people to improvise instead.'

'Not funny,' Polly pulled a face at him.

'They're all in the box in the car, I'll fetch them in in a second. I just wanted to see if you needed some help first.'

'All done in here. Go and get them, and I'll make a start with the tea.'

Harry blew her a kiss and went back out to the car to bring the box in.

A short while later the others started to drift in. Valerie and Gerald were the first to arrive, followed very soon after by all the others. Like a new class of schoolchildren, they all stood around nervously, not really knowing what to say to one another. Some of them clutching pencil cases, others just holding onto their scarves tightly like their lives depended on it.

Polly had made the tea in a big teapot she'd found in the kitchen, and had used seventeen teabags, which had mean it was a little on the strong side. When Patricia questioned her about it, Polly said she was working on the philosophy of one for each of them, plus one for the pot.

'Right everyone,' said Harry warmly. 'Come and take a seat and I'll dish out the scripts to you all.'

'Want a hand, Harry?' Helen asked.

'Yes, please. Hand these around if you would,' Harry said, passing Helen a pile of scripts, which had been hole-punched and put into yellow folders.

Andrew also picked up a small pile and helped pass them around.

'Welcome everyone, great to see you all,' Harry began. 'The aim of this evening is to just read through both of the acts, so that you all get to know your characters. As they're both here this evening, shall we all just say a big thank you to Polly and Valerie for putting it together so expertly.

Helen started the clapping off, much to Polly's embarrassment, whilst Valerie looked like she'd just been elected as Prime Minister.

Over the next couple of hours, they read through the script together, each actor reading out their own lines, familiarising themselves with their characters and the general stage directions. Some of the more organised ones amongst the group had brought with them different coloured highlighting pens, so that they could mark out their own sentences for easy identification. Darren had brought along a whole packet of different coloured pens and was marking out the stage directions in a different colour to his lines, which Polly noticed caused a few knowing winks and grins between Andrew and Leo.

Sat opposite Polly was Valerie, her glasses perched in their usual position at the end of her nose, following the lines as they were being spoken with her silver fountain pen, making sure that each word was rigidly stuck to, causing Harry to glare at her every time she interrupted, to which she was totally oblivious.

At the end of the first read through they adjourned for tea and biscuits and Harry spent the last twenty minutes running through the rigorous rehearsal schedule that he had put together. He reminded them all that it was nearly the end of September, and if they wanted to put on the production in January as planned, that they needed to get their skates on and get up to speed, as Christmas would soon be upon them and after that it was show time.

Thirty-Four

Helen

As Helen drew the heavy curtains across the windows in her living room she shivered. 'It's definitely getting cold out now, Mr Darcy,' she said to the cat, as she felt the nearest radiator to her. She withdrew her hand quickly as it was still cold.

She gave Mr Darcy a scratch under his black chin, which he enjoyed now as much as he always did. He'd been her loyal companion for nearly seven years now, after she had adopted him from the local cat rescue centre. When she went to choose a cat, she had walked past his pen and found his soulful eyes looking back at her and she had fallen for him at first sight. One of the staff had pointed out to her the *'danger'* sticker that had been placed in his window, which was because he had taken a couple of chunks out of some poor man's hand a few days earlier. But without hesitation, Helen had opened up the pen door and stroked him and they had become instant friends.

Helen settled comfortably into her armchair and wriggles her toes inside her slippers, which had been a Christmas present last year from one of the mums from school. Reaching for the TV remote control, she looked at Mr Darcy. 'Shall we watch some more Grand Designs tonight, Darce? Hmm?' Taking his purring as validation, she flicked through the channels until she found what she was looking for, and she was just settling into her chair when the doorbell went.

Mr Darcy looked at her as if to say, *Well I'm not expecting anyone, so you had better get it.*

Getting up, Helen put the television on mute and went over to her front door and looked through the spy hole that her husband had put in, on one of his rare outings down from the attic and away from his train set.

Leo's baby face and small fuzzy beard filled the spy hole, and she opened the door to him and welcomed him in with a warm hug.

'Hello trouble, how are you?' he greeted her. He gave her a big grin and a peck on the cheek, then put down the bag he was carrying.

'I'm good thanks stranger, how about yourself?'

'All good thanks, but it's freezing outside, so stick the kettle on.'

'Will do. Come on through to the kitchen with me. Have you eaten this evening, or would you like some leftover lasagne?'

'I'm good thanks H, I had a bite to eat before I came over.'

'Are you sure? It's homemade?'

'Very tempting, but I'm fine, honestly. But thank you.'

'Tea or coffee?'

'Tea, please. Unless you've got any hot chocolate?'

'For you I have.'

Helen opened one of the kitchen cupboards and lifted down two mugs, she then picked up a third, as one of the first ones hadn't been washed properly and still had tea stains around the bottom of it.

'So, what brings a handsome young man like you to my door?'

'Well obviously it's because I've won the lottery and I've come to take you to the airport; we're off to Australia baby,' he spread his arms open wide in mock excitement.

'Can the cat come?'

'Of course he can. And Mr T can as well.'

'Pah, he can stay here and guard the house.'

Leo laughed. 'Alas, there is no lottery win, I've just popped over to drop off the flyers, as we've had the first batch back from the printers.'

'How exciting. How do they look?'

'Amazing, of course. After all, I did do the design.'

'I would expect nothing less, let's have a look then, don't keep a girl in suspense.'

'They're in my bag,' Leo said, nodding towards the living room.

'Great, I'll just do these and then we'll go through and have a look.'

Helen finished making the drinks and handing Leo his mug, ushered him back into her cosy living room, where Mr Darcy was sprawled out on the sofa, one eye opening lazily to watch them.

Sitting down and placing his mug down on a side table that was next to the sofa, Leo unzipped his bag and pulled out one of the flyers and passed it over to Helen for closer inspection.

'This is brilliant, Leo.'

'Ta, H.'

'Very artistic, isn't it, Darcy?' she said, waving it in front of the cat's open eye. Who then tried to swat it with a paw.

'Cheers, I think the printer has done a decent job too, good quality paper and all that.'

'Mmm, very professional looking. Can I have a load to give out to some of the parents when I'm on lollipop duty?' She took a sip of her tea, which was still too hot to drink.

'Yep, I've brought you over a hundred, if that's ok for now?'

'Yep, I can give some out over a couple of days, perhaps morning and afternoons as well, that way I should be able to catch most of the parents.'

'Fab, thanks.'

'I'll put them on the kitchen table, otherwise if I leave them on the floor, the cat will make a nest out of them.' She stroked his tummy.

'But that would give it a more authentic look, it is Dick Whittington and his Cat after all.'

'Good point.'

'It's a shame we can't have a real cat on stage, I think Mr Darcy would play the part eloquently.'

'He would, wouldn't he? He would want to be paid equity rates though, and have a percentage of the royalties, so I'm not sure we can afford him, sadly.'

'Ah well, the people of Taunton must make do with just the amateurs performing then,' Leo said.

'I'm sure it will be just as wonderful.'

Leo's eyes lit up. 'Hey, did you hear about Ben's finger? I'm not sure that's a good sign. Isn't the saying meant to be *"break a leg,"* not hack your finger off and spray blood everywhere?'

'I did, and I saw that his hand was still wrapped up in bandages the other night. Poor bloke.'

'I heard from Andrew that it was because that cleaner, Jenny, crept up on him. She's a bunny boiler if ever I saw one.'

'I'm sure it wasn't intentional.'

'You never know with these bunny boiler type.' He mimed a stabbing motion.

The two of them continued to chat, gossip and generally put the world to rights until Leo had finished his drink and then been given some lasagne to take home in a plastic tub, which regardless of his polite protests, Helen knew that he would devour hungrily as soon as he got home. Probably with a couple of vodka and cokes to wash it down.

Thirty-Five

Harry

Taking a couple of quick big strides, and side stepping a doddering old lady with a trolley full of bottles of supermarket own brand gin and tonic, Harry caught up with Finn and lifted him up into the air, the two-year-old's little chubby legs still doing the running motion as he ascended. Harry's timing had just saved little Finn from running head first into a stack of moronic looking plastic snowmen that were guarding the beginning of the toy aisle at the out of town supermarket.

'And where do you think you're going little fella?' Harry asked the giggling child in his outstretched arms.

Following a garbled response, of which the only understandable word was "bubbles", Harry placed the youngest of his offspring back safely on terra firma and steered him carefully around the snowmen guards and down the toy aisle, an action which Harry was almost certain would end in tears when Finn wasn't allowed to take all the toys home with him.

Harry was joined a few seconds later by his wife and his two other children, Tyler and Arlo, who after only a mere ten seconds inside the supermarket, were already arguing about which of them was going to push the trolley; which today was doubling up as the *starship*, *Enterprise*. A slightly hassled looking Polly was doing her very best to ignore them, putting her purse back inside her large flowery handbag.

'Sorry, I couldn't find my B-L-O-O-D-Y purse in my bag, and then I couldn't find a S-O-D-D-I-N-G old pound coin to put in the blasted trolley,' she said to Harry, whilst the children's squabbling rose up several notches, causing passing shoppers to look and tut. 'I mean,' she continued, while Harry thought that the judgemental shoppers deserved a slow and painful death, involving being surrounded by children on E numbers playing with puppies. 'Does anyone actually steal shopping trolleys anymore? Aren't the kids these days too busy gunning down hordes of zombies in computer games, or glued to their smartphones, which are destroying all their brain cells? Who thought up smartphones anyway?'

'You would be surprised,' was Harry's reply, thinking grimly back to a murder that had happened about a year ago, which had involved a shopping trolley, a couple of pairs of handcuffs, the River Tone and some poor sod who had obviously pissed someone important off. They had eventually caught the henchman culprit, ironically from a sample of DNA from dried blood found on the pound coin in the trolley, that by some miracle the river hadn't washed away.

'Since being a parent, nothing surprises me anymore. Right, where's the shopping list that you wrote out gone?' Polly said, delving once more into her colourful bag of tricks and digging around inside, muttering as she did so. 'Ah, here it is,' she said jubilantly, before popping a carrot stick into her mouth, reminding Harry of a slightly unhinged Bugs Bunny.

'Right boys, we're heading for the fruit and veg section first. So off you go.' said Polly, pointing in the right direction.

The two older boys, who were still arguing about which of them was pushing the trolley, zigzagged off, the bickering continuing into the cold realms of outer space. Once again Harry picked up Finn and he and Polly followed after the *USS Enterprise*, which was clearly being piloted by a very inebriated Mr Sulu. At that point, right on cue, Finn started to cry as he was forced to leave all the lovely and very expensive toys behind.

'I wish I had their energy,' Harry said, nodding towards Tyler and Arlo, with Finn screeching in his ear.

'Me too. I'm knackered by eleven in the morning these days.'

'At least if they burn off their energy here, they'll go to sleep quickly this evening.'

'You think?' Polly said doubtfully as she chewed on a carrot, 'I think that the only thing to get them to go to sleep quicker, would be a tranquilliser dart that was meant for a really big elephant.'

'Good point. And aren't all elephants really big?'

'The baby ones aren't. Still, we were all children once I suppose,' Polly sighed.

'Most of us were, but I'm not sure about Valerie you know. On that note, how do you think the rehearsal went the other night?' Harry asked, as he swung Finn onto his shoulders, much to the toddler's sudden delight, the abandoned toys forgotten about.

'I think it went well, for the most part anyway.'

'For the most part? What do you mean? Finn, don't pull daddy's hair so much, please.'

'What do you think I mean? Ben's not exactly ever going to win an Oscar for his performance is he.'

'Hmm, but what can we do about it? This is only an am-dram thing after all, it's not like we're the professionals and we can sack him and get Jude Law in instead.' Harry said.

'Or Denzel Washington,' Polly said dreamily, which Harry was used to by now. Polly carried on, 'I know, I know. But I really want this to be a success. This is my first go at writing something, and I don't want it to be a giant flop.'

Wiping toddler drool from his face, he said, 'I realise that, darling, and so do I, but I just can't see what option we have. If we say anything to Ben, it could really upset him, and I think the poor lad has enough on his plate. Onions?'

'Yes, three red ones it says on your bit of paper. God, your handwriting isn't getting any better you know. But back to Ben, I think you're just going to have to give him *a lot* of directions, Mr Director,' said Polly.

'Great, so I get to be the bad guy then.'

'You should be used to that, being a policeman,' said Polly, eyeing up some packets of pre-sliced carrot sticks.

'Hey. We're the good guys you know.'

'That's not what's spray painted on the side of this supermarket.'

'Not again. The last lot was only removed a week or so ago.'

'Cheer up, it could be worse.'

'Like having to direct Ben in a leading role you mean?' Harry said, forlornly.

'Something like that, and anyway, I thought you liked a challenge. At least the others seem to be getting into the swing of it ok. Darren was really going for it, wasn't he?'

'True, but I think he's P-I-S-S-E-D off that he didn't get the lead role.'

'What? As Dick?' He's too fat and middle-aged to play that part,' said Polly, picking up some tomatoes that were on offer and giving them to Tyler to put in the trolley, ignoring his whines about Arlo not being old enough to pilot a starship correctly.

'I know that, but I don't think he knows that. Umm, do we need celery? I can't remember.'

'Well, Helen was really good, wasn't she.' It was more of a statement than an actual question. 'And no, we're ok, it's only me that eats it anyway, unless you count the guinea pigs eating the leftovers.'

'That she was, really entertaining. Considering how lovely she is in real life, she doesn't half play a good bad-tempered cook. And that reminds me, add guinea pig food to the list before I forget.'

'Mmm, that's what I thought as well. About her acting I mean, not about the guinea pig food. Shame she's not a bit younger, she would have been an excellent Dick Whittington.'

'Hang on, you can't say that,' said Harry as he caught the dummy that Finn had spat out.

'Why not?' She stopped and looked at him.

'That's ageist, or sexist, or something to do with the whatsit Equality Act,' he said.

'No it's not, no more so than what we were saying about Darren.'

'Well, it doesn't sound right.'

'Why's that, because it's about a woman? Now that's sexist, Mr Police Officer,' said Polly, waving a cucumber at him.

'It's not like that.'

'Alright, calm down, you twonk. I'm not going to report you to inspector thingy, the bald one you don't like. Is that covered by the Equality Act as well? A dislike of baldies?'

'Surprisingly, it's not. Thankfully.'

'Not that you can talk, you're thinning on top.'

'I most certainly am not. Full head of hair me.'

'Oh yeah, sure, sure. Now, we must remember to pick up some of that special shampoo that you secretly buy and hide at the back of the bathroom cabinet and think no one knows about.'

Harry looked at her for several moments, before simply asking her, 'Pick up some courgettes will you.' *And a big heavy marrow,* he thought, *so I can bash you over the head with it.* 'The others were good too. Andrew seemed to love playing the Ship's Captain, even if he did sound a bit like a pirate. It's just Ben that I think we have to worry about,' he continued.

'We have a couple of months, and we have only had the first rehearsal, so it's still early days, isn't it?'

'It sure is. Have we sold any more tickets do you know?'

'A few more now actually, but we've still got loads to shift. Hopefully once we all start dishing out the flyers we will get a few more bums on seats,' said Polly.

'Yep, and I'm going to ask one of the chaps at work if his son can set us up with a basic website. The kid's some sort of computer genius and he's only fifteen.'

'About the right age for a computer genius then. And a website is a great idea, we can link it to the Facebook page Leo set up.'

'Excellent. We'll soon get those seats filled up. Hey, it's going to be a tremendous success you know,' Harry said, putting an arm around Polly's shoulders, but then quickly letting go when Finn began yanking at his hair again.

The Berwicks continued with their weekly shopping expedition, despite the hordes of bloodthirsty aliens that were circling in their ships nearby, poised and ready to attack.

Thirty-Six

The Two Cleaners

Jenny stood impatiently outside of the pasty shop in the High Street. She was waiting for Kelly to stop trying to flirt with the young blonde chap that was serving her - who was in the process of turning an embarrassed shade of red. Normally she would have been egging her friend on, but this morning she had a banging hangover, and really needed the orange juice and bacon roll that Kelly had gone in for. She would also have sold her own niece for a cigarette, but she was determined to give up. Or at least break her current record of three and a half days without one.

Eventually Kelly came outside and joined her, grinning like a dog who's just figured out how to open tins.

'Alright, my lover?' Kelly said.

Jenny just scowled at her. 'You took your bleeding time didn't you.'

Kelly rearranged her cleavage. 'I was just doing my bit for supporting local community businesses.'

'Trying to chat up that bloke more like. He only looked about seventeen anyway.'

'Ahh, he was way older than that, my love. Eighteen at least.'

'It looked like you were terrifying the poor lad,' Jenny said, as she leant up against the brick wall for support. Her eyes looking at the bag of food that Kelly still had in her hands.

'Don't be daft. Just a bit of harmless banter, but come to think of it, he did seem a bit shy when I asked him to squirt his thick juice all over me baps.'

'Jesus, Kelly. You need locking up you do.' Her stomach growled angrily.

'And it looks like *you* need some hair of the dog. Either that or putting in a sack with a couple of heavy stones and chucking in French Weir.'

Jenny rubbed her stomach and screwed up her face in reply. 'Urgh, God no. I'm off booze now for good. I can't keep feeling like this in the mornings.'

Kelly looked at her with genuine concern on her face. 'Are you a raging alcoholic, my love?'

'Course not, you discarded toenail clipping. Alkies don't admit they've got a problem and don't want to give up. I just told you that I'm going to give it up.'

'Hmm, I think we both knows that's not true.' Kelly had her hands on her hips now, still with the bag of food clutched tightly in her hand. The smell of food escaping and wafting up. Jenny could almost taste the bacon.

'Shut your face and pass me my food. If it's not already cold 'cos you was gassing to that spotty teenager,' she thrust out her hand, her patience now depleted.

Kelly tutted and opened the paper bag. 'Here you go, you pile of festering compost. One bacon bap and one orange juice for you to take your happy pills with. Or preferably, choke on.'

Jenny's reply was a universally recognised one fingered gesture. She unscrewed the cap of the orange juice and downed half of the contents straight away and used the back of her hand to wipe her mouth, before biting hungrily into the food. 'Good job it's still hot,' she said with her mouth full of food, the brown sauce tingling her tongue.

'Is that grumpy cow language for thank you?' Kelly said.
Jenny looked at her, her eyes narrowing slightly. 'Thank you, your highness.'

They stood eating their breakfast, leaning against the brick wall, watching the mums drag their kids around the town centre from clothes shop to clothes shop and overhearing promises of sweets and chocolate if they were good little boys and girls.

'If Ben and I was together, we'd make gorgeous kids,' Kelly said thoughtfully, finishing the last bite of her breakfast bap, oblivious to the egg yolk that had dribbled down the side of her chin.

Jenny decided against telling her about the yolk. 'Yeah, so long as they got their looks from their dad that is.'
Kelly stood up straight, one hand on a hip. 'Oi, you repugnant goat. There's nothing wrong with the way I look, thank you very much.'

'Calm down princess.'

'But sadly, despite my devastating good looks, it's not likely is it, now that he's shacked up with little Miss what's her face.'

'You never know, it is coming up to Christmas time. Christmas miracles and all that. Like that film with thingamabob in,' Jenny said, waving her nearly empty bottle of orange juice about as she tried to remember the actor's name.

'Yeah, I suppose so. I mean, I have been a good girl this year, after all.'

Jenny snorted loudly. 'You? A good girl? If you say so, Pinocchio.'

'It's true.'

Jenny pointed at Kelly's short skirt. 'Oh look, someone call the fire brigade as your pants are on fire now.'

'Bugger off and hush your noise. I'm an upstanding pillar of the community, don't you know,' Kelly said, sticking her nose up in the air.

'Upstanding pillars of the community don't spend most of their time trying to chat up teenagers that are barely out of pampers.'

'What time did you say your appointment was?' Kelly was glaring at her now.

'Eh? What appointment, I haven't got no appointment?'

'Well you frigging need one, to get your head seen to. You're on one today, my love,' Kelly said, fishing about in her yellow handbag for something.

'Sorry, me head's killing me this morning'.

'So then,' Kelly said, lighting up a cigarette from the packet she had just retrieved from her handbag and inhaling deeply, causing the end of the cigarette to glow a bright red. 'Talking of Benny boy, dish the dirt, Florence Nightingale,' she continued, taking a swig from her can of cherry flavoured pop.

Jenny looked at her nails, pretending to be shy. 'I'm not one to kiss 'n' tell.'

'Uh-huh. So nothing happened then?' Kelly said, taking a knowing drag on her cigarette.

'No. Not a bastard thing. He barely said *thanks* when I dropped him home. Even after I offered to go in and make him a cup of tea.'

'The ungrateful sod.'

'I know. He's still beautiful though, isn't he. I certainly wouldn't push him out of bed in the morning.'

'He is that. Perhaps he was delirious and not in his right mind?' Kelly said helpfully, picking at a scab on her elbow.

'Yeah, that must be it,' Jenny said thoughtfully. 'I mean, who wouldn't want me?'

'Oh well, it's the silly boy's loss. Come on then, let's do this shopping and then we can get off home and you can get some kip. Try and become human again, rather than a miserable cow bag with a face like Theresa May.'

Stuffing their litter into the already full rubbish bin, they made their way down the High Street. Kelly linked arms with Jenny as they walked away, already moaning about the price of vodka in supermarkets these days. Flaming Brexit.

Thirty-Seven

Harry

'Okay everyone, let's try that scene again,' Harry said, sitting back down in his chair once more and rubbing the sides of his temple with his index fingers in a circular motion. He'd read somewhere online that doing this was meant to relieve stress and tension almost immediately, but the evil cretins had been lying. 'Right,' he continued, 'from the top of page, uh, twenty-one please everyone. And, Ben, I think you should slow down a little bit when you're speaking, as you're rushing it slightly. Remember, we need good clear diction from everyone please.' His last comment was directed at all the cast, to not make Ben feel singled out any more than he already had been that evening. 'Aaaaaand......ACTION,' he said, trying to be full of enthusiasm and motivation like the Internet article had told him to be.

Ben shuffled onto the stage area, with about as much charisma and enthusiasm as a prisoner on death row walking the green mile. 'Oh, how weary I am,' Ben said flatly. 'For I have been walking for,' Ben stopped to check the scrunched-up script that was in his hand, which he did so with some difficulty, as he still had a large bandage around his injured left little finger. 'For days and days now. And night is fast approaching, and, and, and,' he examined the script once more, 'yet I still have no lodgings.'

For the love of God. This is going to take us all night at this pace, Harry thought, massaging his temples with renewed vigour.

'If only there was a place for me,' Ben looked down at the script again, 'to rest my tired feet for the night.'

Onto the stage came Jessica, playing the part of Dick Whittington's Cat. 'Purr, purr, why hello there. And who might you be? Purr, purr,' Jessica said, walking up the stage and in a circle around Ben, before miming washing her paws with her tongue and overacting a little.

Ok, ok, we can work with this, after all panto is all about overacting, Harry thought, but then he saw Ben looking at his script again and changed his mind. *Come on, Ben. It's not rocket science here.* Harry paused his thoughts for a second. *Perhaps I'm being too harsh, this is only the second rehearsal after all....but everyone else seems to have mastered most of their lines already.*

'Hello there, little cat,' Ben said eventually, sounding like the computer voice that professor Stephen Hawking uses. 'I am Dick Whittington of Wellington, on my way to London to find my fame and fortune.'

'To London you say? Purr, purr. Why my big friend, you are very nearly there, for you are on the outskirts of that great city, purr, purr.' There was more mime washing of her face from Jessica.

'Thank goodness, as I have been travelling for,' he glanced down at the script, 'days and days, and I am hungry and tired and need shelter and some lodgings.'

'Why, purr, purr, there is a large mansion house, but not a short distance from here.'

Why do all of the scenes that Valerie wrote sound like ruddy Shakespeare? I thought pantomime was meant to be funny? Harry ran his hands through his hair.

'Is that where you live, little cat?' Ben continued.

'Why no, purr, purr. I too have no home and am looking for shelter for the night, as it is growing cold and the rain clouds are nearly overhead, and if it rains I'll be a wet pussy.'

There was some sniggering from somewhere behind Harry.

'Shall we go there together then and see if the owner will take pity on us?' said Ben.

'Yes, let's. Shall I lead the way, big Dick of Wellington?'

Ben stuttered and once again looked down at the papers that were held tightly in his hand.

Oh for goodness' sake, Harry thought. *Why is he checking the script for the answer, I would have thought it would have been fairly obvious what it would be.* Harry got up and started to pace backwards and forwards, as the drama - or distinct lack of it - unfolded before his eyes.

'Why yes please, little pussy.'

'My name is Patch, purr, purr.'

'It is indeed a pleasure to meet you, Patch.'

The two of them walked a couple of circuits around the stage, until Jessica stopped and turned to Harry. 'Sorry, Harry, just a thought here, but could the two of them hold hands? You know, show to the audience that the two of them have a special bond from the outset?' she said.

Five minutes on stage, and everyone thinks they're a director all of a sudden, Harry thought, but the words that came out of his mouth instead were, 'What a great idea, Jessica, well done. But do you think it might be a little odd for a man to be holding hands with a cat?'

Jessica gave it some serious thought before replying, 'I suppose. Never mind, sorry for the interruption, Harry.'

'Not at all, not at all. And once again…..ACTION.' *Just follow the flaming script pleeeease. Good grief, I'm sure Steven Spielberg doesn't have these problems.*

Ben and Jessica did one more loop of the stage before coming to a halt.

'Ok,' said Harry. 'Imagine there's the set in front of you. There's a porch way and a big wooden door right where you are.'

'Shall I knock at the door?' Ben asked Harry.

'What do the script's stage directions tell you to do?' Harry said, trying really, really hard to keep the sarcasm out of his voice.

Ben checked the script. 'It just says that they knock.'

'Excellent, in that case, you should knock,' Harry said, hoping that his face didn't betray his true emotions.

'Ok, cool, just checking that it wasn't meant to be the Cat knocking.'

'Fine, now that we've got that cleared up, let's continue,' Harry said dryly. *How I am going to find the energy for my night shift at the police station after this, I have no idea. Perhaps secretly raid the seized drugs locker?*

'KNOCK, KNOCK, KNOCK,' said Ben loudly, raising his hand and acting out the motion with his fist.

'That's a big one,' said Jessica.

'Yes, I like big knockers.

'There doesn't seem to be anyone at home this evening.'

'I think you're right, little Patch.'

'But it's starting to rain, what shall we do?' Jessica said, looking up and shivering.

'Why,' Ben checked his script, 'we could sleep here this evening. This porch is big enough for us both to escape the rain and sleep under for the night.'

'What a good idea, clever Dick.'

'If only we could have a wash as well, as I haven't had a shave today.'

'Oh that's alright, I like whiskers.'

Hopefully pause for laughter, Harry thought, *if not, we're really in the shit, as that's one of the better deliberate comedy lines that Valerie's written.*

Ben and Jessica then lay down on the floor of the stage, and pretended to go to sleep.

Harry stopped pacing. 'Thanks, you two, you can get up again now. Alright everyone, shall we take five minutes and grab a drink quickly. We've been going for quite a while now, so let's take a break,' he announced to the room. He then turned and looked over at Andrew for an indication of how he thought it had gone. Catching Andrew's gaze, Harry raised his eyebrows in a, *Well, what do you think?* expression. The look that Andrew gave to Harry confirmed that they were both thinking along the same lines. His suspicions confirmed, he decided to go and have a chat with Ben, who he saw was now sat by himself with his script in his hands. Taking a swig of water from his bottle and wishing it was something stronger, Harry walked over to where Ben was sat, and plonked himself down next to the young man and smiled kindly. 'Hey.'

Ben looked up and gave him a forlorn smile. 'Sorry about that, Harry.'

'Don't worry. So how do you feel that went then?'

'Well I'm not going to win any awards, am I?' he said, resting his head in his good hand and sighing.

Harry stretched out his legs in front of him. 'Look, don't beat yourself up too much about it. It's only our second rehearsal, so we still have plenty of time.'

'I guess,' he looked down at his feet.

'It'll be easier once you have learnt all of your lines. That way it will flow a lot better, as you'll be able to concentrate on your acting and delivery, rather than just trying to remember what your lines are.'

'Sorry about that, work has been a bit manic recently and my boss is on the warpath, so I've not had a lot of time to concentrate on learning them.'

'Just keep going over them whenever you get the chance. You'll nail it, okay?' Harry looked at Ben and winked.

'Okay, thanks Harry.'

'No worries, now go and get yourself a brew,' Harry said, bumping shoulders with Ben gently.

As Ben got up and wandered off, Harry thought to himself, *No wonder the banks caused the global meltdown, if they're all like him.* Standing up again, he said to the room, 'Alright everyone, just a few more minutes then we're going to move onto the next scene. Can we have Ben, Jessica, Darren and Helen ready to start scene four shortly please.' *Unless anyone wants to put me out of my misery and whack me around the back of my head with a shovel?*

Thirty-Eight

Ben

Closing a long email he had just spent five minutes reading, Ben sighed as he sat at his desk at work. He was feeling pissed off. After his incident with the power saw the other week, the bank had agreed that he would be able to continue working, but only on light duties behind the scenes at the office, rather than out the front with the customers. At first, this had sounded like a godsend to Ben. No more whining customers with their kids that grabbed your tie with their dirty fingers. Or emptied out your business cards from their little box all over your desk. Or the ones that crawled under the table and switched the computer off, just as you were about to finalise a long and complicated mortgage application with Mr and Mrs Body Odour of Dimshitvill. However, light duties actually translated to being "the bitch" for his boss. And The Wicked Witch of the West Country was doing her utmost to make his working life as miserable as she possibly could. When he wasn't making her tea and organising her business accommodation for upcoming meetings, she made him do filing. Which because of his injured finger, took an eternity to do and sent his frustration levels up to the stratosphere, where he would rain down cosmic rays on his boss' head. He was craving a cigarette badly, but he couldn't justify spending the money. He'd even resorted to having a sneaky peak in a couple of his colleagues' desks for any, but his search had produced nothing – although he now knew who was pinching all of the Post-it-Notes.

Another thing that was causing his stress levels to rise and make him want to take up smoking again was this pantomime palaver. *Who in their right mind cast me as Dick Whittington?* A thought that he had had on numerous occasions. It was starting to keep him awake at night now, which meant that he was always tired, which didn't aid his line learning abilities. He was spending hours reading and rereading through his many, many lines, but it just didn't seem to be sinking in. He was in most the scenes, and he could barely remember the lines for *one* of the scenes, let alone all of them.

He had hoped that when his finger had been chopped off, that Harry might take pity on him and ask if he wanted to stand down from playing the part, but oh no, he had just told him some rubbish about being lucky that they could sew it back on again. Ben certainly didn't feel very lucky, and was seriously considering feigning some exotic tropical illness to try and get him out of the show; he had even been searching the Internet for the symptoms of the really contagious ones. The only thing was, that in order to be totally convincing, he would have to be off work sick as well, and his Bradford Factor sick level was already looking dire, and the Wicked Witch had warned him gleefully at his last return to work interview that the next time he was off, it would trigger a formal review – which he knew she would take great delight in pulling out of her cauldron.

He continued to stab his stress ball with a paperclip that he had bent out of shape to form a small spear, imagining it was his boss and he was carrying out his own version of a voodoo ceremony. The Wicked Witch wasn't in the office today, as she was out for a couple of days at a new branch of the bank, undoubtedly perfecting her spells. However, she had just sent Ben an email with a great long list of menial tasks to complete by her return at the end of the week. He was really tempted to just delete the email and deny all knowledge of it. But, knowing her, she would get the IT department involved and prove that he had received it and then deleted it. She would then say this was gross misconduct and fire him with a smile on her face, and although he detested her very existence with a fiery passion, he needed this job and the pay that it brought in – or the pantomime would be the last of his worries.

He often dreamt of winning the Lotto, and how he would take great delight in telling her where to stick her job; and if he thought he would be able to get away with it, look at how much the going rate was for a contract killer with a fondness for slow torture. But until that day arrived, he would just have to make do with his voodoo and replace the stress ball once it had too many holes in it.

He looked at his emails, and wondered how hard it would be to hack into the Wicked Witch's email account and start sending rudely worded emails to her boss. If only he'd listened during his GCSE ICT classes all those years ago, instead of trying to chat up the one girl in the class, he might have a clue about where to start. The only lesson he did remember was when the teacher, a Mr Edmund, had been showing them how to operate Google Earth. He had persuaded the class to wave their hands out of the classroom window, and had convinced the dimmer members of the group that he could see them waving their hands from the Google Earth image on the computer. A couple of those class members were now working at a fast food restaurant, so they had obviously put their grade E in ICT to good use.

He looked around the small open plan office that was up on the second floor of the town centre building, since there was no one else here as all his colleagues were downstairs with the great British public. He opened his desk drawer where his mobile phone was hidden and checked to see if there were any messages. There were the usual six texts from Jessica babbling on about going to the Ikea store in Bristol at the weekend to get some ideas for new bedroom furniture and asking him how much his budget was. *About one pound twenty-five to be honest, sweetheart,* he thought, as he locked his phone again. He still hadn't come up with a plan to pay back the money he owed to the loan shark, and he was starting to fear for his fingers and toes; having nearly lost one finger, he certainly didn't fancy permanently losing anything else.

His phone lit up, notifying him silently of a message, and this time it was a text from Chelsea. He grinned to himself as he unlocked his phone again with his fingerprint and tilted back in his swivel chair to give it his full attention. The message contained just one word, "Lunch?"

He quickly swiped out a response. *Sounds good as need to escape this prison. Where and when? X*

As he waited less than patiently for the reply, he worried about whether he should have added the kiss at the end of the text or not.

His phone lit up again with another message. Reading it hurriedly, he grinned, and logged out of his secure banking profile, all thoughts of hacking into his boss' account forgotten. Grabbing his jacket from the back of his chair, he set off for the stairwell and the temporary freedom of the outside world.

Thirty-Nine

Ben

Stepping into the street with other pedestrians shuffling by, Ben automatically felt the pockets of his thick coat for his packet of cigarettes as he always did, before remembering and tutting loudly. *Old habits die hard,* he thought, zipping his black coat up to the top and then stuffing his hands deep into his pockets to save them from the cold October wind, being careful with his injured hand.

He had been feeling a bit morose for the last few days, but the fact that Chelsea wanted to see him had lifted his spirits and his heart was racing and he could feel his face flush, despite the cold air.

Chelsea had suggested that they meet for a coffee and grab a bite to eat from the food to go section at the M&S near to where she worked. The walk wasn't too far for Ben to go, which was just as well as he wanted to use every second that he could of his lunch break to spend with her. He knew that she was completely out of his league, hell, she was out of ninety-nine percent of men's leagues, which probably explained why she was still single. He knew he didn't have a chance with her, but he still was excited that she had asked him to lunch. Oh, and just the small fact that he had a girlfriend already wasn't ideal. Attempting to push the guilty thoughts of Jessica out of his head, he strode quickly on towards his rendezvous point.

Spying her up ahead he tried to control his heart rate; he felt like he was on a first date, feeling the excitement and nervous anticipation flood through his veins like a shot of tequila on an empty stomach. *Shit, I didn't check my breath,* the thought flashing through his brain at lightning speed, along with about a million reasons why he shouldn't have met her, and a billion reasons why he needed to.

Seeing him approaching and waving her hand, a smile growing on her face, Chelsea greeted him, leaning in and kissing him when he finally reached her.

'Hello, you look red, did you run here?' she asked, as they turned up the street together and started walking towards M&S.

'Err, no, it's just hot at work,' he said unzipping his jacket slightly to cool himself down.

'Yeah?'

'Yeah, the air con is stuck at twenty-six degrees,' he lied.

'At least you're not cold, my place is always cold, what with all the sick people coming in and out of the door all the time. I wish they would just stay outside in the cold and die quietly.'

Missing her joke completely, a thousand thoughts flashed through Ben's mind about how he could warm her up and his cheeks started to burn again.

'Mustard be good in the summer though,' he said, his self-consciousness about his red cheeks causing him to jumble up his sentence. 'Must be,' he corrected himself quickly.

'Been drinking at work again?' she asked with a smile, as they turned into the shop's main entrance. Chelsea picked up a shopping basket as they walked past a stack of them and a bored looking security guard, who was looking at the screen of his mobile phone.

'Well, there has to be some perks of the boss being away.'

'Just make sure you get rid of all the empty bottles,' she said, as they navigated their way around a small elderly lady with a walking stick, who reminded Ben of Yoda.

'Oh, that's given me a great idea, I could fill her desk up with empty wine bottles and send a picture to her boss, drop her in the shit.'

'Paving the way for your promotion?'

'No chance. I've got too much common sense to be in management.'

'Are you sure that's what's holding you back?' she asked, as she weaved past another old lady. This one was holding up a giant pair of pants against her, obviously trying to guess her size and if they would fit her.

'Of course. Bloody hell, you could fit the Bake-Off contestants inside that tent she was holding up,' he muttered to her.

'Big pants are back in you know,' she winked at him, which caused his heart to flutter. Not really knowing what to say, he opted to stay silent in case he embarrassed himself by saying anything inappropriate.

Unless she's flirting with me, quick, think of something funny to say back.

Reaching the food-to-go section of the shop, she scanned the shelves in front of them and asked, 'I'm just going to grab a sandwich or something. Maybe a wrap, what are you having?'

You missed your chance, you gert numpty. 'Umm, yeah, I'll just grab a sarnie too. Holy smokes, have you seen the names of some of these? "Shredded caramelised onion, with flakes of goat's cheese", is this for real?'

'Have you not seen grown up food before, Benjamin? What does Jessica feed you? I must have a word with her.'

Ben very nearly replied with "Jessica who?", but managing to stop himself in time, the guilty thoughts returning quickly to the forefront of his mind. Attempting to push them aside, he replied, 'I'll have you know, her spag bol is the talk of the South West.'

Laughing gently, she selected a wrap, checking the calorie count on the front for a brief few seconds, and placed it in her basket, followed by a bottle of sparkling water.

Ben continued to stare at the choice of food, before opting for the cheapest one they had, not even paying attention to what the filling was, picking it up with his non-injured hand.

'Not having a drink?' she asked.

'Na, had a load of coffee before I came on lunch,' he fibbed, not willing to spend more money than he had to, and wanting to buy a scratch card on his way home; just in case it was his lucky day.

'Ah, ok. Well you can always have a swig of my water if you want.'

Is that flirting? I think that's definitely flirting this time, he thought, *quick, you need to say something funny - NOW.* 'Err, thanks.'

'I'll pay,' she offered.

'No, no, I couldn't let you do that,' he replied, hoping that she did, as he only had a few pounds left in his bank account overdraft.

'My treat, you can get them next time, after you've set up your own Christmas business and are rolling in money.'

There's going to be a next time. 'Deal, thanks Chelsea,' he said gratefully.

They queued in silence, along with all the other shoppers, edging closer and closer like a solemn funeral march to the front, paying the overly enthusiastic employee and then finally leaving the shop. The big pants lady wasn't there on their way out, so she must have made her selection. Ben shuddered at the thought.

Pointing at a vacant bench that thankfully wasn't covered in pigeon mess, Chelsea led the way over and they sat down, with only a small gap between them, as if a magnet were pulling them together, his planet caught in the gravity of her celestial body.

Handing him his food first, she then opened her chickpea wrap and looking hungry, bit into it. Glancing at him and his sandwich carton she nodded, 'You need a hand opening that?' she asked.

'Na, should be fine, I've kinda become used to it now,' Ben said, as he gingerly opened his sandwich, trying to avoid the carton touching his bandaged little finger. He took out one half of the sandwich and took a bite. Grated cheese fell onto his jacket and he felt like a slob in front of her. He quickly brushed them away, cursing that he had bought a cheese and pickle sandwich. But at least it wasn't egg mayonnaise – that could have been worse.

'So, Ben,' she said, after a few more bites of her wrap, with not a single crumb or morsel of food dropping onto her coat.

OMG, what is she going to say?

'I've been thinking.'

Yes, yes, I will marry you and father your children. We should have four I think. Two boys and two girls. I can take the boys camping and you can teach the girls all the clever things you know.

'Are you ok?'

What? 'Umm, what?'

'Are you ok? I've noticed that you didn't seem to be yourself at the last rehearsal.'

Oh bollocks. That's what she's wanting to chat about. He could feel himself deflate inside, as if someone has burst his heart with a knitting needle made of cold, cold steel.

He gave a little sigh. 'Yeah, I'm ok, I guess.' *Go for the sympathy vote.* 'It's just that I've got a lot on my plate at the moment.'

'If you want to talk, you know where I am.'

Breathe, breathe. 'I know, thank you. I guess it's just a few things really.' *Don't tell her about the loan sharks, she'll think you're even more of a loser than she already does.* 'I must admit, I'm feeling really out of my depth with the panto.' *Which is true.*

'I was reading through your lines. It is a lot to learn, isn't it?'

She was reading my lines? Perhaps she does like me after all? Why else would she want to read through that crap? He felt his heart flutter. 'It is, yeah. A hell of a lot.' He looked at her with what he hoped were puppy-dog eyes.

'I'm sure you'll get there, and if you ever need a hand practising your lines, I'm more than happy to help you know,' she said as she took a delicate sip from her bottle of water, before offering it to him. He shook his head slightly.

Cha-chink. She does like me after all. Ed Sheeran's song *kiss me* filled his head.

'But I'm sure Jessica is helping you out anyway, as you're both in a lot of the same scenes,' she continued before he could answer.

Unfortunately. 'Yeah, we have been going over them together, but it might help to go through them with someone else as well.'

She checked her watch. 'Well the offer is there, so just let me know if you want some help, and I'll happily do it with you.'

I'll happily do it with you too. I'd do anything with you. 'That would be great, thanks,' he said, biting into his sandwich again. He chewed and swallowed before asking, 'How are you getting on with your lines?'

She bobbed her head up and down, which caused a strand of hair to fall onto her cheek. 'Yeah, getting there I think. But I'm only in a couple of the scenes, I'm not the star, unlike you.'

'No pressure then.' *She thinks I'm a star...*

She brushed the stray hair up behind her ear. 'You'll be fine, you'll see,' she said, and gently swatted his shoulder. 'How's the finger?'

He held his hand up. 'Yeah, it's ok. Still throbs quite a bit and I'm on antibiotics to fight off any infections, but the docs seem to think it's healing ok. I'm just glad they managed to sew the thing back on to be honest with you.'

'You were very lucky. Who was your doctor?'

'Um, Doctor Berry.'

'Oh yeah, I know her. She's good.'

Checking her watch for a second time, Chelsea said, 'Blast it, look at the time, I've got to go. We're short staffed today, and they've sent us a useless locum to help out. He's already dropped half of our stock on the floor this morning. It's playing havoc with the paperwork.' Leaning in, she kissed Ben on the cheek and put a friendly arm around his shoulder. 'You take care of yourself, and if you need a hand with your lines, you know where I am. Just believe in yourself and you'll be fine. Just don't cut off any more of your body parts.'

Shall I kiss her, shall I kiss her? 'I'll try not to,' he managed to stutter. Standing up and brushing yet more stray cheese off his jacket he followed suit.

'See you later, Ben. Have a good afternoon and don't forget to hide those wine bottles,' she said. Giving him a hug, she then crossed over the road, waved at him and re-entered her pharmacy, pulling the door firmly shut behind her.

He checked the time on his phone and swore. He rushed back to the office, aware that he was now a few minutes late. He suddenly remembered that he still hadn't replied to Jessica's texts from earlier and made a mental note to reply when he got back upstairs to the office; which he promptly forgot to do when he logged onto this emails and saw how many he had been sent in the short time that he had been away at lunch.

As Jessica watched Ben rushing back into the bank, a single tear rolled down her pale cheek and landed on her stripy scarf, the one that she had chosen herself after Ben had forgotten her birthday back in July.

Forty

Polly

The COBRA (Children Ordered to Bed Right Away) meeting was taking place at the Berwick's house, as Polly couldn't find a babysitter for the three children. She did feel bad about the last one, who had quit after having Sellotape wound around her head, resulting in a very painful two hours trying to remove it from her hair. Polly shared Harry's worry that they had been put on some sort of babysitting blacklist, as they hadn't been able to find a replacement. This was despite a number of pleading phone calls to their friends who had children of an appropriately responsible age to babysit their monsters. The children had been sent to their rooms, which after tears, tantrums and the paint that had been thrown down the stairs had been cleaned up, had now been successfully achieved.

In preparation for Valerie's arrival, Polly had cleared away the toys, the carpets had been vacuumed and Harry had been made to trim his beard, as she had told him that he looked like a vagrant, but with only *slightly* better dress sense.

Polly was now sat on the recently vacuumed sofa drinking her second vodka and tomato juice of the evening, seriously wondering if she could run away to her friend Sue's house. Sue wisely didn't have children. Sue also always had a large supply of vodka. *The great thing about vodka*, Polly thought, swirling the thick red liquid in her glass around, *is that you can put it in almost any drink and no one knows it's there.*

She downed the rest of her drink, letting the warm haze that the couple of drinks had given her wash over her and she could feel her stress levels falling. She then remembered that Valerie was due to arrive in the next five minutes or so, so she got up and headed for the kitchen and the half empty vodka bottle, not even caring that it wasn't even seven o'clock yet and she was about to have her third drink of the evening. It was nearly the weekend after all.

Harry came downstairs and stood at the bottom of the staircase, looking at her quizzically. She grinned at him, knowing that her eyes would give her away.

'Are you pissed?' he asked, raising an eyebrow.

'Not yet I'm not,' she toasted him with her glass and took a big sip.

He looked at her for a few seconds before saying, 'You've remembered that the Ice Queen is about to arrive any second?' He put his hands on his hips.

She nodded. 'Yep. And you've trimmed your beard like I asked. Well done, Harry.'

'Thanks. Why are you talking to me like one of your schoolchildren?'

'Why are you talking to me like PC Plod?'

'Because you're drunk and disorderly,' the doorbell went. 'Now just behave when she's here. I'll go around the back and let her in.'

'We should have met her at the pub,' Polly called after him, putting her drink down. She then picked it back up, had another sip, before placing it back down carefully on the coaster.

'I don't think she knows what one of those is,' he called back, as he went out of the back door and along the side of the house to show Valerie in.

Polly went to stand up, but felt a little light-headed, so decided to sit back down. This was one of the dangers of being just an occasional drinker; when she did drink, she was a complete lightweight. *Come on, focus, focus, focus,* she thought, trying to work out what to do with her hands to try and act like she wasn't half cut on cheap vodka and not-from-concentrate tomato juice. The approaching muffled talking announced their arrival, and she put on her best welcoming smile.

Forty-One

Valerie

With her hands resting in her lap, Valerie sat on the sofa wondering why Polly was grinning so much and had said "hello" to her three times. She had dealt with many different people over the years and was accustomed to dealing with most situations. This had ranged from aggravated parents, to children with broken arms on the school playing field, to cleaners falling out with each other over someone else using their precious mop and teachers being caught sleeping at work because they had been kicked out of the marital home; but she was starting to feel uncertain about the woman that was sat opposite her, especially since Polly had started rubbing her hands together menacingly.

She had read in *The Times* about these serial killer types, the ones that befriend you first and slowly pulled you into their web of lies and deceit, making you trust them, before they struck, and a body was being fished out of a manhole with important bits missing. She felt inside her handbag to see if she still had that mobile phone contraption in there that Gerald insisted she take with her "in case of emergencies". Yes, it was there, but she couldn't remember if she had charged the blasted thing recently or not, or even which of the buttons it was that switched it on. If she made it out of here alive, she would instruct Gerald to show her.

Harry was in the kitchen finishing off making the drinks, and she was suddenly struck cold by a thought that sent a shiver down her spine. *What if he's poisoning my drink? Lacing it with a barbiturate of some sort? Being a police officer, he would surely have readily available access to such things? And of course, no one would suspect a policeman of being a serial killer.*

It was just then that Harry came into the room with a tray in his hands with all the drinks on. He was also grinning like a hyped-up toddler at a petting zoo.

'Here you go, Valerie. Earl Grey tea as ordered,' he said, putting down a cup and saucer on the small coffee table that was next to the chair that she was sitting on.

'Thank you,' Valerie replied uncertainly. She looked at the liquid in the cup to see if it looked a strange colour, but couldn't quite tell in the lamplight.

'And another tomato juice for you, darling,' he said, handing Polly a tall glass. Sitting down next to her, he leaned the tray up against the side of the sofa and took a sip of his drink, which looked like either blackcurrant squash or a very weak red wine.

'Are neither of you having any tea?' Valerie asked hesitantly.

Harry looked shiftily at his wife for a few seconds before answering her question. 'Polly's had enough.....tea for today. And I try not to drink it after lunchtime, otherwise the caffeine keeps me awake at night. My body clock is skew whiff enough with the shifts I do, without confusing it with excess caffeine.'

A plausible answer, Valerie thought, but still not trusting her drink entirely just yet, she picked up her cup and pretended to have a sip, but gave it a good sniff, to try and detect any unusual aromas coming from it. Alas, as Earl Grey is scented anyway, she was none the wiser. Instead, she placed the cup back down on the saucer and decided to get down to business, so that she could escape this madhouse as soon as possible. She would then speak to Gerald, and demand that he got in touch with his old workplace and have these two thoroughly vetted. After all, there had to be some perks of being married to a retired spook.

'Thank you both for agreeing to meet. I think we all know what it is we need to talk about,' she said, examining them over the top of her glasses that rested on the end of her nose.

'Is it the tea making incident?' Polly said, and Valerie froze. 'As if it is, I am sorry for putting so many tea bags into the pot, I'm not sure what I was thinking really, putting seventeen teabags into the pot – ha! I will of course pay for a new box of tea myself.'

Harry took another sip of his drink, trying to hide a smile, but Valerie had clocked it.

'What? No, no, it's nothing to do with that. Why on earth do you think I would want to call a senior executive meeting to talk about something as trivial as that?'

Polly just looked confused, and as Harry wasn't volunteering to speak either, Valerie sighed and filled in the blanks for them. 'Ben. We need to talk about Ben.'

'Good grief, he's not suing us over his chopped off finger, is he?' Polly said, raising a hand to her mouth.

Valerie felt inside her handbag once more, and this time held onto her mobile phone in case she needed to summon help in a hurry. It also crossed her mind that she might be able to inflict some damage with her fountain pen. 'No, he most certainly isn't doing that. And I think it wise that no one should put that idea into his head either,' she said dryly. 'What we really need to discuss is Ben's acting ability.'

'Ahh,' said Harry and Polly at the same time.

'I think we can all agree that his acting is quite evidently substandard. Which is why we originally cast him as the

Island King in the first place, so that we would only have to endure him in a couple of scenes and his dialogue was purposefully minimal. Quite frankly, if it was anyone else then they wouldn't have got a part at all.' She pulled her handbag an inch closer to her.

'I wish we had found out who changed the casting list that the vicar read out,' Harry said shaking his head.

Valerie shifted slightly in her seat. 'Yes, quite. If only that error had been spotted before it was handed to the vicar to read out, then we wouldn't be in this situation at all, would we?' Valerie said accusingly.

'Well I didn't realise that the list had been sabotaged with Tipex, and I didn't think that anyone in a church would do such a thing,' Harry said quickly.

'Yes, it's not Harry's fault,' Polly said in agreement.

Valerie looked from Harry to Polly and back to Harry again. 'I'm not saying it is. Anyway, what's done is done and we need to discuss what we are going to do about it.'

There was silence.

'Any suggestions?' she said, feeling her tolerance running out.

Harry shrugged his shoulders, 'I'm not sure there is anything we can do is there? Surely, it's too late now to do anything about it?'

'I think the time to replace him has come and gone, perhaps we should have taken action straight away after the service where it was announced,' Polly added, obviously trying to be helpful, but failing.

Valerie clenched her teeth before speaking. 'As I said just now, what's done is done. But I really think it would be to the detriment of the production if we left him playing the lead role.'

Harry held his hands up, 'I just don't see what other options we have to be honest with you. I think it would be cruel to take this part away from him, regardless of how frustrating it is that he doesn't know his lines yet. I think he will get better, he just needs a bit more time, and he'll get there.'

Valerie looked at Harry, hoping that her face portrayed that he had just suggested something as ludicrous as invading France and claiming it as an extension of the British Empire. 'Do you really think that, Harry?'

Harry looked at his feet for a few moments. 'I'm not sure, but really, Valerie, what can we do? And who would we replace him with? The girl that we originally cast in the role, Kate Taylor, is now apparently starring in Chicago, with one of the local am-dram groups. None of the others we auditioned were up to the part.'

The silence echoed around the room for a few seconds and on top of the piano, Valerie watched as the cat stood up on all four legs, stretched, turned around a few times and then settled back down on top of a small fluffy blanket that had perhaps been placed on top of the piano to stop it being scratched. Valerie sighed dramatically, went to pick up her cup, before retracting her hand at the last moment.

Harry tapped his finger on the side of his drink a couple of times, his wedding ring dinging against the glass as he did so. 'Look, we've still got some time. Perhaps I'll suggest to Ben that I give him some extra rehearsal time with a couple of the other characters. Or perhaps even with just me or Polly reading the lines. Practice makes perfect and all that jazz.'

Deciding that she was getting nowhere and that it was time to make a sharp exit, Valerie smiled thinly at him. 'You're the director, Harry. I just want this to be successful.

But if you're confident that it will be fine, I will leave it in your hands.'

'Let's just give him a little more time, eh,' he smiled back at her, clearly misreading the look she had just given him.

'As I said, Harry, you're the director, so I will leave the decision up to you. I just wanted to air my personal thoughts on the matter.'

'I do share your concerns as well, I'm just trying to deal with the situation as sensitively as I can.'

'Quite. Now, I will get going and leave you good people in peace to enjoy the rest of your evening,' she went to stand up.

'You're not fishing your tea? I mean, *finishing* your tea?' Polly asked, slowing down her words as she spoke.

'I'm, umm, fine thank you, Polly.'

'Are you sure, you've gone a little red?' Polly looked at her, concern on her face.

'Yes, yes, quite sure. I've just decided to take some of Harry's advice and not have any caffeine this time of the evening, what with bedtime only a few hours away.'

Valerie stood up fully and brushed the creases out of her thick woollen skirt and placed her mobile phone back into the recesses of her handbag, but she didn't zip the bag up, just in case. She wasn't out of the woods yet. 'Harry, would you be so kind as to fetch my overcoat for me.'

'Yes of course,' Harry stood up too, and looked at his wife. He then went off to fetch her coat from wherever he had hung it up. He returned quickly and handed Valerie her coat.

'Well, goodbye Polly, Harry, I'll see you both soon,' and with that she marched off through the kitchen and out of the back door to her freedom.

Harry looked at Polly, and he went to open his mouth.

'Well that was weird,' Polly began, beating him to it.

'I think we pissed her off about saying to leave Ben where he is,' Harry said, scratching his beard.

'Oi, less of this "we" business. You did all the talking there, mister. You can take full responsibility for pissing her off.'

'Oh. Well that's great, now you too.'

'What do you mean?' She looked at him.

'She was clearly passing the buck with her speech at the end, saying that I'm the director so the decision lies with me. In other words, if it all goes tits up, then I'm the one that the fingers get pointed at, not her,' he sighed, wishing he had a beer in front of him.

'Oh, I hadn't noticed that.'

'And what was it with her not drinking her tea? Normally she gulps it down and then is quick to tell me that I haven't made it to her exact specification.'

'Yeah, that was odd. Perhaps she just wasn't thirsty after all. Crazy old witch.'

'I don't know. I saw her reach for it a couple of times and then take her hand away.' Harry walked over and picked up the cup and saucer and looked at it. 'Well it's not chipped or anything,' he continued. 'I thought perhaps she had a bag on because I had dared give her a chipped cup.'

Polly plumped up the cushion that he had just been leaning against. 'Well, whatever it was, let's make sure that we do it again when she next comes around. I think that was the shortest visit by her majesty ever.'

'Do you want her tea? Seems a shame to let it go to waste,' he said.

'Are you serious? I don't want her leftover tea. I might catch some old lady disease from her or something. Besides, it smells like potpourri that stuff.'

'Oh well, I'll just chuck it away. Strange woman.'

'I tell you what, I will have another vodka and tomato juice though,' she said, waggling her empty glass at him and grinning.

Forty-Two

Harry

Yawning, Harry slumped down in his seat and rubbed his eyes, wishing that he had stopped off and bought some paracetamol from the shop across the way before coming to tonight's rehearsal. He picked up his battered copy of the script, opened it, and flicked through the pages that had notes scribbled all over them, until he found the one that he was looking for.

On the make-shift stage at the end of the room, the set door swung open wide, and onto stage right proudly stomped Darren, looking as masterful as he could muster. He theatrically looked around the stage before putting his hands up to his mouth, miming a megaphone and bellowed out loud.

'Fair daughter, young Dick, my household staff, I have returned from my meeting with Captain Shaw and I have good news to share.'

There was a pause for a few seconds, before the trudging of feet could be heard coming from the stage left area. Shortly after, Chelsea and Ben appeared together as their characters.

'Father,' said Chelsea, running up to Darren and embracing him.

'Mr Fitzgerald,' said Ben, who walked awkwardly up to Darren and shook his hand.

'Good morning to you both and goodness me, brrrr, it's cold out there this morning. Which reminds me, the new instructor at the ice cream parlour in town is also a sundae school teacher,' Darren looked out at the audience, then back at Ben and Chelsea.

Off stage, Harry started to rub his temples with his fingers.

'What news do you have from Captain Shaw, father?' Chelsea asked.

'I met Captain Shaw by the seesaw on the sea shore front, as he has finally returned from his voyage and come ashore.'

'Was his voyage a success?' Ben asked as Dick Whittington, trying to sound enthusiastic.

Harry mentally cheered that Ben had opened the set door the right way this time and remembered both his first and second lines. Perhaps this scene would finally come together - and it would be about time, as this was the fifth time they had rehearsed it this evening, and he could tell that frustration amongst the group was growing.

'It was, my boy, but it was first struck with tragedy.' The hall was then filled with the music of Steps and their late nineties hit for a very long five seconds.

'It sounds like that adventure's better best forgotten!' said Ben with gusto.

'What tragedy befell them, father?' Chelsea asked, returning to Darren's side and putting her hand on his arm.

'Captain Shaw and his gallant crew were shipwrecked on the shore, after their ship ran aground during a violent storm.'

'Goodness, were there any injuries?' Ben asked, concern etched on his face.

This is good, we're getting there this time, Harry thought, his knees jigging up and up.

'Thankfully not. And as luck would have it, they happened upon an inhabited island kingdom.'

'Full of rats you say? That's a long tail indeed,' Ben said.

Uh-oh, Harry thought, putting his head in his hands.

Darren put one hand on his hip and the other covered his eyes and he sighed dramatically. 'Ben, you've jumped lines yet again. We're not at that bit yet.'

'God, sorry Darren, sorry,' Ben said.

'You keep saying sorry, but we are just not getting anywhere, are we?'

Harry could see that Darren's frustration was getting the better of him, and his normally calm and placid voice was now building up in a crescendo, and his face was getting redder and redder, which was in contrast to his pale bald head.

'I'm, I'm doing my best,' Ben stuttered.

'Uh-huh, uh-huh, but are you actually listening to the dialogue?' Darren now had both hands on his hips, and as he spoke his podgy tummy was wobbling up and down, like an aftershock to the words that were being spat out of his mouth like volcanic fireballs of destruction.

'I am.'

'Well, were we talking about rats yet?'

Ben shifted his eyes downwards, 'I don't think so, no.'

'You don't think so? So, you weren't actually listening then?' Darren hissed.

Sitting in the row of chairs behind him, Andrew nudged Harry, reminding him that he was meant to be in charge of this rabble and that perhaps he ought to step in. Harry sighed and stood up wearily. 'Ok, ok guys, let's just take a quick break shall we, then we can start again from the top of the scene.'

'Harry, I'm sorry but what will that achieve? We've gone through this scene countless times now this evening, and previous evenings I might add,' Darren had turned his wobbling tummy in Harry's direction now.

'Yes, Darren, that's the point of rehearsals, to rehearse scenes and to iron out any issues.' Harry said as diplomatically as possible, no matter how valid Darren's point was.

'Iron out any issues, Harry? This is a joke, it's a big rip in the shirt, not a small crease that needs ironing out!' Darren's face was getting redder and redder. It would be just Harry's luck that the silly sod would give himself a heart attack.

Harry held out his hands. 'All right, Darren, let's just calm down and take a few moments, shall we?' he said.

'Harry, we're just going around in circles here,' Darren paused for a few moments, 'I think we need a new shirt.'

'What? Leo's still working on the costumes,' Harry said, confused.

'It's a metaphor.'

'Oh. Right.'

'We are making progress, and Ben is doing well,' Chelsea spoke up, putting an arm on Ben's shoulder. 'Why don't we have a rest, I'll go through the lines again with Ben during the break, and then we can pick it up again and do another run through.'

'Good idea, Chelsea,' Harry quickly piped up, wondering whether he needed to read up on negotiating tactics again in his police manual.

Darren turned and walked off the stage, slamming the set door behind him, causing the whole thing to wobble. He then had to shuffle alongside the wooden set so that he could reach the front where the other cast members were sat pretending to look at their phones and trying not to snigger.

Ben stood looking dejected on the stage, and Chelsea put her arm around his shoulders in comfort. 'Come on, I'm sure he doesn't mean it really. We're all a little tired and stressed,' she said.

'Yes, try not to worry, Ben. We'll get there, you're coming along well,' Harry said. *You just need to hurry up and remember your lines in the right order...*

'Thanks guys. I'm sure I'll get it next time. Shall I go and apologise to Darren again?'

'I think it might be best to leave him for a few moments to be honest with you, Ben,' Harry said, as he turned and saw Darren stomping his way to the back of the hall where the kitchen was.

'Let's go and find a quiet corner to run through our lines,' Chelsea suggested again, and she led Ben off, her arm still around his shoulder.

Harry blew out a stream of air and felt in his shirt pocket for the packet of painkillers that he thought he had, before remembering he didn't have any. Sensing someone approaching behind him, he tried to hide his own frustration before turning around, expecting to have another battle with Darren about why they should recast Dick Whittington.

Seeing it was Andrew, he smiled wearily, a wave of tiredness suddenly hitting him.

'That was certainly interesting,' Andrew said quietly. 'I thought Darren was going to launch at him, and I'd finally see PC Berwick in action as the hero of the hour.'

Harry chuckled. 'Give me psychotic chainsaw wielding maniacs over flaming melodramatic actors any day of the week.'

Andrew held up a finger at him. 'And you want to know why I work with the dead, there's your answer; they don't have hissy fits and stomp their feet like toddlers.'

'Mm, you're not wrong there.'

Looking behind Harry at the stage, Andrew said, 'I think I'm going to have to take a look at this set again, make sure it's still structurally sound after little Miss Shouty pants used it.'

'Ok, thanks Andrew,' Harry reached out and gave his friend's shoulder a gentle punch.

'It's the only bit of set that we've finished so far, so if he's bust it, there may well be a murder this evening, and I'm expecting you to provide an alibi for me, officer.'

Harry nodded. 'Consider it done, just tell me what to say. In fact, I'll help you hide the body as well. I know a few good spots.'

'Ta,' Andrew started to walk off, before turning back around and taking a step towards Harry again. 'I think we both know what his problem is though.'

'Darren?'

'Yeah, he clearly wants the lead role as he thinks he's the only *"professional"* actor,' Andrew said, using his fingers to create the quotation marks.

'Ha, well he's not getting the part, no matter how much he stomps and shouts. He's too old for a start, and I know I can't talk, but he's not exactly a sex symbol with that little podgy tummy he's got.'

Andrew pretended to look thoughtful. 'Oh, I don't know. I don't think the ladies of the Flower Arranging club are too picky.'

'Polly's thinking about joining that club, so she can escape from the kids one night a week.'

Andrew looked at Harry's stomach and said, 'See, point proven.'

'Oi. Carry on like that and there might be a second body that needs hiding tonight.'

'As yes, but who would provide you with an alibi, eh?'

'Fine, I'll let you live a little longer. But only if you fetch me a coffee. Oh, and you don't have any headache tablets, do you?'

'Thought you were off caffeine in case it turned you into a zombie?' Andrew said, as he dug in his pockets and pulled out a half-used packet of pills and passed them over to Harry.

'I have a feeling it's going to be a long night.'

'Aye, aye skipper,' and Andrew walked off towards the set and gave it a shake. Nodding his head he made off for the kitchen area at the back of the church hall, where Polly and Leo were dishing out cups of tea and coffee and broken chocolate digestives that had been bought on the cheap.

Harry looked at the packet of painkillers and popped two out of the pack, chucked them into his mouth and dry swallowed them, half hoping he would choke and have to be taken to hospital. Anything to escape this madhouse.

Forty-Three

Harry

It was the night of the annual Christmas lights switch on in the town centre, which was the second most exciting event that happened in the town on an annual calendar basis. The most exciting occasion in the yearly diary was the carnival, which brought with it a good variety of floats of all shapes and sizes; and of course, lots of loud music and flashing lights, as well as the odd cursing pensioner who had been hit by a stray twirling baton let loose by an overly excited performing child.

The best places to watch it would quickly be snapped up, with some people getting there in advance and setting up an arrangement of camping chairs and banners and looking smug with their thermos flasks of tea, coffee and hot chocolate. Although, by the time the floats went past several hours later, no one was sat in the chairs, as the bitter cold normally forced people to stand up and hop from one foot to another in a bid to keep the circulation going.

As Christmas was six or so weeks away now, in recent months the local council had been busy putting up and installing the lights ready for the big day. Although the same lights had been used for the last twenty years or so, there was usually a good turnout for the event. The centrepiece was the grand fir tree that stood on the paved area next to the roundabout in the centre of the town. This year, as with every year, the tree was adorned with, as yet, unlit lights, swaying ever so gently in the November breeze, ready to dazzle and sparkle.

In years gone past, the tree had stayed up until twelfth night, but as this included New Year's Eve, this had been quickly changed after several intoxicated men had tried to climb to the top of the tree in a bid to prove their manliness and lumberjack skills to their equally as intoxicated girlfriends; fallen off and then been carted off to accident and emergency by a paramedic with no sympathy, with a variety of broken bones and an epic hangover the next day to match.

This year's star attraction was Foxi Wootton, who was due to turn on the Christmas lights at six o'clock. Foxi had come seventh in last year's X Factor competition, but had so far been far more popular than any of the other contestants that had gone further than she had in the competition. It was a small miracle that the town planning committee had managed to secure her acceptance to attend the switch on, but it probably helped that Foxi was a local girl, having grown up in the nearby town of Chard.

Harry had persuaded the key members of the Book Club, some more willingly than others, to meet in the town centre at five thirty, so that they could hand out some leaflets for the upcoming pantomime. Harry had suggested that they come in costumes, but this had quickly been vetoed as some of the costumes were still to be made and the ones that had been made were not particularly warm. When it was pointed out to Harry that most of his cast would be off with pneumonia if they did go dressed up, he quietly backed down admitting defeat. Instead, they were all wrapped up against the cold; fitted out with thick winter jackets, gloves, scarves and bobble hats, looking more like a North Pole expedition team than the cast and crew of a local pantomime.

Harry had only been there a few minutes, and already Leo was complaining to him about the cold.

'But I don't see why I'm needed here, I'm the costume department, I should be at home, in the warm, sewing buttons onto costumes,' Leo said, with his arms crossed, reminding Harry of a gobby teenager.

'You're here, because you're a part of the key management team, Leo,' Harry replied, in what he hoped was a motivational tone.

'Ha! Don't try and flatter me, Mr B. I know my place, I'm just the wardrobe department.'

'Oh, Leo, you're much more than that.' said Helen, rubbing her owl patterned gloved hands together, her cheeks made rosy red by the cold.

'I just don't see why I have to be out in the cold.' Leo whined.

'Because,' hissed Harry, whose patience was now starting to wear thin, 'if we have to be out here, then you bloody well have to as well. So, pipe down, look sodding jolly, and hand out some leaflets.' After a forlorn look from Leo, he then decided to adopt a tactic he used with his own children. 'Look, the sooner we're done, the sooner you can go home.'

With that, Leo grabbed a handful of the pamphlets, put on a smile that would have had dentists lining up around the block to use him as their model and set off handing them out to passers by

Helen gave Harry a knowing smile, and Harry just shrugged at her, before turning to the rest of the small group that had assembled.

'Right you lot,' he said loudly. 'Time to get these handed out. Helen, can you dish them out in roughly equal amounts, please?'

'Sure, Harry.'

'Ok, Polly and Ben, would you like to go up by the McDonalds area please? Jessica and Chelsea, can you go up to the High Street, Andrew and I will go up to the Debenhams bit of town, and the rest of you can just mill about here with Leo and make sure that he doesn't throw his flyers in a rubbish bin. Ok everyone?'

There were nods from everyone, their steamy breath quickly disappearing into the cold air.

'Good. Let's say meet back here in about an hour or so, then I'll treat you all to a mulled wine from the takeaway van over there,' he said, hoping that the prices weren't stupidly expensive.

Everyone sauntered off towards the area that they had been assigned, some blowing into their hands to warm them up and get the blood circulating once again, until only Andrew and Harry were left.

'Pub then?' said Andrew with a mischievous grin on his face.

'Don't you start as well. Although it's a wonderful idea, and it would really annoy Leo if he found out, which makes it doubly tempting, but...'

'But you're going to be a good boy and set a fine example?' Andrew said, slightly tilting his head to one side.

'Something like that. Plus Polly would kill me if I stayed in the warm and sent her out into the cold.'

'You're a scholar and a gentleman, sir.'

'No, just anything for a quiet life, Andrew.'

'Good point. Come on then. Lead the way, chubby'

Harry raised an eyebrow at him. 'Chubby?'

Andrew shrugged his shoulders. 'I didn't realise we had to leave our sense of humour at home this evening.'

Harry swatted his shoulder. 'I can see how your clients are charmed by your winning personality. Oh wait, perhaps that's why they died?'

The two men weaving their way in and out of the crowds down the packed street, families with pushchairs causing regular roadblocks and temporary roundabouts that they had to navigate. Andrew nearly fell over a darkly dressed toddler and then was glared at by a teenage mother with a glowing cigarette in one hand and a can of cheap cider in the other.

'Charming,' Andrew muttered to Harry, after apologising politely to the glowering mother.

'Perhaps she should keep more of an eye on her kids,' Harry agreed. 'And I think that was a herbal cigarette she was smoking. Shall I go and ruin her evening?'

Andrew shook his head. 'No, leave it. It'll only be more hassle than it's worth. And besides, you're not getting out of handing out these leaflets that easily you know.'

'You spoil all of my fun.'

'That's life, sunshine.'

The two men continued to negotiate their way along the pavement towards the big department store.

'Remind me, why did you assign us to the furthest end of town again? Not that I'm not enjoying your enthralling company of course,' said Andrew.

'I'll let you into a little secret,' Harry said, sidestepping a screaming child.

'Oh, goody, I love secrets, do tell.'

'When I was a beat copper, I discovered that throughout the night this department store keeps its fan heaters above the doors on full blast, and as there's a good half inch gap between the glass doors, you can stand guard outside the store and keep your hands warm whilst they're behind your back.'

'Genius.'

'Yep, it's the most heavily guarded shop in all of Taunton during the chilly winter months.'

'In between all of the doughnut eating you fuzz do.'

'Ah, see, there's no doughnut shops open during the night around here, otherwise we'd all be guarding that,' said Harry.

'I see, we're off to hand out flyers and pinch a bit of their heat at the same time, I love it. Leo will be so pissed off when he finds out.'

'That's why it's a secret, and he won't find out, *will he*, Andrew?'

'Scouts honour.'

'Right then, here we are. You take this entrance and I'll take the other one. If we get this done quickly, we can have a swift half before going back and meeting the others.'

'Now there's motivation for you.'

'Good man, now let's crack on. Don't forget to smile.'

'Are you sure you should be handing these out, haven't you heard that men with beards shouldn't be trusted? You might scare the children away.'

'Haven't *you* heard, beards are back in again.'

'God help us all. Right, enough jibber-jabber, catch you in a bit.'

With friendly smiles adorned on their ruddy faces, the two friends warmly greeted the passers-by and hand out the flyers.

Thankfully no children were sent running for their parents due to any beard related issues.

Forty-Four

Peter

Stepping outside, Peter breathed in the fresh afternoon air deeply, and then sparked up a cigarette. The exhaled smoke mixing with the cold air and forming a miniature cloud for a brief time.

He had finally admitted defeat and had decided to get a cleaning company in to try and help him spruce his ageing house up a bit, as burning it down may have prompted too many awkward questions from both the authorities and the bishop; and Peter knew who he was more afraid of.

After the first two cleaners had both left quickly, not even unholstering their cans of Vanish and attempting to start on the mammoth task that lay before them, Peter had managed to secure the deal with two Polish cleaners that had come highly recommended from one of his chess playing friends at the local pub. This friend had once been an esteemed bank manager, so Peter had come to the conclusion that if an ex bank manager recommended people, then they must have high standards and be trustworthy.

Peter liked the Poles. His father had served in the Royal Air Force as a pilot in the last couple of years of World War Two and had flown alongside the Polish pilots of 303 Squadron. His father had commented that they were the most ferocious and determined fighter pilots he had ever known, and was glad they were on the side of the Allies. As a young teenager at the time, Peter had met most of his father's pilot friends, and always remembered the smiles and tiny pieces of chocolate the Polish pilots gave him; it was always so sad when one of them didn't return from a dogfight, and was one of the reasons Peter had entered the service of the church, to try and spread a little love and peace.

The Polish cleaners, Lukasz and Marta were now into their fifth hour of employment with him and in the front garden was a growing wall of black rubbish bags. This presented Peter with his next issue, and he was seriously considering employing little Billy to have a bonfire.

Next to the wall of black plastic bags, was a green army of empty wine and whisky bottles, all lined up in smart rows, like a well-disciplined army regiment waiting for the battle orders to be given and ammunition handed out.

Peter had been shocked, but not altogether completely surprised at the volume of empty bottles that were currently paraded in front of his house. And although they hadn't made any comment, he did wonder slightly what the two young cleaners thought of it all?

He had tried to make conversation with both of them earlier; and they were incredibly polite and courteous, but they seemed more interested in completing the task at hand. So here he was, standing outside in the still frosty garden in December trying to work out which he had drunk more of in his lifetime, tea, whisky or wine. He wouldn't like to put a safe bet on any of the answers, as the number of cups of tea that he had drunk whilst at the homes of his parishioners over the years must be very close to the amount of whisky that he had guzzled by himself in the comfort and sanctuary of his own home. Not to mention the pub; although he didn't like to be seen too regularly there, in case word got back to the bishop. He shuddered involuntarily.

'Good afternoon, Peter.'

The greeting came from the front garden gate, bringing the vicar out of his day dreaming state and back to the here and now. He looked over at the gate and squinted slightly. 'Ah, hello there, Valerie, Gerald. How are you both?' he said, internally summoning the energy needed to deal with this woman from his reserves, and quickly flicking away the cigarette he had in his hand, which pinged against an empty bottle.

'I'm very well, thank you. Goodness me, are you having an early spring cleanout?' Valerie said looking around the garden like a startled owl. Gerald stood just behind her, like a personal assistant who knows when to be quiet and let the master speak.

'What? Oh, you mean all this? Well yes, actually. Just having a little tidy up,' he said, as Lukasz came outside once again and deposited another three black bags of rubbish onto the growing wall of bagged refuse. He smiled politely at the newcomers, then nodded and returned to the house.

'Got some help I see.'

Peter sighed quietly. 'You're as observant as ever, Valerie. Would you care to come in and have some tea?' he said, sending up a small prayer that they would decline his invitation, as the only milk he had was four days past its use-by date.

Thankfully she shook her head. 'Thank you, no. We won't keep you, as I can see you're busy. I did however want to speak with you to confirm the dates we can put the play on in the hall?'

'Yes of course. Do you want to come into the garden to speak, it seems odd talking to you both over the top of the gate?' He gestured for them to come into the garden.

'Gerald, open the gate,' Valerie commanded, and the order was obeyed without hesitation. Peter couldn't help but chuckle to himself.

Valerie and Gerald walked into the garden, Gerald carefully shutting the gate behind him.

As they passed the wall of bags, Valerie spied the whisky bottle army and couldn't hide the astonishment from her face.

'The dates?' Peter said, pleased that Valerie had reacted the way he hoped she would, but pretending to divert their attention away from the obvious.

'Umm, yes. The dates. Gerald, do you have the dates?'

'Yes, my dear,' he replied, efficiently pulling out a folded piece of lined paper from one of the pockets of his long black overcoat. He held out the piece of paper to his wife, who was still distracted by the sight in front of her. Coughing to catch her attention, he passed the paper to Valerie. Perhaps glad of something new to focus her eyes on, she unfolded the paper and faced him.

'I understand when Harry first spoke with you, he suggested the ninth of January until the fourteenth? I know it's a little late to be confirming, now that the flyers have been given out and tickets are being sold, but as we're about six weeks away now, I just wanted to finalise the arrangements.'

Peter considered toying with her and feigning confusion about the Flower Arranging Club needing the space for an emergency Pansy and Wallflower convention, but he wasn't sure if God would forgive him if he sent Valerie to meet Him early if she had a fatal heart attack at the news.

'Absolutely, it's all been entered into the church diary, so the other groups know not to meet in the church hall that week.'

'Marvellous, thank you,' Valerie said, continuing to look around her, trying to hide her astonishment, but failing miserably.

'Was there something else I could help you with, Valerie?' Peter asked.

'Umm, no, thank you, vicar. I can see you're busy, so we'll leave you in peace now.' She started to turn around to leave.

Gerald coughed. 'What about the chairs, my dear?'

Valerie looked at him blankly. 'Chairs?'

'Yes, we're borrowing some extra chairs from the primary school, and you were going to ask the vicar if it's alright to leave them in the hall in between the performances during the week.' Gerald rocked on his feet slightly.

'Oh, yes. I'd quite forgotten about that,' she turned back to face Peter.

To quicken the conversation so that he could have another cigarette, he said, 'That wouldn't be a problem, Valerie. No one else will be using the hall during the day, so you may leave the chairs and scenery and what-not in the hall. It'll be perfectly safe there.'

'Thank you, that's most kind. Well, uh, good luck with your, uh, pre-spring clean,' Valerie started walking backwards, as if she might get ambushed by the bottle army if she turned her back on it.

'Cheerio, Valerie. Take care and mind how you go. Bye, Gerald. See you both on Sunday.'

Valerie did a half wave, before turning and making for the garden gate. Gerald lent in slightly towards Peter. 'By the way, good choice of single malts, old boy,' he whispered to Peter, winking as he turned and walked back up the pathway to the gate, after his disappearing wife.

Smiling, Peter decided it was time for a mid-afternoon snifter and shuffled back towards the house, wondering if Polish vodka was as good as he had heard.

Forty-Five

The Two Cleaners

'I told you that we should of got here earlier. But do you listen? No,' Jenny said, looking through the smoke-stained car windscreen at the queue of cars in front of them trying to get into the multi-story car park in the centre of town.

'Don't you start on me again,' Kelly warned her, wagging her finger. 'I told you before that I had to fetch the newspapers and milk and that for the old bat that lives next door.'

'You should of told her to get it herself.' Jenny tapped her hands on the steering.

'You've no heart.'

'Well, we're late now, ain't us.'

'You can't say no to that woman. She don't give you the opportunity neither. She spies you coming from her window and pounces out of the front door at you. Honestly, when I get back from work, she keeps me chatting on the doorstep for at least half an hour before I can get in. I try to get in before she sees me, but for nine hundred odd years old, she's surprisingly quick,' Kelly said.

'She should be able to get her own ruddy milk and newspapers then. And who still buys newspapers anyway?'

'Old folk and people with nothing else better to do with their time. Oh, and smart arses who like to boast about doing the crossword thing.'

Jenny sniffed. 'They should get on the Internet and read the news and whatnot on Facebook, like normal people do.'

'I don't think she's on Facebook.'

'Why not? What's wrong with her?' asked Jenny, feeling confused.

'Nothing, I don't think. She's just old and that.'

'She's selfish too, making us late for our Thursday night Christmas shopping exposition.'

'Expedition,' Kelly looked at her.

'Eh? That's what I said, clean your ears out.'

'Me thinks someone needs a ciggy. Like right now.'

'I think I need a pint of strong cider,' said Jenny edging the car forward towards the back of the car in front. 'And none of that fizzy flavoured shite, proper cloudy cider.'

'More like a pint of vodka, the mood you're in, my love.'

'Exactly,' she sighed again. 'We should of caught the bus in, I knew it was going to be mental tonight. What's this joker in front playing at? Come on you wanker, move it.'

As another Christmas song came on the car's radio, Kelly turned up the volume and started bouncing up and down in her seat like a hyperactive Duracell bunny. Jenny just glared at her and then continued to shuffle the car forwards in the queue, muttering all kinds of dark spells and curses under her breath. Thankfully, for all of humanity, she didn't know any actual spells, other than the ones she'd learnt from watching the *Harry Potter* movies time and time again.

Twenty-five long minutes later and after scraping the side of the car on a concrete pillar, they were parked up.

Kelly looked at her cautiously, perhaps expecting a torrent of swearing, abuse and having the finger of blame being pointed at her after the concrete pillar incident. But all Jenny did was take out an 'emergency' packet of cigarettes from the glove box and lit one up, smoked it all in silence, before calmly getting out of the car and heading for the lifts to the ground floor.

The lift was full of parents and overly excited children - the latter screaming about what toys they wanted for Christmas and the former doing their best to persuade them that in order to get said toys, they would need to be good, which had no effect what so ever on the children. This would normally have caused tutting, muttering and eye rolling from Jenny, but still she said nothing, keeping her eyes glued straight ahead at the lift door in front of her like a model on a catwalk.

Reaching the ground floor, they were met with a tidal wave of shoppers trying to get into the lift at the same time as everyone was trying to get out. Eventually the two of them managed to wrestle their way out of the crowd to safety and made for a quiet spot on the pavement, where Jenny promptly lit her second cigarette with a hand that was shaking ever so slightly. Kelly opted to stay silent and found a sudden interest in the lamppost that they were stood next to.

A couple of drags of her cigarette later, she turned to Kelly and said, 'I is never coming flaming Christmas shopping with you again. Or if we do, you need to learn to drive first, so I can at least have a drink to calm me nerves.'

'Ok, my love. But if I'm driving, you might need to have a lot more than one drink, as your nerves will be done in after a trip with me,' she grinned.

Jenny could feel a smile forming on her hardened face. 'Okay. Since we're here, we might as well get on with it.'

'Come on then, you old barndoor.'

'Where are we going first?' Jenny popped her lighter back in her handbag and zipped it up.

'You need to even ask? Wilko, where else?' beamed Kelly, taking the lead and walking past the fresh doughnut seller and down towards the Old Pig Market. Christmas music was playing over the array of loudspeakers that had been erected around the tall Christmas tree in the centre of town.

'God, you are a proper classy bird, aren't you?'

'What? I got loadsa people that I need to buy for this year, and I ain't made of money you know.'

'That's cos you spend it all on fags and booze.'

'It's my hard-earnt money, so I can spend it on whatever I want,' said Kelly, playing along with her teasing. 'And you can talk, Mrs I've got a bag full of condoms and Viagra. I'm still surprised you haven't got rohypnol in there as well to be honest with you, my love.'

'I told you, I don't need that stuff, I've got me natural charisma and legs to die for.'

'And like I said before, have you been taking your own rohypnol?'

'Shut your face. Are we going to actually do some shopping or what?' Jenny huffed, as she narrowly avoided being taken out by a large framed lady carrying armfuls of bags and rolls of wrapping paper sticking out in all directions. 'Rude!' she called after the departing backside of the woman, who either didn't hear her, or just didn't care.

'Nearly there - nowoooooh my God! Look who it is,' Kelly hissed at her, grabbing her by the shoulder.

'Is it baby Jesus?'

'No, you gert wazzok, it's Ben!'

Jenny looked around her, but couldn't see him. 'Where to?'

'Over there, at the jewellers, looking in the window. Red scarf on,' Kelly said, hoping up and down.

Jenny still didn't see him. 'You sure?'

'Yes, of course I am,' said Kelly excitedly, her fingernails digging into Jenny's shoulder.

Finally spotting him, Jenny said, 'Oh yeah. Has he got that field mouse of a girlfriend with him?'

'Not that I can see. He must be out Christmas shopping for her.'

'Looking at jewellery? Don't mice eat seeds and shit? Oh, and cheese, he should be buying her a nice block of cheddar and saving his money to buy me a nice Tiffany ring.'

'Hey. I saw him first, so he's out buying *me* an expensive ring,' Kelly protested to her.

'What, are you like twelve or summat?'

'Come on, he's walking away. Let's stalk him,' Kelly said, her eyes fixed on Ben.

'What about your shopping?'

'Screw it, I don't like most of me family anyway,' said Kelly, almost hysterical.

'Off we go then, before we lose him.'

The two women pushed their way through the crowds, not wanting to lose sight of their prey. If a riot were to ever break out in the town, these two would be able to handle riot control all by themselves.

Ben was walking along at a steady pace, stopping to glance in shop windows that took his fancy and occasionally pulling his mobile phone out of his pocket to check for messages and then quickly stuffing it back inside one of his jacket pockets again, appearing to be totally oblivious to the tail he'd picked up.

'He keeps checking his phone. Perhaps he's waiting for an important text, or summat?' Jenny whispered.

'Eh, what did you say? I can't hear you over this flaming Christmas music they got blasting out,' Kelly replied.

'You liked the Christmas music just now. Anyway, I said, he's checking his phone a lot, he must be waiting for a call.'

'Eh?'

Jenny rolled her eyes. 'Oh forget it. You'd make a shite spy you know.'

Following at a respectable distance behind him, the women darted, ducked and wove behind and between the other shoppers, like a Christmas shoppers' version of ballroom dancing, without any of the grace, style or fancy costumes. Seeing him heading towards the entrance to a large department store, Jenny nudged her fellow sleuth.

'Look, he's going into Marks and Sparks.'

'Them do nice food. He's got good taste that one.'

She looked at Kelly. 'Of course he's got good taste. Well, apart from his current girlfriend anyway.'

'Good point. Come on, let's follow him in,' said Kelly, making for the automatic doors that were constantly open, due to the steady flow of festive shoppers entering and departing the store.

After pushing their way in, they both did a striking impression of Meer cats, scanning the sea of faces for the one with a red scarf tied around his neck. Spotting him heading towards the lingerie section, they once again set off in hot pursuit.

As Ben glanced around, he slowed his walking down, and eventually stopped. With a quick embarrassed look around to see if anyone was looking, he started looking at some of the garments on offer.

'What's he looking at?' asked Kelly excitedly.

'Undercrackers.'

'The dirty pervert. That said, he's welcome to look at mine anytime he likes, if you know what I mean,' Kelly dug her in the ribs with her elbow.

She looked at Kelly. 'Do you wear big pants?'

'What?'

'Do you wear big pants?'

'That's a bit personal, like. And I may be getting on a bit, but I ain't resorted to granny knickers just yet, you cheeky mare.'

'It seems our Benny boy is into the larger sized panties, if the ones he's looking at are anything to go by,' said Jenny, who in her head had already gone out and bought an entire drawer full of big knickers, if that's what Ben liked.

'You what? Shift over, let me take a peek,' Kelly said. As she shifted around to look, the mannequin that they were hiding behind wobbled slightly as she knocked against it. 'Sorry,' she muttered to the plastic figure. 'Oooh, yeah. What's he looking at them for then?'

'Perhaps the field mouse likes them like that,' Jenny replied, in her head already cancelling the order she'd made earlier.

'She needs to get out more then, if that's the case. Oh look, someone's talking to him now.'

'Who is it?' Jenny said.

'Dunno, they've got their back to us, so I can't see. Long hair, so it's a woman.'

'Sales assistant?'

'Na, they're wearing a coat,' Kelly said, squinting her eyes, her head bobbing from left to right, as people walking past got in her line of sight.

'Let me see then,' Jenny demanded, and once again the mannequin rocked slightly as the two of them swapped positions, along with another whispered apology to the inanimate object. 'Yep, defo a girl. Oh, wait. She's turning around. It's what's her face, the chemist lady?'

Kelly scrunched up her face, 'Chelsea, I think. Shame she doesn't work at Boots, otherwise she'd be Chelsea Boots. Ha-ha!'

'Hilarious,' Jenny said dryly.

'You really do need that drink, don't you?'

'Shhh, I'm trying to lip read what they're saying.' She squinted for a few seconds. 'No, it's no good, he keeps scratching his nose and his hand is covering his mouth, so I don't know what he's saying. Bloody hell.'

'Perhaps the big pants are for her?' Kelly suggested, causing Jenny to turn and face her.

'What? You reckon he's knocking her off on the side? He is a naughty boy, I thought he had higher morals than that.'

'You're a fine one to talk about morals. If you had the chance, you would have your wicked way with him.'

Jenny looked at her. 'But that's different.'

'Why?'

'Why? What do you mean, *why?* Because I want to father his children, not just have a quick leg over in the bushes behind the pub.'

'Speaking from experience, are we?'

'Don't you forget, Kelly my love, that I know a thing or two about you and your extra curricula activities, before you start getting all high and mighty.'

'Easy, easy, I'm only pulling your leg,' Kelly said, backing down.

'Hmm,' and with that, Jenny turned back around in Ben's direction again. 'Shit,' she exclaimed, far too loudly, causing an elderly couple to look her way and glare. 'What?' she said to them, and they both shook their heads and walked off.

'What? What is it?' Kelly asked.

'He's gone. I can't see him anywhere. This is your fault, wench. If you hadn't of been yapping on as usual, we wouldn't have lost him. Now we'll never know what those two are up to.'

'You sure? Come on, we can take a wander around and see if we can spot them.'

'Do you know how big this store is? They could be anywhere by now,' she said miserably, feeling as if her entire world had just imploded.

'Well, my lovely. It's either try and find them in here, or back to Christmas shopping we go. You decide,' Kelly said, folding her arms.

'As you put it like that, let's have a look, see if we can see him. Oh. Perhaps we could split up, like in the movies. You stay on this floor, and I'll take the escalator upstairs to the menswear section. He could be looking at men's undies and I'll follow him into the changing room, ka-ching.'

'Right you are, my love. Good plan,' Kelly replied eagerly and they went off in their separate directions.

With the throng of customers in the shop and each wrapped up in their own little worlds, neither Ben and Chelsea, or Jenny and Kelly had spotted Jessica standing near the secret Santa gifts section of the shop. Watching all of them.

Forty-Six

Harry

To try and heal the professional differences of opinion between some of the cast members, Harry had suggested that they should all go out for some food and drinks and have a night off from rehearsing. This had been widely welcomed by the group, especially by Darren, who had told Harry in confidence that he was feeling a little foolish after his outburst at Ben, although his frustrations remained.

However, trying to find food that everyone liked was a completely different story. The Chinese food lovers hated Indian food, and the Indian food lovers hated Chinese. Only a couple of people liked Mexican, so in the end, and nearing the end of his tether, and almost regretting suggesting the idea in the first place, Harry had suggested that they all go for pizza at an Italian restaurant in town. This had been met by only one objection, who after they had been glared at by Harry, had quietly said that the lasagne the restaurant did would be fine.

It was agreed that they would meet at the restaurant at around seven in the evening, have some food and then go to one of the nearby pubs for a couple of drinks. Valerie and Gerald had sent their apologies, along with Patricia, but otherwise everyone else had said that they would be attending. In fact, several people confirmed their attendance with Harry after the apologies had been given.

Harry had made the booking a couple of days ago and had been relieved that it hadn't been fully booked with Christmas parties. He had arrived there early this evening so that he could greet everyone as they arrived and thank them for all of their hard work and support so far. He'd been reading that people that feel appreciated will always go out of their way to help more, so with the recent tensions, he'd decided to give it a shot.

As he stood outside in the cold, waiting for the first people to arrive, he looked in at Polly - who had opted to wait inside in the warm - as she spoke to the waiter, probably ordering a Bloody Mary. She was looking a bit less stressed, now that Valerie had started to miss coming to the rehearsals recently. She had been insisting on either directing the actors herself, or making last minute changes to the script. This was much to the annoyance of both Polly and the actor concerned, as it was mostly Polly's work that Valerie amended and the actor had to relearn the line. And it had really annoyed Harry too, after all, he was meant to be the sodding director.

He was glad that Valerie wasn't coming tonight, as he wanted the group to relax and enjoy themselves this evening. Gerald was a decent enough bloke, just hen pecked, and everyone knew who wore the trousers in their relationship. He'd heard from one of the chief inspectors at work, that Gerald used to have some secret job for the Foreign Office. Harry couldn't see it himself, unless the job was as a handyman fixing broken lightbulbs for the spooks' offices. Still, it was always the quiet ones you had to watch.

Hearing approaching footsteps, he brought himself back to Earth from his daydreaming and turned to see Leo fast walking towards him and the restaurant, the bobble on his bobble hat swaying in time to his footsteps, his hands stuffed deep inside his thick jacket.

'Hiya Harry, how are you doing? God, I'm freezing my tits off out here this evening.' Leo said, taking out one of his hands to shake Harry's outstretched hand.

'Hey Leo, I'm good, you? Yeah, it is nippy this evening.'

'Good ta. Glad work has finished for the day. You on guard duty out here, or what?'

Harry shuffled his feet. 'Ha, no, just wanted to welcome everyone as they arrived.'

Leo grinned at him. 'Ah, you're a good one you are. Well, I consider myself welcomed, so I'm going to head in out of the cold and get a vodka and Coke to warm myself up.'

'Sure, Leo, head on in,' he nodded his head towards the restaurant. 'Polly's holding the table for us and she's by herself, so I know she'll welcome the company.'

'Righto, see you in a bit. Oh, you want me to order you a drink?' Leo said, his hand resting on the door.

'I'm good thanks, I'm driving this evening anyway, so I'll just grab an orange juice and lemonade later when I come in. But thanks.'

'No worries, see you in a sec.' Leo darted inside and Harry saw that he spent quite a while giving an attractive waiter his drink order.

Ah, what it is to be young and single, Harry thought, and he smiled.

'Smiling at the voices in your head again?'

Harry turned and faced Andrew, who he hadn't heard approaching. 'Yes, actually. They were telling me to report you to Customs and Excise.'

'Lock up the Ship's Captain only a few weeks before the performance? You wouldn't dare.'

'You're right. But as soon as the show is over, the call is going in; understand?'

'Loud and clear. The others in there already are they?' Andrew said, squinting through the glass window.

'Polly and Leo are, still waiting on the rest of the mob to get here.'

'Ah, looks like that's them now,' Andrew said, nodding towards the group of people that were heading their way, giggling and laughing.

'They sound in good spirits already. Perhaps they all met earlier and went for a drink somewhere first?'

'Jealous that they didn't invite you?'

'Not in the slightest, a general shouldn't mix with the troops too much,' he grinned.

'Ha-ha, a general? Oh Harry, you do make me laugh.'

'Sod off and get inside, you're making the place look untidy and scaring away the punters.'

'Fine, I'll go and order a bottle of champagne. You're paying tonight, right?'

'Now who's being the comedian, eh?'

As he entered the restaurant, Andrew just stuck two fingers up as his reply.

Harry turned and faced the oncoming group, and put on his best welcoming smile.

Forty-Seven

The Restaurant

The manager had placed the group in the centre of the dining area, which she was regretting. They had only finished their starters and some of them were clearly drunk already. They weren't being obnoxious, rude or even demanding to her staff, just very loud and giggly, which was very similar to the children's parties they did on Saturday afternoons.

She checked the name of the reservation again, and it was under 'St Jude's Book Club', which to her sounded very much like a church organisation. This explained why they weren't rude, but she was surprised at the racket coming from them. Weren't church clubs meant to be full of knitting and praying, not getting drunk on overpriced, weak restaurant booze? Perhaps they didn't get out much, and besides, drunk people normally over tipped, so unless they started chanting and crucifying the children at the table next to them, she'd keep topping up their wine glasses and leave them to it.

At the table, Harry took a sip of his drink, the cold liquid setting one of his sensitive teeth on edge. He'd been meaning to go to the dentist for a while now, as it probably needed a filling. Leo had just finished his one-man impersonation of both Valerie and Gerald, and although he'd nailed it to a T and had the rest of the group in stitches, Harry was wondering if he should try and move the subject along. Thankfully the conversation switched directions naturally as

Helen regaled the group about an occasion when she had been home alone taking a shower and her cat had snuck into the bathroom and launched itself at the shower curtain. Helen had thought a serial killer was trying to attack her, which Leo thought was so funny that he sent a volley of wine shooting out of his nose as he tried to stop himself laughing mid-gulp, which sent the rest of the group into hysterics.

Harry decided *not* to be the adult and intervene, this was clearly what the group needed to bond, relax and unwind. He had seen Darren topping up Ben's wine glass and smiles exchanged between the pair of them, so hopefully that little episode had been put to bed.

One of the waiters was at the table again, asking if any more drinks needed ordering. Harry was certain that that was the third time in the space of half an hour that they had been over checking on drinks. The table quietened slightly, so the orders of prosecco, bottled beer and the house red could be given. Harry made a mental note to check the bill at the end and make sure no extra drinks had been charged to them.

'So how are ticket sales doing, Chelsea?' Ben asked, and Harry once again concentrated on the conversation.

'Not too bad,' she replied, taking a delicate sip of her red wine before placing her glass back down on the table and then smoothing out her napkin that was resting on her lap. 'We've sold out completely for the Saturday matinee and the evening, which is great news.'

Cheers erupted around the table, with lots of glasses clinking and smiles all round.

'That's fantastic,' Andrew said, when the cheering had started to subside. 'How about the rest of the nights, how are they looking?'

'The Thursday and Friday nights are about two thirds booked each, and the Tuesday and Wednesday nights are roughly half sold.'

'Looking positive then,' Harry said, feeling upbeat.

'Absolutely,' replied Chelsea, taking another sip of her wine. 'But it would be good if we could fill up a few more of these empty seats.'

'Agreed,' Harry said. 'Make all your hard work worthwhile with packed houses if we can get them.'

'Anyone got any clever ideas about how we can get some more bums on seats?' Polly asked the group, as a waiter reappeared with their drinks order.

'Other than drag people out of their beds at the YMCA, I think we've exhausted everything, haven't we?' said Leo.

'Oh, there must be something else we can do.' said Helen, playing with her napkin.

'I would put some leaflets up at work, but I'm not entirely sure that's appropriate,' said Andrew.

'No, maybe not for you, but the rest of us can,' said Harry.

'Yeah, I'm sure I can sneakily put a few up at work,' said Ben. 'The Wicked Witch is off this week, so I should be able to get away with it,' he said, playing with his fork.

'Good man.'

'Yep, I can do that too,' said Leo, with the rest of the group then nodding along.

'Ok, so what else can we do, gang?' Polly asked once again.

'Well we have the Facebook page, have we all shared the page with our friends?' A normally quiet Jessica spoke up.

'Another good idea, Jessica. Yes, everyone, let's do that as well please.' said Polly smiling.

Andrew cleared his throat. 'It's a bit late to suggest this now, as I know the schools break up soon, but we should have gone to some of the local primary schools and put on a ten-minute performance. One or two of the scenes perhaps, try and drum up some excitement from the kids, who in turn could have nagged their parents to take them along,'

'Yep, good idea mate, but as you said, perhaps a little late in the day. Go back to sleep and we'll wake you up again when it's home time,' Harry teased.

Andrew sneered at him, picked up his bottle beer from the table and leant back in his chair, feigning that he was sulking, but the twinkle in his blue eyes gave him away.

'How about we all go carol singing? That could be fun,' suggested Helen.

'Like I told you before, sweetie, you don't wanna hear me sing,' said Leo. 'And where are the main courses? I'm wasting away here.'

'If they're not here in a few minutes, I'll chase them up,' Harry said, looking around for a free member of waiting staff to wave at, but typically, they all seemed to have disappeared.

'I think carol singing might be a bit of fun actually,' said Darren, with Ben quickly nodding in agreement with his new friend.

'And me,' said Jessica, who so far this evening had laughed at all of Ben's jokes and agreed with everything her boyfriend had said.

'You guys go ahead, I'll sit this one out, unless you want to frighten people away that is.' Leo said, brushing a strand of hair away from his face.

'Perhaps you could give out the leaflets, Leo?' said Polly.

'Yeah, yeah, happy to do that, so long as it's not cold out. But you're not going to get me to sing in a million years. My performing arts A level teacher tried and failed, and if she couldn't teach me to sing, then none of you are,' he said, before taking a big gulp of his depleting wine and then straightening the paper Christmas cracker hat that was sliding down his forehead.

'There we go then, that's settled,' said Polly. 'Harry, can you speak with Patricia about trying to arrange some sheet music?'

'Will do, darling,' Harry replied.

'Great, we've still got a tonne of leaflets left, so we won't need to spend any more money having more printed out,' Chelsea said.

'Excellent, and I'll speak to one of the inspectors at the police station, see if I need to liaise with the council about getting a permit or whatnot,' Harry said, his stomach beginning to rumble. Spying a waitress, he waved at her to come over.

'Lovely. Does anyone else have any other ideas? We've got more promotion on our Facebook page, and the carol singing,' Chelsea asked.

The group continued to talk, as Harry spoke with the waitress, who apologised profusely and scurried off to the kitchen.

'Nothing really springs to mind,' Darren said.

'Well perhaps after some more wine we'll think of some more promising ideas,' said Andrew, leaning forward and joining back in the conversation once again.

'Now that's a splendid idea. Where's that cute waiter gone again?' Leo said.

'I think you've frightened him off. And anyway, I thought you were dating that maths teacher; Mark, or Matt, or Martyn?' said Helen.

'Marc. Marc with a C. And yep, I am, but he's not here and it's nearly Christmas and a little flirting is allowed at this festive time of year, it's the law,' Leo replied with a mischievous look on his face.

'Is he coming to see the show?'

'Yep, and he's bringing some of his work colleagues as well. Make sure you all put on a good show, and don't cock anything up.'

There was a slightly awkward silence around the table, and everyone tried not to look in Ben's direction.

'Err, anyway,' said Helen. 'What are you all doing for New Year's Eve? I was thinking of having a bit of a do at my place, and you're all very welcome to join me, if you're at a loose end,' she said, playing nervously with her napkin.

'That sounds fun,' Polly said. 'We'll get a sitter, if we can that is, and come along. Won't we, Harry?'

'Yep, I'm pretty sure I'm not working the night shift, so count me in,' Harry confirmed, as he played with one of the small glass pepper shakers that were on the table.

'I'd be delighted to come along, thanks Helen,' confirmed Andrew.

'Ooh, marvellous. Will there be food?' asked Leo. 'As I don't think we're going to get any here at this rate.'

'Ha, yes, I'll do some nibbles and bits and pieces. Just bring your own booze, as if we touch Mr T's gin, we'll be in trouble.'

'Smashing, I'll be there,' Leo said.

The others also chipped in and said what a lovely idea it was, and how pleased they would be to come along. A few seconds after Chelsea said she would be going, Ben also said that he would be going as well. Several very long seconds after that, he remembered to check with Jessica that she could go as well, and another slightly awkward silence ensued, with several knowing glances being exchanged amongst the rest of the table. Thankfully, several apologetic waiters arrived with the food and more drinks, and the party was soon back into full swing, with Leo's impersonation skills turning to imitate Harry. Harry, being a good sport sat there, sipping his orange juice and lemonade, and considered asking the drug squad to raid Leo's house in the early hours of one morning.

The evening was deemed a success by all those that attended, until the next morning, when some pretty epic hangovers kicked in.

Forty-Eight

Christmas Day, Late Morning

The house was unusually quiet and still. The central heating had switched itself on automatically at six, and then off at just after nine, with neither of the house's current inhabitants having woken to feel the benefit of its maximum warmth and comfort. Clinking radiators the only evidence that the old boiler had once been in the throes of life, and was now slumbering like an elderly dragon in its cupboard cave in the kitchen.

In the kitchen sink were two used wine glasses, with just the undrunk dregs remaining at the bottom. Alongside the fingerprint and lipstick stained wine glasses were two small shot glasses, with some of the clear liquid from the blue agave plant with which they had once been filled numerous times clinging to the side, and filling the stale kitchen air with the sweet smell of alcohol.

The kitchen worktop was a drinker's Stonehenge of empty and part full wine and spirits bottles, with the silver foil from a mince pie utilised as a fire pit come ashtray as the centre piece. An assortment of discarded chocolate wrappers were randomly scattered around like magic fairy dust, with all of the uneaten coffee flavoured chocolates pushed to the back of the work surface, resembling an earthen pagan burial ground.

Back in the living room, the lights on the Christmas tree continued to gently fade up, and then down, and then back up again, before manically strobing away to a classic nineties rave track that only the tree could hear. The cheap tinsel cheerfully reflecting the different coloured lights and radiating the light out into the known universe to last for all eternity; or as far as the drawn curtains at any rate.

The reflective Christmas morning stillness was interrupted by a loud noise emanating from the rear end of Jenny, who was lying on the sofa on her front. Her right arm was dangling down towards the floor and a trickle of drool was coming from her open mouth and collecting in a small puddle on the pink and fluffy Poundland cushion that was under her head. She had been thoughtfully covered in a *Minions* duvet, which had helped to muffle the foghorn noise to some extent, but it had still been loud enough to stir the sleeping West Country girl as her heavy eyelids flickered to life, and her brain coughed, spluttered, stalled, then dimly wavered into first gear.

Looking around at her surroundings, at first she didn't recognise where she was, and wondered which halfwit of a bloke's house she had ended up on this occasion. About at the same time as the pounding sledgehammer headache started, she remembered where she was, as glass splinters of last night's events were recalled by her memory.

With the hand that was already dangling on the floor, she felt about for her phone on the ground to see what the time was. Not finding it, she rolled onto her side to see if she was lying on it, the movement of her head and body sending mayday calls and distress flares up her nervous system and into her head, which had only just engaged second gear, causing the pounding sensation to intensify.

Counting to ten slowly, she lay very still and started praying to any deity that would listen to please stop the pain. If they did, she would then become an immediate convert to that religion and go and live in a secluded cave, far, far away from any alcohol. More importantly, she would be far away that gurt numpty Kelly who had forced her to continue their drinking binge when they had got back to Kelly's place after the pub had eventually kicked them out - which wasn't very hospitable in her opinion.

She heard footsteps coming delicately down the stairs towards the living room.

The footsteps reached the bottom of the stairs, and the living room door started to quietly open, the bottom of the door brushing against the carpet as it was opened just enough for a head to appear around the side of the door.

'That had better be Brad Pitt coming to wake me up with a cup of tea, some paracetamol and going to look after me until me headache's gone,' Jenny said to the floating head.

'Oh, you are awake then, love. I thought you might be still asleep.' Kelly said, opening the door wider and filling the doorway with her frame, the alcohol fumes coming off her at light speed and pinging around the room in all directions.

'Jesus, you stink of booze. Away with you.'

'You can talk. Smells like a tequila factory in here. Oh, and mixed with stale farts if I'm not mistaken.'

'That's the chimney for the factory.'

'I'm sure it is. God, your head as bad as mine is?'

'If your head feels like there are angry ants crawling around inside of it, and they're all wielding chainsaws, then yeah, mine feels the same.'

Kelly lent against the doorframe and rubbed her eyes. 'I told you not to have that last glass of wine.'

'You did not, forcing it down me neck you were.'

Jenny shuffled slightly underneath the blanket. 'Urgh, my mouth feels like the inside of a Russian gymnast's knickers. Get us a brew and some toast, will you love? Oh, and if you have got any painkillers, let's be having them and all.'

'What did your last slave die of?' said Kelly, continuing to lean against the painted doorframe for support to try and slow her spinning head down.

'I'm a guest, if you hadn't noticed. You need to be attentive.'

Kelly sighed. 'Alright my love, alright. I'll go and stick the kettle on and have a rummage about for some tablets,' she said, as she turned around and made for the kitchen.

'And some toast,' Jenny called after her.

Forty-Nine

Christmas day, Lunchtime

Sat upright in her usual dining room chair around the circular table, Valerie put her reading glasses on and once again looked over at the time on the silver carriage clock that was on top of the mantelpiece. Underneath, the log burner gave out licks of red, yellow and orange flame as it greedily ate up both the kindling and the seasoned logs that were sitting in its mouth, the bark on the logs causing the fire to spit and pop loudly. This made Valerie even hungrier. Gerald had been instructed to have the Christmas dinner prepared for one p.m. exactly, so that they could enjoy their dinner, he could do the washing up and both be settled back into their armchairs with plenty of time for the Queen's speech at three. It was now several minutes past one, and she was not impressed.

Admittedly, the salmon and scrambled egg on toast that he had prepared for breakfast had been first class, but that had been several hours ago, at eight thirty sharp, and now she was hungry and getting impatient. When Gerald had retired, he had insisted on taking on most of the kitchen duties, which Valerie didn't mind in the slightest. In fact, she actively encouraged it, but what she did mind was tardiness of any kind. She had fired teaching staff for lesser crimes.

Tapping her fingers on the linen table cloth briefly, she then took off her glasses and called through to the kitchen, 'Are you quite all right in there, Gerald?'

'Yes, fine my dear, I won't be a moment,' came the muffled voice through the closed door.

'You are taking quite a while in there.'

'Sorry my dear. Be with you in just a few moments more.'

'Hmmm.'

Valerie glared at the kitchen door and continued to drum her fingers on the table cloth, like an executioner's drum roll.

Through the door and in the steamy kitchen, Gerald's stress levels were rising rapidly. It had started when Valerie had asked him to put on one of her classical music CDs, and he had put a Handel one on, rather than something by Arlo Rutter.

His bad luck had then followed him through to the kitchen; first his potato peeler had snapped, which had meant he had to peel the rest of the potatoes and then the carrots with a knife, which meant that he chopped off too much potato and carrot in the process. He had broken one of his favourite knives, trying to chop up the swede, and just now, the food processor that was meant to mash the swede and carrot together had died, and the smell in the air indicated that the motor had burnt out. Lastly, after scooping out the swede and carrot and mashing it by hand, he had ended up bending the metal masher out of shape, so he now had a collection of broken bits and bobs that he was going to have to carefully dispose of, without his darling wife finding out what he'd done, otherwise he would never hear the end of it. In the interest of simplicity, he did consider just disposing of her instead, somewhere over the North Sea would have done nicely. There was a group captain in the RAF that owed him a favour; but no, this was Christmas time after all. Peace and goodwill and all that.

As he placed the different vegetables into ranks in the serving dish, he suddenly realised that he hadn't made any stuffing balls, which were one of Valerie's favourite. He wondered if he could delay lunch by another thirty minutes or so, to give him time to cook some? But by then the rest would be cold, so she would just have to live without them; she was going to find fault with something he did, so it may as well be that.

The dish of vegetables ready at last, he took a final large mouthful of the five-fingered single malt whisky he had secretly poured himself about an hour and a half ago, after potato peeler gate. He then put on his best smile, and started taking through the various dishes of food, with the cooked goose being the centrepiece to his Christmas arrangement. All of which was met with a deadly glare by the vulture that was sat at the table, and Gerald wished he had bought a second bottle of the whisky that had been on offer at the supermarket.

Fifty

Harry

As the various cast and crew shuffled into the hall, Harry occasionally looked up from the amended notes that he was reviewing from his copy of the script and smiled or nodded a greeting at the latest person to have come shivering through the door to the hall. One evening over the Christmas period, when the kids had been in bed and he had a free evening from being on shift at the police station, he had gone over the typed script and the pencilled in stage directions that he had previously given the characters. Whilst mulling it over with a lager shandy and a couple of mince pies, a slice of Yule Log, a box of Maltesers and a couple of assorted Quality Street that Polly had left, he had come up with a few minor amendments to his stage directions, which he was planning to run through at this evening's rehearsal.

As he looked at the changes he had made for Ben's character, Harry kept all his fingers and toes crossed that Ben had now learnt all his lines, as even though the pizza night out had served its purpose, he didn't want any more flare ups between the actors this close to the live performance. He sighed to himself, and thought about what his Welsh coal-mining father would say about all of this. However, as his father had a very strong accent that even he struggled to understand sometimes, thankfully some of it would be lost in translation, if his father ever were to voice an opinion to him on the matter. He was glad that he hadn't mentioned it to his parents when he'd taken the kids over to Newport in South Wales to see them yesterday. The kids had told their grandparents that they were in a pantomime and that they were little rats, but thankfully his parents had assumed it was a school thing, and neither he nor Polly had corrected them.

He picked up his mug of tea that was on the seat next to him and took a sip, the hot liquid warming up his insides. Harry looked down at his tummy and decided that perhaps he had eaten one too many chocolates over Christmas, and that he might do a few sessions at the gym that was at the police station. The only trouble was that the gym was next to the staff canteen. This usually meant he made a last-minute diversion and ended up munching on a cheese and salad sandwich with salad cream and then a Bounty chocolate bar. Although in his head he counteracted the cheese with the few shreds of lettuce that were also in the sandwich. And the walk from the police station through the carpark to get to the outbuildings that housed the gym and canteen must have burnt off the calories in the chocolate bar. Plus, it had coconut in for goodness' sake, that must count as one of his five a day.

However, after Polly had not so subtly bought him a rowing machine for Christmas to go in the garage, he decided that perhaps he should start doing a bit more exercise; but that was easier said than done, working changing shift patterns, looking after three young children and doing this as well. He just didn't feel as though he had any spare time to do any, but he had made a conscious decision to cut down on the amount of junk food that he ate and to start taking a packed lunch and dinner to work instead of calling in at the dreaded canteen and hopefully that would do the job.

Placing the half full mug back down on the vacant seat next to him, he uncrossed his legs and reviewed his edited stage directions once again and glanced around the room to see if all were assembled. There were still a few missing faces, so he decided to take a quick trip to the toilet, as this was his second mug of tea, then hopefully make a start on tonight's proceedings. Standing up and stretching his arms above his head, he made off towards the gents, saying "hellos" to the people he passed and pulling a funny face at Andrew as he caught his eye.

Five minutes later, after the last few group members had shuffled in and taken their seats in the first couple of rows, Harry got up on the stage and addressed the group.

'Evening all, thanks for coming tonight. I hope everyone had a good Christmas and got all the presents they wanted from Father Christmas this year?'

There were murmurings, grins and nods of agreement from the cast sat below. Sat at the back Andrew made the international sign for "wanker" at him, which Harry just ignored.

'Good, good. I don't know about you lot, but I think I've eaten my own body weight in Twiglets,' he continued.

This was met with more smiles, as the cast continued to remove scarves, hats and warm coats, with a couple of them then putting their scarves back around their necks, as they acclimatised to the temperature in the hall, that the clanking radiators were trying their hardest to increase.

'Ok, so we seem to have the first act nailed, which is excellent; good work everyone. What I would like to do this evening is run through the second act in its entirety, so that we get that one polished off as well. In addition, I've made a couple of changes to some of the stage directions, which I'll go through with you all as we progress through the act. Don't worry, most of them are minor, and it's just about bringing your characters further forward on the stage, and trying to fit in the odd "it's behind you" gag as well.'

Harry looked around at the faces below, pleased to see that most of them were still looking positive after his announcement. One of the things he'd noticed early on, was that it was relatively easy getting people to walk about on the stage. It required a little more effort for people to learn their lines. But getting people to walk and talk at the same time could prove difficult to accomplish.

'Ok, so unless anyone's got any questions? No? Good, then positions please for the start of act two, scene one, where we see the Cat being sold to the Ship's Captain ahead of their voyage. Let's start in five please everyone.'

Harry felt a surge of pride, as with the minimum of fuss and almost no confusion from anyone, people started getting themselves ready and in position to start. He thought he might have a bit of a battle on his hands, what with dragging them in for an extra rehearsal in the week between Christmas and New Year, which most people normally reserved for watching old episodes of Dr Who, eating leftover turkey sandwiches and trying to remember which day the recycling bin had to go out.

Seeing Ben about to go past him, Harry half raised his arm to stop him, wanting a quick word. 'Ben, how are you? Nice Christmas?'

Ben stopped and put his hands on his hips. 'Hey Harry, yeah good thanks, but, err, you might not want to ask Jessica that. I, err, didn't get her what she wanted, or, err, too much at all. She's a bit pissed off with me.'

'You rotten sod. Ok, I won't mention the C word to her. You're ok though? How's your finger now?'

Ben held up his left hand, which still had a bandage around his little finger.

'Yeah it's better than it was thanks. The doc said that it normally takes up to four or so weeks on average to heal, so I'm going back next week to have the bandage taken off, as that will be about six weeks, 'cos of Christmas and whatnot.'

Harry smiled. 'That's great. And it's feeling ok?'

'Yep, just itching quite a bit, so I'll be glad to get the bloody thing off to be honest,' Ben said, as he turned his hand around so his palm was facing him.

'I'm not surprised.'

'I also wanna see what it looks like.'

'The scar you mean?'

'That, and also it's going to be shorter than it was,' Ben said, more theatrically than any of his acting had been to date.

'Oh, really? Why's that?'

'From what I can remember the doc saying whilst she was sewing it back on, they shorten the bone a little bit, so that the nerves aren't under tension when they sew them back together. Or something like that anyway. I wasn't listening too much as there was a bit of a looker in the room, if you catch my drift,' he winked.

'Ah, huh,' Harry said, thinking that only Ben would be concentrating on women during minor surgery.

'Well, I think she was anyway. She had one of those facemasks on, but she had lovely eyes.'

'Well, I can see how that could be distracting for you.'

'Yep,' Ben leant in towards Harry slightly. 'Err, perhaps that's something else to just keep to ourselves and not mention to Jessica, eh?'

Harry mimed zipping his lips shut. 'My lips are sealed and I will take your secret to my grave.'

'Thanks Harry. Right, I better go and get ready for the first scene.'

'Great, off you go and catch you in a bit.'

It wasn't until Ben had disappeared around the corner of the set that Harry realised that Ben wasn't even in the first scene. Shaking his head and wondering what mishaps lay before him this evening, he made his way back towards the rows of seating that served as the auditorium to get his script and get act two underway.

Fifty-One

Helen

New Year's Eve

Helen had been thrilled that everyone had been so interested in coming to her New Year's Eve gathering when she had mentioned it at the meal. She was glad that apart from one ruckus between Darren and Ben, the pantomime was forging firmer friendships between them all and she now considered them all friends.

Friendship hadn't really been something that she had been missing from her life, as she did have the odd friend here and there. She had also got on well with Leo before the pantomime got started and she always had her cat to keep her company anyway. That being said, she was pleased at the response to her party invitations.

She put frozen sausage rolls onto a baking tray, alongside trays with quiche, mini cheese and onion rolls, chicken kiev bites and several small pizzas. She stood there for a minute scratching her head, wondering how she was going to fit all of this into her small, two-shelved oven.

The hot food was in addition to the stacks of crisps, nuts, cheeses, fruit, bread, breadsticks, fun sized bags of chocolate bars and several bottles of wine and lemonade that she had bought first thing this morning from the local supermarket. She had been so focused on buying all the necessary food and nibbles for the party this evening, that halfway home, she'd realised that she had forgotten to buy both cat food and something for her husband's dinner.

When she had arrived back home, temporarily put the food and drink away and had a quick sit down and a cup of tea, she got stuck into some housework. Several hours later her cottage was spotless and supposedly smelt of *summer lawns*; or at least according to the can of air freshener that's what it smelt like; she wasn't so sure. Just to be on the safe side, she had lit a few joss sticks and strategically placed them about the downstairs rooms as well as the bathroom.

Now, as she stood in her kitchen, mentally juggling different baking trays around in her head, she couldn't be happier. She loved entertaining, and always enjoyed it when it was her turn to host the Book Club on a Wednesday evening.

Her husband had come down from the attic and his beloved train set earlier in the day, to see if she needed any help tidying up or arranging any of the food, but she had politely declined his help. She was more than happy to sort things out herself, so she had sent him back upstairs to his railway tycoon empire with a mug of tea and a sandwich. Like most days, she hadn't heard from him since.

A few years back, after reading a crime novel with the Book Club, she had briefly wondered what he was doing up there and if he was really playing with his train set? Or, did he have naked women swinging from the rafters with gags in their mouths, as he slowly and silently tortured them, before feeding their remains to the cat. After plucking up the courage, she had stuck her head up in the attic one Thursday afternoon when he was at work, and had been almost disappointed to find just the train set and a stack of railway based magazines. The only thing she spotted that was out of sorts was the half-empty coffee mug with mould growing in it that he had forgotten up there.

After deciding the order in which to cook the party food, she checked the kitchen clock, pleased that she still had a couple of hours before people started to turn up. She could cook all the food now, and then just zap it in the microwave to warm it back up before people would start arriving.

As a favourite festive song of hers came on the radio, she turned the volume up a little. She didn't care that Christmas was now over, she was just happy to be in her element.

In the front room, Mr Darcy opened one eye as the noise from the small box got noticeably louder and he decided to get up and look for the fuse box; but then tiredness overtook him and he lay back down again under the Christmas tree. It was damned hard work being a cat.

Fifty-Two

A couple of hours and an outfit change later, Helen and her party food were almost ready to rock and roll, despite her nearly blowing up the microwave by forgetting to take the silver foil from the mince pies she was warming up. Crisis averted, she was putting the finishing touches to the buffet spread when there was a knock at her front door and Leo's voice called through the letter box.

'Only me. I come bearing gifts of wine. And it's cold out here, so come and let me in.'

'Coming,' she called out, as she wiped her hands on a tea towel that was on the kitchen worktop, and walked through the living room to let him in.

As she opened the door, he shot in and shuddered. 'Brrr, it's cold out there this evening,' he said, giving Helen a kiss on the cheek and then handed her a bottle of wine. 'Here you go, present for you. Well, actually, it's for me to drink, so get it open.'

'Come on through to the kitchen. I'm just finishing off the last few bits before the rest of the gang turn up.'

'Will do, just going to nip and use your loo first, as the cold always makes me need to go for a tinkle.'

'Yep, you know where it is,' she called after him, as he took the stairs to the first floor two steps at a time.

She had just returned to the kitchen and was putting the mini sausage rolls in the microwave, when there was a knock at the door again and this time when she opened it, it was

Andrew. He was very smartly dressed and holding a bottle of champagne, as well as two bottles of wine with fancy looking labels on.

'Hello, Andrew. Come on in,' she said grinning, stepping back to let him in.

'Good evening, Helen. This is for you,' he said, bowing slightly and handing her the bottle of chilled Bollinger champagne.

She didn't know much about champagne, but she did know that Bollinger was a decent one and must have cost Andrew a few quid.

'Oh, why thank you, Andrew. This is really lovely of you.'

Andrew wiped his feet on the doormat. 'Think nothing of it. It's not a vintage one I'm afraid, so just a little something from me to thank you for hosting us all this evening.'

'Honestly, it's my pleasure. Come on in and let me take your coat. I'll hang it up in the utility room.'

'Lovely, thanks,' he said, putting the wine down on the sofa and slipping off his jacket.'

Helen led Andrew through the kitchen, where she carefully placed the bottle of champagne and the two bottles of wine that he had given her. She nodded in the direction of the utility room for him to hang his coat up in.

After he re-emerged she asked, 'What can I get you to drink?'

'Just a glass of wine, if you please.'

'One of the ones you brought with you ok?'

'Great,' he said, looking at the plates of food.

Helen lifted down from the shelf one of the wine glasses that were reserved for best and poured Andrew a party sized measure and handed it over to him. Then, lifting her own half full glass that she had poured herself earlier, clinked glasses with him.

'Cheers.'

'Cheers.'

'Started drinking without me I see,' Leo said as he bounded into the room and the two men hugged in greeting and exchanged pleasantries about how their Christmases had been. Andrew told them both that he had visited his parents for the day, along with his brother and his brother's family. He joked that he got on well with his family, but that he was ready to go home by the end of the afternoon and had had a large gin and tonic when he had got home. Leo had also spent the day with his family, and had driven over to Kettering in Northamptonshire on Christmas Eve after he had finished work; as that's where his family lived, including his brother and sister in law and their young daughter, whom Leo doted on. He was busy regaling them with the list of noisy presents he had bought his niece for Christmas, mostly to annoy his brother, when there was a knock at the front door. This heralded the arrival of Polly and Harry, Darren and Patricia, who had all arrived at the same time, with a various assortment of wine bottles, vodka, fruit juice and a bag of carrot sticks.

Within fifteen minutes, they were joined by the others. Helen was both surprised, flattered and horrified that Valerie and Gerald had turned up, as she was certain that they would cancel at the last minute.

Being a dutiful host, Helen went around making sure that everyone's glass was topped up, and that the bowls and plates of food and nibbles were not running low.

The party was soon split into two camps, with Valerie, Gerald, Patricia, along with Harry and a very bored Polly in the living room and the others in the kitchen. Polly had tried sneaking off to the other room on a couple of occasions, but Harry's stare had quite clearly told her that if she did abandon him here, her remains would only be discovered in several decades time, after he had died and the new owners had dug up the patio to build an extension. She had stayed, but the ferocity in which she crunched on her carrot sticks hopefully told Harry that he was lucky to be married to her and that he most definitely owed her one. Which is why when half an hour later he offered to get everyone a top up and disappeared she could have quite happily poked both of his eyes out with the blunt end of one of her carrots.

Valerie was self-importantly telling them how to discipline children to get the best out of them, and making an example out of children that weren't performing well could be a motivational tool, if used correctly. Both Gerald and Patricia were nodding in agreement with Valerie. Polly rolled her eyes and wished that Harry would hurry up with her drink. She would down it, and go for a half an hour refill and join in with the laughter and merriment that was coming from the kitchen. She had not signed up to have to listen to this old dinosaur prattle on all evening about archaic teaching methods. It was New Year's Eve and she wanted to enjoy herself.

Helen took a bite out of a sausage roll. In the kitchen the wine was flowing and the more wine that Leo had, the more animated he became. 'Well,' he said dramatically, waving his wine glass about in his hand, 'probably the time I was most embarrassed was about ten years ago. When I was younger, I very occasionally used to sleepwalk. Anyway, I was living in a ground floor flat at the time, and one morning I woke up to find myself standing in the car park for the apartments, stark bollock naked.'

The kitchen filled with laughter and Helen topped up Leo's glass again.

'Thanks love. Now, that's not the best bit either. I had only gone and locked myself out of my flat.'

'God, what did you do?' asked Jessica, as some of the others giggled away.

'Thankfully it was still quite early in the morning, about five ish I think. I had some friends that lived a couple of streets across and we had spare keys for each other. I started creeping up towards their house, crouching down between the cars as I went. And then what happened? A police car pulls up alongside me as I'm sneaking along.'

Guffaws of laughter exploded from everyone and Leo now had the attention of the whole room and he took a gulp of his wine before continuing. 'They had received reports of a flasher in the area and had been sent to investigate.'

'And what did they say?' asked Darren, halfway through a mini quiche, with pastry crumbs down the front of his jumper, intermingled with different shades of cat hair.

'Thankfully, once I had told them my story and they eventually realised I was being serious, they became quite sympathetic and wrapped me up in one of those silver tinfoil blanket things and drove me round to my friends' house. They were rather confused to be woken up by a couple of coppers and me wrapped up like a kebab. Since then I've always had a spare roll of tin foil hidden somewhere in my garden, just in case.'

As Leo continued to hold court, Harry chuckled to himself and returned to the funeral in the front room with the fresh drinks that he had offered to get about twenty minutes ago, not daring to look in his wife's direction, for fear of seeing a jet of flame come out of her nostrils and head his way. He'd got her a very large measure of vodka and tomato juice to help make amends, but he wasn't at all surprised when after a mere few seconds, she made an excuse to leave the room and disappeared. He just sat there nursing his own drink, listening to Valerie talk about how Ofsted are incompetent and how she could do a much better job at improving the country's teaching and learning standards. He stopped listening after she mentioned that she would bring back the use of the cane and decided that she was a bat-shit crazy megalomaniac.

Eventually others came into the living room. More to sit down somewhere than anything else he guessed, but it meant that there was an alternative conversation to join in with, rather than just Valerie's sermon.

The clock continued its march ever closer to midnight and the New Year, somewhat faster now that there were other people in the room.

Out in the kitchen, accompanied by several empty wine bottles and half eaten food, Helen was with Ben, Leo and Chelsea. They were having a drunken conversation about a documentary programme that Helen hadn't seen, but the others had. It was supposedly on Netflix, and was about a man who had been accused of murder. They had differing opinions on whether the man was actually guilty or not. If it had been up to Ben and Chelsea, the man would have been released with a full pardon by now, but Leo was seemingly convinced of his guilt.

'The problem is that if they, you know, *zap* you, then that's it, isn't it,' Ben said, leaning against the sideboard, with a bottle of beer in his hand.

'Yes, but he clearly did it,' Leo said.

'Yes, but what if he didn't, eh? Then there would be a dead innocent man.'

'But that's the law of the land. Plus, they had him bang to rights.'

'Aw, no. They stitched him up good and proper. They didn't find half the evidence until something like the fortieth search and then it was planted there.' Ben continued, looking at Chelsea for support, who nodded in agreement and took a sip of her wine. She looked a little worse for wear and Helen noticed that she briefly held onto Ben's arm for support, before steadying herself on her feet again.

'If only you were so passionate about learning your lines, Ben,' Leo laughed.

'Hey. It's difficult you know, remembering all those lines and where to stand and who to look at.'

'I know, it's so difficult talking, isn't it?'

'Ah, shut your face. I didn't even want the part. I thought I'd get cast as one of the villagers.'

'Or the village idiot.'

'Oi, Leo, that's enough,' Chelsea pipped up, swatting Leo's arm, but then having to hold onto him for support.

'I'm only teasing him. Love you really, Ben,' Leo said, blowing him a kiss.

'Well if I'm the village idiot that makes you one of the village people.'

'Very good. Perhaps you have got a sense of humour after all, cheers!' said Leo, clinking his wine glass against Ben's beer bottle.

'What time is it anyway, is it midnight yet?' asked Ben, putting the bottle down on the worktop.

'God knows, my phone's run out of battery, from all the knob-heads texting me "Happy New Year" since about two o'clock this afternoon,' Leo replied.

'It's, err, coming up to eleven fifty,' said Chelsea, after looking at her watch for about ten seconds and squinting her eyes.

'Fabo, shall we go and join the rest of them in the front room?' Leo asked.

'You two go ahead, I'm just going to grab a drink of water,' said Chelsea.

'I'll stay with her and join you guys in a second,' said Ben, looking around for a glass that wasn't half full of alcohol, so that he could get her some water.

'Here you go,' Helen said. She then followed Leo into the living room.

Leo bounced into the living room and announced that it was getting close to midnight. Helen picked up the remote control for the television and on came the TV, and they waited for twelve o'clock and the chimes.

Returning from the upstairs bathroom, Jessica came down the stairs one at a time, careful not to fall, as she was feeling a little tipsy. Looking around the crowded room, she looked for Ben, as she wanted to be with her boyfriend when New Year arrived.

'Leo, have you seen Ben anywhere? He's not outside having a crafty fag is he?' she asked.

'No, flower. He's in the kitchen getting some water with Chelsea. You know what a lightweight she is at the best of times.'

Jessica made off for the kitchen to grab Ben and drag him into the room to be with her. The kitchen door was slightly ajar, so she pushed open the door, and after a quick gasp, she grabbed the nearest thing to her, which was a mince pie, and threw it at her boyfriend.

Then, to the sound of Big Ben's first *Bong* she went over and punched him. Hard.

Fifty-Three

The Two Cleaners

The blackbirds sang in the trees nearby as they woke up, stretched their wings and peered outside their nests to check the weather.

Kelly yawned loudly and continued tapping her foot. She checked her phone again for both the time, and for a message from Jenny to say where the hell she was.

Her friend normally picked her up for work, but Jenny had been on a date last night and wasn't sure if she would be the right side of town in the morning to pick her up.

As she stood outside the church, the cold attacking her feet and face, a prang of jealousy pricked at her heart. She hadn't been on a successful date for a couple of months now and was getting fed up with the whole dating scene, especially on-line dating. She would spend a few days exchanging messages with some bloke that she had met on one of the many dating apps that she was on, Tinder, Plenty of Fish, Match and eharmony, and the chap would come across as funny, charming, attentive and normal and she would allow herself to become excited at the prospect that this might be the one.

Then she would meet them. Then everything changed.

They would spend all evening looking at her breasts, trying to stroke her leg and expect a snog at the end of the night in exchange for a couple of glasses of cheap white wine. And to make things worse, they never, ever looked like their profile pictures. Either that, or they had aged ten years, lost their hair and put on three stone overnight.

She had even turned up to one lunchtime date, to find her date five drinks ahead of her and slurring. Thankfully, after fifteen minutes the drinks had worked their way through his system, and he had to go to the toilet. She had made her escape from the pub and quickly blended in with the Saturday lunchtime shoppers and blocked his number.

She glanced down at her phone once more and shivered in the cold. She would give her another ten minutes, then as she didn't have the keys to open up, she was off home to warm up and ignore the world for the day. looking up the road and saw a figure approaching.

The figure got closer and closer and Jenny strode to a stop next to her; cheeks red and flushed.

'Morning. Why are you walking?' Kelly asked her.

'That lazy bastard wouldn't get out of bed to give me a lift in, would he,' Jenny replied, sniffing her nose that was running from the cold.

'What a git,' Kelly said, feeling a *bit* guilty about feeling smug.

'I know. He had his wicked way with me last night and promised me a lift in in the morning. Then can't be bothered getting out of bed, claiming he's too knackered from a long week at work. I felt like saying I was knackered from holding me legs in the air all night, but then I remember it weren't all night, it were only about thirty seconds.'

'Sounds like a real catch you got there,' Kelly said.

'Hmm. I don't think I'll be seeing him again anytime soon.'

'Need the Viagra?'

'Yeah. And like waiting in line for an hour for a rubbish rollercoaster, it wasn't worth the ride.'

Kelly shivered and looked at her friend. 'Come on then, let's get inside. Although I doubt it will be much warmer in there to be honest. You know how tight they are with the heating.'

The two of them made their way up the path to the church hall that they had been asked to clean before the pantomime's opening night in a few days' time. Jenny fiddled with the key in the lock for a couple of seconds and they were soon in the dark hall. Kelly turned the lights on and the room flickered to life, revealing the scenery propped up at the stage end of the hall and plastic seats stacked up in piles around the sides of the room.

'Get us a brew on, and I'll dig out the brushes and mops from the cupboard.' said Jenny, yawning.

Kelly paused. 'You sure no one will notice? I wouldn't be surprised if they counted the flaming teabags you know.'

'Don't be daft, no one will find out. Besides, it's cold in here and there must be some health and safety law about not working when you're cold. Get that kettle on, love.' Jenny said to her, chucking the bunch of keys over. 'It's the small silver one to get into the kitchen.'

'Ok my love, on your head be it.'

A few minutes later she brought the piping hot mugs through into the hall and they both stood there sipping their tea. Kelly could feel the warmth slowly return to her body.

'OH MY GOD,' burst out Jenny suddenly, nearly causing Kelly to drop her tea in fright.

'What? Jesus, you scared the hell out of me.'

Jenny looked at her, excitement plastered all over her tired looking face. 'I just remembered what I was going to tell you. You'll *never* ever guess who's now single.'

'George Clooney?'

'No. You silly sausage. *Ben!*'

Kelly stopped, her mug halfway up to her mouth. 'You're winding me up?'

'Nope. At least, that's what it says on Facebook'

'Bloody hell. I didn't know you was friends with him on there?'

'Err, I'm not. I was just doing some looking about, like you do.'

'Oh yeah. Stalking you mean.'

Jenny shrugged. 'Well, he's got an open profile hasn't he. And it's not really stalking, I call it *investigating*.'

'Hmm. Go on.'

'I was doing some *investigating* before my date last night, and I saw that his status had changed. And you'll never guess what's also happened.'

'Tell me, what? What?'

Jenny took a step closer to her. 'One of his friends put a picture up on his Facebook wall, showing him with a proper black eye.'

'Never?' Kelly felt shocked. Ben was gorgeous, who would want to hurt him like that?

'Yep. God knows what happened. But I'm guessing someone's clouted him one.'

'Yeah, that's generally where black eyes come from, Inspector Clouseau.'

Jenny crossed her arms. 'He could have walked into a tractor door,' she said, like it was obvious.

'I suppose. But I doubt there are many tractors at his bank. I wonder what happened?' She took a sip of her tea, her mind going over all the possibilities.

'I reckon he must have been chatting up some bird, and her fella thumped him one,' Jenny said.

'Or it could have been the field mouse?'

'What? Jessica lamp him one? Come on, be serious.'

She pondered it. 'Good point. I don't think she could fight her way out of a paper bag,' she said, before thoughtfully slurping her tea.

'And you know what this means now, don't you?' said Jenny animatedly.

'What?'

'He's single.'

Kelly laughed. 'Going to make your move on him then, my lover?'

'You never know. I'd take good care of him and his black eye, nurse him back to health.'

'And keep him locked up in your bedroom as well?'

'Uh-huh. Just for his own safety you understand.'

'Such a caring and considerate person you are.'

'I know. I should have gone into nursing really.'

'You're a real-life Florence Nightingale. Only with Viagra instead of antibiotics.'

'I most certainly am. I'd cook him fresh chicken soup to help him feel better.'

'Cook? You, cook?'

'Opening the tin and stirring it on the hob counts.'

'Sure.'

Jenny started to pace up and down in front of where Kelly was standing. 'I wonder if he likes watching *Real Housewives*? We could snuggle up on the sofa together and watch it in the evenings.'

'Hmm,' was all she replied, as she shook her head.

Jenny stopped pacing and stuck an index finger into her ear and gave it a wiggle. 'I wonder what happened though? And is he going to be well enough to do this play thing in a couple of days?'

'I didn't think of that, my love. I guess they'll have to put some make up on him, to hide the bruise. Is it a big one? Get your phone and show us a picture.'

Jenny fished her phone out of her pocket and managed to unlock it on the second attempt. Clicking on the Facebook app, she found Ben's profile and handed her phone over.

'Ouch. That's a right shiner, isn't it.'

'The poor lamb, who would do such a thing?'

'You should speak to that cleaner that you know at the bank, see if she knows the gossip. Come on, we had better get started with this lot, otherwise we're never going to get home today.'

Kelly looked around the large hall. 'That's true. We should finish in a couple of hours. You fancy a quick half up at the Shepherds Rest after?'

'You buying?'

'You're a tight arsed duck, you know that?'

'Yep, that's how I got me millions stashed away in a Swiss bank account.'

'Millions? You could have splashed out on some plastic surgery.'

'You're definitely buying the drinks now. And I feel a full pint is in order, not just a half.'

'Jesus. Alright, alright, deal. You can leave me some of your millions in your will.'

'You think you're going to outlive me?'

'I'll have you assassinated,' Kelly grinned and passed Jenny a plastic broom. 'Come on then, let's get cracking shall we,' she said downing the last dregs of her tea and looking around for somewhere to put her mug.

The two of them went about sweeping up the large hall and continued to gossip, and by the end of their cleaning shift, Jenny had planned her wedding to Ben, knew where they were going on their honeymoon and what each of their five children were going to be called.

Fifty-Four

Harry

As the scene played out in front of him – the cast more or less sticking to the script and stage directions - Harry sat with Polly, Valerie and Gerald at the back of the hall deep in conversation.

Patricia had been left in charge of the direction, which she had looked thrilled about. So thrilled that she had just muttered under her breath when Harry had asked her to step in for a few minutes, so that he could have a quick chat with the others.

'It's a week today that we open, so I don't see what we can do about it,' hissed Polly, looking over her shoulder to make sure no one was in earshot. Apart from a couple of young children dressed as rats laughing at something they were watching on a mobile phone, there was no one nearby.

'That may be all well and good, Polly, but he does have a black eye. What kind of a message does that send to all of the families that have paid good money to come and watch a *family friendly* play?' Valerie said over the top of her glasses that were resting in their customary spot at the end of her nose.

'Well what's your suggestion then?' Polly fired back.

'I'm not suggesting anything, I am merely highlighting that there is an issue. Perhaps, Harry, if you had replaced him as we discussed a few weeks ago, we wouldn't be in the predicament now,' Valerie said looking at him.

He just about resisted the urge to respond with Welsh swearwords.

'You were right, Harry, she is making sure you take the blame for this,' Polly said.

Harry went to open his mouth, but Valerie spoke first.

'You mistake me again, Polly. I'm not blaming anyone for anything, I'm simply saying that if Harry had have listened to the opinion that I voiced a while ago and acted upon it, then we would be facing an alternate of circumstances now.'

'But how could we replace him, then, or now? We don't have anyone to replace him with. Should we just call the whole thing off, Valerie, is that what you would like?' Polly's hissing had become louder and Harry was certain that if she had been a snake, her tail would have been rattling as well.

'Absolutely not. I am simply stating the facts and voicing my thoughts on the matter. I would have imagined that my opinion as the primary writer and my extensive management experience as a headmistress should be taken into consideration.'

'Primary writer? Are you having delusions of grandeur? You're a co-writer. And no one likes your scenes anyway, they aren't funny and the language is like being in the sixteenth century.'

Gerald stood up. 'I'll just, um, make some tea for us, shall I?' He practically ran to the kitchen.

Harry wondered if he could get away with going to help him.

Valerie glared after him disdainfully, like a general watching her cowardly troops retreat on the battlefield. 'I think you'll find,' she continued, her voice icy cold and her eyes narrowing, 'that it was I who had to correct the majority of your work. But thankfully for you, that's not what we're meant to be discussing here.'

'There was nothing wrong with my work, thank you very much,'

'Ok, ok, let's just take a minute and all calm down,' interjected Harry, not wanting to witness a fight between the two of them in the middle of a church hall. Besides, he was afraid that Polly would win and then he'd have to arrest her for beating Valerie to a pulp; and that certainly wouldn't go down well. 'It's far too late to replace Ben, there's no one else available. And as we've already said, it's only a week to go until we open, which wouldn't give anyone enough time to learn the lines.'

Valerie folded her arms and stared straight at Harry, her beady eyes fixated on him, unblinking, like a wolf before it pounces mercilessly on its prey. 'Correct me if I'm wrong, Harry, but are you saying that you're happy for him to be the lead role in a *church* pantomime aimed at young *children* and *families*, when he's got a black eye?'

'No, Valerie, I'm not saying that. What I am saying is that we need to show a little compassion here and consider what all of our options are. Valerie, as you know, the church next door is called Saint Jude's. Do you know what Saint Jude is the patron saint of?' Harry said slowly and calmly.

'I don't recall at this exact moment.'

'Let me enlighten you. Saint Jude is the patron saint of lost causes. Ben is clearly having a hard time at the moment, so as his friends and colleagues, why don't we show him a little compassion, eh?'

Valerie took her glasses off the end of her nose and sighed. 'I leave the decision to you then, Harry. I'm sure you'll do what's best for the play.' She stood up, dusted down her skirt, nodded curtly to both of them, and then walked off, nose stuck up in the air.

'Well done, darling, one nil to you I think that is.' Polly said, ruffling Harry's hair.

'Thanks. Still not sure what we're going to do about Ben though. Good grief, this is a nightmare.'

'Oh, give it a week and it will have gone down quite a bit I'm sure. Stick a load of stage make up on him and people will never notice. Besides, it's only his right eye, so we can always just change the stage directions and have him only ever showing his left side or something.'

'Good thinking. He's just come so far, and we don't have much time, so I don't want to get someone else in the role unless it's absolutely necessary. Unless, you fancy playing the part? In which case, I'll fire him right now.'

'Good grief, no way. I can't get making the tea right, I'd totally sod acting up.'

Gerald walked back over with a tray and four mugs of tea on it.

'Has she popped out for a minute?' he asked innocently.

'She's, umm, yeah, popped out. Not entirely sure she's coming back this evening to be honest.' Harry said, aware that the poor guy would probably be bearing the brunt of Valerie's wrath later.

'Ah. I see,' Gerald said, placing the tray down on the seat that Valerie had vacated. 'Tea?' he asked them both, as if he didn't have a care in the world.

'Err, yes please, Gerald,' said Polly.

'And for me please. Thanks.'

'Should I presume that she's left as she didn't get her own way? Well, can I just say well done for standing up to her. No one's done that in years, so good for you. I would stay and chat, but that mightn't go down too well. But well done

277

all the same. See you at tomorrow night's rehearsal.' With that, Gerald grinned at them both, did a mock salute and then walked over to the door, turning and waving at them before closing it behind him.

Harry and Polly just looked at each other.

'Did that just really happen?' Polly asked.

'Yep. Unless he spiked both our drinks with something and we're hallucinating.'

They both sniffed their mugs of tea.

'Right, I suppose I had better get back to directing, and make sure that Ben doesn't sod anything up,' Harry said, getting up and rolling his head around his shoulders to try and relieve some of the tension in his neck.

'Catch you later.'

Harry walked up towards the front of the rows of chairs where he had left Patricia standing in for him as director, and took back the helm.

Fifty-Five

First Day of the New School Term

The outside evening air was starting to chill and the street lights were just starting to flicker on up and down the quiet road outside of St. Jude's. All was quiet on this Wednesday evening, until the front door of the church burst open and out peered a deranged mad woman with venom in her eyes. A mad woman dressed in an apron and bright pink cleaning gloves.

'Oi, Kelly, you skinny witch. Get your arse in here now,' Jenny screeched, feeling really annoyed, sweat gathering on her forehead and starting to trickle down the side of her face, causing her to dap the torrents with the back of her gloved hand. Pausing, she then sniffed her glove and promptly turned her nose up and away from the offending hand. Jenny looked around and couldn't see her friend, strike that, her lazy, good for nothing friend anywhere.

'If you don't get back 'ere now, I will shove this can of Fabreeze up your...'

At that moment, Kelly's head popped up from behind one of the gravestones, fag in mouth, her wide eyes looking quizzically at her, so that she resembled a type of manic looking Jack-in-the-box that would scare the hell out of even the most hardened of horror film fans.

'Alright my love?' Kelly asked her, her head tilted to one side and raising one eyebrow, which didn't improve her less than sane appearance.

'Jesus, Mary and Joseph,' Jenny exclaimed. 'What the hell are you doing hiding behind a bastard gravestone for? You very nearly gave me a heart attack!'

'And what a loss you'd be to the single men of this world, my love.'

'And you should take up a career in comedy.'

'Oh yes, I can just see myself on some comedy show-whatsit. I'd be such a hit, and I'd be famous. Perhaps then Ben will realise that I am really the woman of his dreams, and lust after me, a deep longing in his loins.'

'I take it back, you can tell a joke after all,' she said, facing Kelly and feeling like murdering someone.

Kelly looked at her and said, 'What's up with you, my love, you are not looking the happiest of bunnies at the moment?'

'I most certainly am not a happy frigging bunny. The kids are all throwing up in the toilets at the moment, and there are more kids than sodding toilets, so it's going everywhere.'

'You're having a laugh, love?' Kelly asked her cautiously. 'I know you're the Queen of practical jokes, but you didn't look like you're joking at the moment. In fact, you look like a thermonuclear warhead about to explode and cause the landscape to be decimated and uninhabitable for the new few generations, if not until the end of time itself,' she sniffed.

'Do I look like I'm having a laugh? Now get your backside in here and give me a hand cleaning it all up. Oh, and see if you can't find some buckets or summat. It's starting to look like the scene from the Exorcist in there, and I can't see the vicar being able to sort it out with a few flicks of Holy Water.'

With that, Jenny gave her friend a final glare before turning back inside the church door and headed in the direction of the toilets, the putrid smell hitting her like a freight train as soon as she heaved open the door.

Fifty-Six

Gerald

Later That Evening

Gerald swallowed nervously. Valerie wasn't looking happy at all. Even the clip-clop of her high heels on the pavement had attitude.

'But what are we going to do? We have our opening night in less than a week.' she exclaimed to Gerald, continuing to pace up and down outside the front of the church, the door wide open in an attempt to dissipate the smell of bleach, vomit and a hint of stale cigarette smoke.

'Yes, this is quite a predicament indeed,' added Gerald slightly nervously. He didn't like it when his wife's voice started rising through the octaves, as the outcome was generally not a positive one. Over the years, he'd learnt that the best thing to do was to say as little as possible and let Valerie boil away and hiss out steam until she eventually simmered down. In the early years of their marriage, he'd tried to be helpful and regularly suggest solutions to whatever the ensuing crisis was. Unfortunately, this just had the same effect as throwing a vat of petrol onto a bonfire.

'Predicament? Predicament?' snarled Valerie, her eyes dangerously close to turning red and have fire seep from her mouth. 'You say that like you're in Waitrose and you're trying to decide which on-offer whisky you're going to buy.

This is more than a predicament, this is a *crisis* Gerald Theobald Charles Makepeace.'

'Yes, my dear, of course, it's a crisis,' said Gerald, remembering fondly some of the more real impending-doom world-ending crises that he had help avoid during his time at GCHQ. The one with the boxes of Russian Dolls had been his personal favourite.

'And...?' Valerie stopped pacing and stood there facing him, her eyes open wide like a demented owl.

Even though it was only January, a trickle of sweat navigated its way down Gerald's back. 'And.... what, my dear?' He took a small step backwards.

'Where on Earth are we going to find another twenty children from to play the rats? The food poisoning has spread throughout all the school now and it's been temporarily closed. Can you believe it? It's only their first day back at school after the holidays. Goodness me. Nothing like this happened on my watch, I can tell you that for nothing. I blame that smarmy Jamie Oliver.'

Gerald decided it was best not to ask what part Mr Oliver had played in the outbreak of food poisoning that had spread throughout St. Jude's Primary School like the black death, causing the majority of the pupils and teaching staff to be off sick and have to stay within three metres of a toilet at all times. Gerald did have a solution in mind, but what would his wife's reaction be? Persuading a loyal Chinese spy to defect would be an easier conversation to have, rather than to offer his wife a solution that she hadn't formulated herself. Summoning all the courage he had, Gerald cleared his throat and said, 'How about asking the headmaster of Clear Lake School to help?'

Clear Lake was a private school about two miles away from St. Jude's, which educated the sons and daughters of

Somerset's more well-off residents, as well as some international students, including the son of a high powered Russian businessman, whose room had been *modernised* by some of Gerald's old colleagues. Clear Lake had once been a large stately home, but during the 1930s it had been transformed into a grammar school, with entrance examinations that determined that only those who donated stupidly large amounts of money to the school passed.

During the Second World War, much to the horror of the teaching staff, it had been seconded by the War Office and had housed evacuated children from London and Coventry. After the Nazis had been kind enough to call it a day, the school turfed out the strangely spoken evacuees and once again it returned to being a prestigious place of education; for children aged three to eighteen, whose parents were happy to pay three thousand pounds a term.

'Gerald,' scorned Valerie, 'what a…' her eyes shifted from left to right, then back to the left again like a 1980s doll with a toggle in the back of its head. 'Actually…' Valerie coughed a little, giving her a few more seconds to compose her thoughts. 'That's not such a bad idea. The head there owes me a favour. I could have a word with him and see if he could lend me some of his year threes.'

'What a splendid idea. Excellent thinking,' said a relieved Gerald, clapping his hands together. He would live to fight another day.

'Yes, yes, I'll give him a call now. Gerald, fetch the car.'

Fifty-Seven

Harry

Harry muttered under his breath for the third time in as many minutes, and tried to remember if his passport was still in date.

Rats were running wild everywhere. And not the small furry kind, but the excitable two legged, seven and eight-year-old, public school kind, that had been asked to dress up in rat costumes. The headmaster of Clear Lake School had agreed to Valerie's request for help, following the outbreak of food poisoning at St. Jude's Primary School. The school had organised and brought down a minibus full of excitable upper-class rats, who, much to Harry's dismay, were now running riot around both the church and the hall. They were squeaking away in excitement, pleased to not be under the watchful eye of one of their school masters. Harry had wondered why the teacher had wished him luck before hopping back into the minibus, wheel spinning out of the car park and tearing up the road like an overly excited getaway driver after a bank robbery.

For the last twenty minutes, Harry had been doing his best to round up the children. He approached Valerie and wiped the sweat from his forehead.

'I thought these private school kids were meant to be better behaved?' he said, putting his hands on his hips. 'I've seen better behaved EDL supporters.'

Valerie pursed her lips. 'Yes, quite. I too am rather surprised at their behaviour. Of course, you'd never see this sort of thing in my day.'

'Do they not let them out much up at Clear Lake? It's like they've never seen daylight before.'

'I think….they're just getting used to their new surroundings.'

'New surroundings? Don't you think -' Harry was cut off by the church bell in the building next door ringing erratically. Harry just looked at Valerie and sighed. 'Can you ask Andrew to try and keep these ones here under control? I'll go next door and try and flush them out. I think real rats would be easier than this lot,' he said, shaking his head.

As he stomped off for the church next door, the bell ringing increased in beat, sounding to him like a fire bell, a really loud fire bell. Wishing he had his police issue CS gas with him, he broke into a jog until he reached the door, pulled it open and gazed into the darkness that lay before him. He then wished that he also had his police torch and possibly his extendable baton and riot shield. It was going to be a long, long night.

Eventually, all the schoolchildren had been rounded up and bribed with sweets to behave, with Jessica having been sent by Harry to the nearby shop to buy a selection of confectionary - and sedatives if they had any. Jessica looked like she hadn't been one hundred percent sure if Harry was joking about that bit or not, so had just smiled nervously at him and set off for the shops.

'Ok everyone. Now that we're all in order, let's run through act two, scene eight, where the rats make an appearance on the island, and the Ship's Captain offers up the services of the Cat to the Island King. OK? Good. Right, positions please everyone,' Harry said, rubbing his temples with his fingers.

The door to the hall flung open, causing it to crash on the wall, making everyone jump.

'The bells! The bells! My Lord, is she dead? When did the news come in?' shouted Peter, looking like he had been struck by a thousand volts of electricity.

'Vicar? Err, are you alright?' Harry asked, looking at the others in confusion and then back to Peter.

'When did it happen? I can't remember the precedent for this. Do I need to do a special church service?'

'Peter, what is it? What's happened?' asked Harry, going over to the vicar and holding his arm, genuinely concerned that Peter had finally gone mad; or worse, was blind drunk in front of half his congregation and a bunch of rabid schoolchildren.

'The bells ringing like that. When were we told that the monarch had died?'

It finally clicked in Harry's head. 'Peter, no, don't worry, all's fine. It was just one of the new schoolchildren messing about with the church bell. The Queen is still very much alive.'

'You're sure?' Peter asked, his eyes open wide.

'Yep, I promise you, vicar. Everything is fine. I'm really sorry for having worried you, and I'll make sure that the little bast- children don't go anywhere near the church bell again.'

'Oh, thank goodness for that. That's a relief. Oh, my goodness me,' Peter said, holding his head in his hands.

'Do you want to sit down, vicar?' Harry looked around the room. Catching Chelsea's eyes, he motioned for her to come over and help.

'No, no, I'm ok, just a little shaken,' Peter said. 'I think I had better get back home. I think I need a whisky. Err, for medicinal purposes. To calm my nerves, you understand.'

'Of course, great idea. Chelsea? Could you go with him please and make sure he gets back home to the vicarage alright?'

'Sure, Harry, happy to.'

'Thanks, you're a star. Peter, again, I'm extremely sorry about this. I'll make sure it doesn't happen again.'

Chelsea guided Peter back out of the hall and Harry shut the door gently behind them. He then slowly counted to ten, before turning around and marching over to the rats, and making it quite clear that if that happened again, he would take them to their parent's house in a police car and see what their darling mummies and daddies had to say about them scaring a vicar half to death.

Fifty-Eight

Polly

The Night Before the First Performance

Polly looked out of the window at the snow as she unpacked an electric fan heater. She called over to Harry, who was on the other side of the church hall. 'Typical. There's no snow at all over the festive Christmas period, but as soon as the Christmas trees are taken down and put back up in the attic and everyone is back at work, it snows. Heavily.'

Harry grunted in agreement and carried on unpacking another fan heater.

Polly carried on. 'And this being the UK, it brings the entire country to a halt. Cars skidding off roads, airports cancelling flights, people being stuck in their cars overnight and motorway chaos. This wouldn't happen in Canada.'

Harry looked over at her. 'The Canadians have huskies. And what is it with you English and talking about the weather and the havoc it brings? I think it is one of your favourite things to do. Second only to queuing and quietly tutting at the person in front that's holding up the line.'

'You can talk. You were about to attack the man in front at Tesco the other day.'

Harry chose to ignore her, instead he concentrated on picking up the stray bits of polystyrene that had escaped from the packaging.

Polly and Harry had arrived early, and whilst Tyler and Arlo attacked each other with snowballs outside in the car park, they continued unpacking and plugged in several portable fan heaters around the large space and turned them up to their highest heat setting, in an attempt to get some warm air circulating around their makeshift theatre.

'I think we're going to have to put the central heating on at least three, if not four hours before the show starts every night this week,' Polly said, as she looked back out the window at the boys playing, winding her knitted scarf around her neck and then rubbing her hands together.

'You're right, otherwise our audiences will freeze up. We should sell soup during the interval, rather than ice cream. We'd make a killing,' Harry said, standing up and blowing into his hands.

'Hmm. We might also kill off a few of the deaf-old pensioners that come to watch it, not sure that would go down so well, Mr Policeman.'

'Talking of deaf, did I ever tell you about the time that we found a severed ear outside of a theatre? We thought it belonged to a bloke that had been involved in a punch up that we'd nicked and was at the hospital. But when we took the ear along, it was the wrong one. The bloke had had his left ear bitten off in the fight and the ear we found was a right ear.'

Like most of his stories, Polly had heard this one before. 'Lovely. Don't let the children hear you tell your *hilarious* stories, or they'll have nightmares,' she said, looking over to where their youngest Finn was, still strapped into his portable car seat, wrapped up in a red all in one body warmer suit making him look like an imprisoned lobster.

'He's asleep anyway,' Harry said, whilst angling the fan heater so that it directed its hot air towards the middle of the room. 'Right, you staying in here while I bring the boxes in?'

'Yep. Oh, could you grab my handbag please? I left it in the car and it's got my carrot sticks in.'

'Uh-huh, will do,' Harry said, patting his jacket pocket for the car keys and pulling his hat firmly down on his head.

Polly hummed to herself as she pottered about looking for little jobs to do. As the first performance was tomorrow evening, they had decided that they would leave all the props and costumes in the hall for the duration of the pantomime's run, as well as the programmes that they had had printed out as well. They had also bought enough teabags, coffee, bottles of squash and biscuits to sink the Russian aircraft carrier, the *Admiral Kuznetsov,* should she ever decide to stray up the River Tone.

After ferrying the boxes inside and telling Polly that he had checked that their two eldest children hadn't killed each other, or any innocent passers-by, Harry shut the outside door and stamped his feet to get the snow off them.

As he sorted through the boxes, Polly looked around the church hall in its theatre form and smiled. They hadn't done a bad job at all. Thick heavy curtains had been pulled across the large windows that ran along one side of the hall, shutting out all outside light. There were rows and rows of chairs, making up the auditorium. They had hired some small platforms, and the last couple of rows were elevated by about two feet, so that all of their paying audience would be able to get a good view of the performance; whether that would be a *good* thing or not, time would tell. Still, she felt pleased with everything that had been accomplished so far.

At the stage end, sat an interchangeable constructed set, with red curtains at either side, to give it as much of a theatre feel as they could. Above the set, they had rigged up some basic lighting, with an assortment of theatre lights. Harry had reeled off the names to her and she thought they were called Fresnels, or Shakespeares, or something like that. They had borrowed them from the drama department at Clear Lake School; who after Harry told them about the bell ringing incident, decided to waive the loan fee that they would normally charge.

At the back of their theatre to the left of the kitchen, perched in a lookout tower made of borrowed scaffolding, sat the lighting booth where Harry would sit, following the lighting cues that he had pencil written in the margins of the script and adjusting the lighting accordingly.

Running behind the stage area, was a two-metre-wide gap, which was hidden by the set pieces and a blackout curtain, which ran the full length of the set. This ran all the way behind the stage, so that if needed, an actor could exit one side of the stage in a scene and then appear from the other side in the next scene. In this alleyway, was a small table with all the props on, as well as a couple of portable clothes racks, which held all the actors' many costumes. This is also where the actors not on stage would squeeze in, waiting for their turn in the spotlight.

Due to the recent rat problem, Harry had said that he wanted them behind the stage for the minimum amount of time possible, so during the first act they would be holed up in the church next door, under the guard of the actors that only appeared in the second half as well – with the bell rope tucked away out of reach.

As she picked up one of the nearby boxes that Harry had put just inside the door, she just hoped they had thought of everything.

Harry yawned and hoped that he would sleep better this evening, but he doubted it. The dress rehearsal for the first act didn't go too badly. Ben had remembered all his lines and his black eye was *barely* noticeable. At least the bandage was off his finger now, so that was something at least.

The set changes had gone smoothly and he was sure that he would be able to get hold of another old-fashioned milk bottle from somewhere, after the one that he had found had rolled off the stage and smashed. Harry had to give it to the actors on stage at the time, they had carried on not letting the mishap throw them. He had even considered writing it into the script so that it happened in the show for real, but he quickly realised what a health and safety nightmare that would be, so he soon dismissed it from his thoughts.

The only real thing that Harry was concerned about at the moment was Jessica spending most of her time on the stage looking like she would burst into tears at any moment. But again, she had stuck to all her lines and the glares she gave Ben weren't noticeable from the fifth row and beyond. With any luck, the first rows would be full of half blind pensioners wanting to sit near to the toilets anyway.

As everyone took a break and stuffed as many biscuits as they could in their mouths before rehearsing act two for the final time, Polly swept up the broken glass from the milk bottle and Harry and Andrew got the set ready for the opening scene.

'So, what do you think?' Andrew asked, as he helped Harry get the boat scenery and props into position.

'Yeah, good,' he replied, manoeuvring the ship's mast into position, which was held up using the concrete base from his garden sun shade.

'Good? Just *good?*'

'Sorry, this thing is heavy. No, it's great, I'm pleased with how it went.'

'Mmm, agreed. From the bits I saw and heard, it went well; apart from the bottle rolling off and smashing that is,' Andrew said as he helped Harry with the mast.

'These things happen and best it happens now, rather than tomorrow evening. Stuck to their lines though, didn't they,' Harry said proudly.

'I know. I thought that would have thrown them, but they did well. Still, did you see the face that Jessica was pulling half the time though?'

Harry looked about, making sure no one else was nearby. 'I know. If looks could kill, Ben would be six feet under by now, pushing up daisies.'

'Or maybe weeds, considering what he did.'

'Good point. I know most young men are clueless when it comes to women and love, but Christ on a broomstick, did he have to kiss another woman? In the next room, for goodness' sake,' Harry whispered.

'Not the most honourable of things to do, granted. Good for Jessica belting him one, I didn't know she had it in her. Ouch, I've just got a splinter,' Andrew said, examining one of his fingers.

'I know. It must have been quite the punch to give him a shiner like that. I've seen police officers throw weaker punches. Want Polly to look at your finger?'

'Really? I thought your lot were just a bunch of paid thugs and tyrants?'

'Only on Wednesdays, when the Police Federation rep is in Bristol for a meeting,' Harry replied, attaching the ship's rigging. 'It's a shame you can't bleed to death from a splinter.'

Andrew looked at his finger. 'I think I'll live.'

'Right, I think that's all set now. I'll round the mob up, then we can get going and get this show on the road. You got your costume ready for the next act, Mr Ship's Captain?'

'Aye-aye, admiral. All ship shape and ready to go. Just give me second to nip to the loo.'

'Good man, and will do. Break a leg and see you afterwards.'

'Catch you later. And make sure the spotlight centres on me, so that everyone knows who the real star of the show is,' Andrew said, grinning.

'Uh-huh, now bugger off.' Harry made a loudspeaker with his hands, and gave the cast and crew five minutes' notice, and told Patricia to release the rats.

Later that evening, after everyone had left to rush home to their nice warm houses, Harry locked up the door as the snow continued to fall all around. As he shook the door to make sure it was secure, he was certain that all would go well tomorrow evening.

Fifty-Nine

Opening Night

'Well, the sodding rats' tails were in the box last night when we left, so can you *please* go back and look again.' Harry whispered to the stage hand, who was one of the five A-level performing arts students he'd managed to persuade the local college to lend to him as "work experience".

The spotty teenager nodded enthusiastically and shot off, as Harry stood there shaking his head and wondering if he had time to nip to the shop over the road for a small bottle of whisky. The evening had started off so well.

He checked his watch again. Time was marching steadily on, edging nearer and nearer to seven thirty, when the curtain was meant to go up. He wondered why he had elected to do the lighting himself, instead of getting someone else to do it so he could stay here behind the scenes and make sure everything went according to plan. Perhaps he could get one of the smelly teenagers to do it? But probably that wasn't such a smart idea, they'll only end up electrocuting themselves, or burning the place down.

He crept over to the curtains at the front of the stage and gently pulled back on one of them, so that he could take a peek out at the audience. It looked busy already and they still had another fifteen minutes until curtain up. Deciding that he would quickly check on Polly and her friend Sue in the kitchen before climbing up to his perch in the lighting box, he set off around the back of the stage.

Ben was pacing up and down the walkway behind the stage, muttering his lines to himself and trying to avoid both Jessica and Chelsea - which was easier said than done in the confined space that they all shared backstage. It was bad enough that he still had to share the apartment with Jessica, as neither of them could afford to move out. Sleeping on their small sofa was far from comfortable, and she seemed to be deliberately making as much noise as possible when she got ready first thing in the mornings.

He had considered pulling out of the pantomime and going over to Spain to stay with his friends Jason and Cris over there, but he couldn't leave the others in the lurch like that. Or, if he was being truthful, he knew that Harry would probably hunt him down and kill him slowly if he did. But if he messed this up, he was almost certain that Harry would kill him just as slowly.

'And,' said Darren, in a loud whisper so that his audience could all hear him, 'when I was in Casualty, I met all the stars of the show and now know them all on first name terms.'

'Wow!' said one of the rats. 'How awfully exciting.'

'What part did you play?' asked another rat, his face-painted whiskers slightly smudged where he'd been rubbing his face to get sugar off his lips.

'I was the main character of the episode that I was in,' Darren proudly announced, puffing his chest out.

'Didn't you say that you were the extra that got run over at the beginning of the show?' said Helen, who was leaning against the nearby wall, in her full 'bad tempered cook' outfit. She had been bribing the rats to behave with sweets that she had secreted in her cooking apron.

'Err, well, *technically*, yes. But the main plot of the episode focused around my character, and his serious injuries.' Darren defended himself.

'Weren't you in a medically induced coma for the rest of the episode?' Helen continued, tossing a lollypop to a nearby rat, who snapped it up greedily, with the others that were nearby squeaking and pawing at him.

'Well, yes. But without me, there wouldn't have been an episode. And I'm a professional actor who's been on television.'

'That's splendid. Got any sweets?' asked a rat, who was rubbing her big fluffy ears.

'Umm, not on me, no.' Darren said, at which point all the rats lost interest in him, and the swarm surrounded Helen, who opened a bag of Jelly Babies as she winked at Darren.

'I'm just going to, err, find my script and go over my lines once more,' he said, and scuttled off.

Andrew readjusted his Ship's Captain costume and briefly wondered if there was a market for fancy dress funerals; perhaps something farmer related? As he debated whether having a toy tractor next to a graveside was appropriate or not, Patricia marched over to him.

He greeted her with a nod. 'Everything ship shape with you?'

'Yes, the seats are filling up nicely out there.'

'Excellent. Not too much longer until curtain up,' he said, checking his watch.

'Have you seen Ben? I'll let him know.'

'He's round the other side of the stage. Hey, have you seen the makeup that he's put on to cover his black eye? He's put so much on, it looks like he's about to do a drag show. All we need is a glitterball and some Abba music.'

'I did his makeup for him,' Patricia said without blinking.

Andrew paused for just a millisecond, 'And what a lovely job you did too. I'm just going to nip to the DIY shop and buy a bigger spade to dig this hole with,' he grinned.

Patricia looked him up and down and didn't reply before walking off.

'What do you mean the hot water urn isn't working?' Harry said, his eyes moving from Polly to Sue and then back again.

'Like I said, I switched it on at the wall when we arrived earlier, and when I checked it just now, the water is still cold,' Polly said.

Sue nodded in agreement.

'What did you press?'

'Just the switch on the wall, like I always do, so don't blame me,' Polly said, crunching on a carrot stick menacingly.

'I wasn't blaming you. I was just trying to work out what the problem is,' said Harry, as calmly as he could, even though he was having a meltdown in his head. 'There wasn't a bang or a hiss, or a spark or anything?'

'Nope, and if there had been, I would have told you. I'm not an idiot you know.'

'I didn't say you were, I'm just thinking,' Harry said, scratching his head. 'Ok, perhaps it's the fuse. Sue, can you find my toolbox? I think it's backstage, somewhere. I've got a screwdriver and some spare fuses in there.'

As Sue exited the kitchen stage left, Harry looked at Polly and smiled weakly.

'What?' she snapped, pointing a carrot at him like it had the potential to be an easily disposable murder weapon.

Sixty

Act One

As the lights went down, a quiet hush descended upon the hall, with just the odd sweet being unwrapped making a noise.

Harry licked his lips nervously and brought up the stage lighting slowly. As he did so, the curtains drew back, revealing Ben in his spot at the centre of the stage.

Silence.

Below where Harry was sat in his perch, he could hear people moving in their seats, waiting for something to happen.

More silence.

Come on Ben, say something, anything, just open your mouth and let words come out. Harry thought at a hundred miles an hour, his brain processing a thousand options all at once if Ben continued to say nothing. Harry's favourite option would be to dim all the lights and then leg it out to the car, off to the pub, and let the buggers sort it out for themselves.

'It's just not fair, having to stay home all the time. There's nothing to do here and I've watched everything on Netflix,' Ben spoke his first line and the trembling in Harry's finger that was poised over the light fader on the board stilled itself, and he retracted his hand and remembered to breathe again.

They were off.

Backstage, Helen looked sternly at Patricia, who was acting as prompt, as if to say, *Why didn't you prompt him?*

Patricia looked back at Helen, a mixture of relief and smugness on her face, as if to say, *He didn't need prompting anyway.* Helen looked down at the script in front of Patricia, and then back up at her again, her eyes saying, *Perhaps you should concentrate on the script, rather than on giving me evil looks.*

Patricia glared at her one final time, before looking back down at the script in front of her, her eyes quickly finding where they were up to, as Ben continued his monologue about deciding to travel to London, as he'd heard the streets were paved with gold and that in moving out of Wellington, he might finally be able to get a good Sky signal for his widescreen television.

Jessica was still fuming. In the last day or so, she had moved from being upset to damn right pissed off.

Who the hell does he think he is? Snogging Chelsea bloody O'Sullivan in the kitchen on New Year's Eve, when he should have been with me, welcoming in a New Year together, and planning the next year of our lives as a couple. I should have punched him in the other eye as well, so he had a matching pair. Then I should have taken a huge knife and chopped off his b-

'Jessica, you're on in a second, you should be over on the stage left side,' someone whispered to her out of the blackness. Coming back to Earth, she heard where they were, picked up her cat tail and legged it over to the other side, her blood boiling as she weaved in and out of the other actors as they paced up and down in the dimly lit walkway, each of them muttering their lines and looking to her like they were waiting for a dental appointment for a wisdom tooth extraction.

Ben wearily walked around the set, making sure that he kept his black eye that was heavily covered in stage makeup towards the back of the stage whenever he could. Thankfully, because of the stage lights, he couldn't see any of the audience, so he had started to relax a bit.

'Oh, how weary I am, for I have been walking for days and days now. And night is fast approaching, and yet I still have no lodgings. If only there was a place for me to rest my tired feet for the night.'

Jessica entered the stage, looking more like a lioness spoiling for a fight, than a cute cat. Ben started to feel nervous, the enjoyment now gone.

'Purr. Purr. Why hello there. And who might *you* be?' Jessica said, swinging her tail around in circles with one hand, the other hand on her hip.

'Hello there, little cat, I am Dick Whittington of Wellington, on my way to London to find my fame and fortune.'

'To London you say? Why, my *little* friend, you are very nearly there,' Jessica said, waggling her little finger. 'You are on the outskirts of that great city, and you would know something about being around skirts, wouldn't you?'

'Umm. Err, well, umm, thank goodness, as I have been travelling for days and days, and I am hungry and tired and need shelter and some lodgings.'

'Why, there is a large mansion house, but not a short distance from here. And in there lives a man and his *tramp* of a daughter, with only a face a mother could love.'

'Is that where you live, little cat?' Ben said warily.

'Not a chance, sunshine. Not with that hussy.'

'Umm, Ok. Right, well, shall we go there together then and see if the owner will take pity on us?' said Ben, his mouth dry.

'Knock yourself out *little* Dick.'

Ben stuttered as Jessica had gone way off script, and not fed him his next line. 'Oh, err, why don't you lead the way, Miss Kitty,' he said, trying his best to improvise, sweat building up on his forehead.

'Sure. Why not.' She was still glaring at him.

'So, what's your name then?' Ben said, trying to stay on track.

'I'm not surprised you can't remember my name. I'm amazed you even remember I exist,' Jessica spat out, twirling her tail menacingly.

'I think your collar says you're called Patch,' stammered Ben, the sweat now running down in to his eyes.

'Whatever,' said Jessica, before walking over to the wooden door. Ben hesitated for quite a while before walking over and joining her.

Up in the lighting box, Harry put his head in his hands and silently screamed.

Backstage, Patricia was looking very worried. For a woman that normally didn't do emotions, this was really concerning her. She was trying to follow the script with her finger, but they kept jumping about all over the place with their lines. Ben was trying to stick to the lines, it was Jessica that was all over the place. What had got into her? She was normally such a quiet, well-spoken girl and she had always got her lines right before this evening.

Darren turned to Helen, his script still clutched tightly in his hands. 'What's she doing?' he whispered, his eyes wide open and darting around. 'She's all over the place.'

303

'I think she's, err, improvising a little bit,' Helen replied.

'She's not allowed to do that. Tell her, she's not allowed to do that. We have a script for a perfectly good reason, so that everyone knows what everyone else is saying and when to say it,' Darren continued, his grip on the script tightening and his knuckles going white.

'As soon as she comes off stage, I'll have a word with her, if Harry doesn't beat me to it that is,' Helen promised. 'Anyway, you're a professional, Darren, so you'll be fine.'

'But she's not sticking to her lines!'

'Darren, you're on shortly, get moving,' Patricia hissed, with all the compassion of a scorpion.

'Oh, right. Yes,' he said, moving towards the stage, looking like he was about to face a room full of gargantuan actor-eating lizards.

'Break a leg,' Helen whispered at him. And with that, hearing his entrance line, he was gone. 'Oh, f….fruitcake,' Helen said.

Patricia looked at her alarmed, 'What?'

Helen just pointed on stage at Darren, who was stood opposite Ben and Jessica, his bright yellow script still firmly in his hands.

'Oh.'

Onstage, Darren could feel his throat going dry, and he was very aware of what he was holding. He cleared his throat and reminded himself that he was a professional. He had been on *Casualty, Eastenders* and a children's programme that hadn't gone past the first season and not even he could remember the name of it.

He was a professional. He could do this.

'Greetings, travellers,' Darren said in his character of the Wealthy Merchant.

'Good day to you, sir,' said Ben, the sweat visible on his forehead.

'Alright,' said Jessica.

'How can I help you fine fellows? said Darren, feeling one of his knees begin to tremble.

'We are hoping that you might be able to provide us with some lodgings for the night, kind sir. My name is Dick Whittington and this is Patch the Cat. We have travelled far, and the storm clouds are gathering overhead.'

'What he said,' Jessica spat out.

'Certainly. I was just, um, reviewing my accounts, as it's nearly the end of January, and I need to submit them to Revenue and Customs,' said Darren, waving his script about and improvising.

'Err, right,' said Ben, looking a bit confused. 'Shall we, err, come in then?'

'Why, yes, yes, I will give Dick and his wet pussy a bed for the night.'

'He prefers kitchens for that sort of thing,' Jessica said snidely.

'Ah. Well, there is a kitchen at your disposal as well,' said Darren, anxious to finish the scene and get the hell off the stage so that he could look at the possibility of moving abroad tomorrow.

'Thank you, sir, you're most kind.'

'Just lock up your daughter. He's got a reputation you know,' Jessica said to him. With that, she marched off the stage and into the wings.

Ben and Darren just looked at each other, both relieved that she had finally left the stage, but also both unsure what to do next, as there was supposed to be another four lines before they were meant to exit.

'Well,' said Darren, taking the lead, 'shall we get inside, before the storm arrives and we both get soaked?'

Ben gave an audible sigh of relief. 'What a splendid idea. I'll follow you.' And with that, they both scarpered off the set and the lights went down for the scene change.

In the kitchen at the back of the hall, Polly put the big stainless-steel lid back on the hot water urn. It still wasn't heating up after Harry had changed the fuse.

'What are we going to do?' asked a nervous Sue.

'We are...' Polly began and then faded out.

'Yes?'

'We are going to... Hang on, give me a minute.'

Sue started to bite one of her nails. 'God, I'm going to drink a bucket full of vodka when I get home. This is far too stressful.'

Polly looked at Sue, and a synapse fired in her brain and she looked at Sue with determination.

'What?'

'I've got it. I'm sure that old Eileen lives in that row of houses opposite here. We can use her kettle and ferry hot water back here. In fact, I think a couple of the old dears from the church congregation live over that way.'

'That sounds promising.'

'Yes, we'll do that. Sue, fetch the rats.'

'The rats?'

'We're going to put the little darlings to good use. They're going to be our chain gang.'

On stage, Helen, dressed in her character's bad-tempered cook outfit, was delivering her lines with the camp bitterness that Harry had directed her to have. She wasn't a mean person in real life, but she was enjoying this; even if she did always have to apologise to Ben after their scenes together were over.

'Come on, you lazy boy. You haven't cleaned those pots yet,' she said with her hands on her hips.

'I'm trying, but I cannelloni do so much,' Ben replied to her.

'Well hurry up. I need to make the pastry soon. This isn't a game of scones you know!'

'Yes, cook. Sorry, cook.'

'Then I have to make a pie. And there's only one of me, not three point one four. Fetch the flour for me.'

'I'll get it for you now, cook.'

Ben made his way over to one of the cupboards on the set and took out the bowl of white flour, which he placed on the table in front of Helen.

'Now get back to work, or I'll cut your celery,' she said.

Ben scuttled off, and resumed his pretend pot washing over in the corner of the stage. Helen picked up the big wooden spoon that was on the table and began to stir the flour while she gave her next line. She could feel something tickling her nose and realised a second too late that it must be one of her cat's stray hairs. Her sneeze echoed around the hall like a Swiss yodeller let loose on a maintain range.

Harry looked up from the lighting board he was priming for the end of this scene. Helen was standing in the centre of the stage covered in flour, with specs of the white powder still falling to the ground all around her, reminding Harry of a snow globe. He swallowed, unsure what to do next. Thankfully, he was saved from devising a plan by the raucous laughter that filled the hall.

Sixty-One

The Interval

After just over an hour, and to the sound of clapping, the red curtains swept across the stage meeting in the middle. The main lights flickered into life, signalling the start of the fifteen-minute interval, and the end of part one of Harry's nightmare.

Two of the A level performing arts students appeared with snack baskets and parked themselves at opposite ends of the hall. The kitchen's metal shutter clanked up, revealing Polly and Sue surrounded by an assortment of kettles.

As soon as he had brought the main lights up, Harry had clambered down from his lookout tower and shot off for the backstage area. He didn't want to hear any of the audience's half time opinion on how it was going, as he had a pretty good understanding on how it was going himself. He was going to share his thoughts in no uncertain terms once he reached backstage.

If they had any audience at all joining them for the second half, it would be a miracle.

In the seventh row from the front, Gerald held his breath and gripped his knees with his hands.

And waited.

Not breathing.

He tried to gauge Valerie's facial expression with his peripheral vision, but couldn't really assess her reaction. Sensing that she was turning to face him, he turned his head.

She looked at him.

He looked at her.

She raised one eyebrow.

'Well, that was certainly *interesting*,' she said.

Not being entirely sure what she meant by that, Gerald opted to tilt his head to one side, nod slightly and said, 'Mmm,' in agreement, leaving Valerie to respond.

'Gerald, I think I'm in need of a nice cup of tea.'

'Let me fetch you one, my dear,' he replied, and stood up, ready to make his way to the back of the hall, glad to be escaping for a short while and hoping that there was a long queue in front of him when he got there.

When the lights had gone up, most of the first and second rows of the audience had made a dash for the toilets, and as there were only a couple of cubicles for each gender, there was now a growing line. Waiting for their turn were pensioners Fred and Beryl, who had come out for the night. Beryl had been an enthusiastic amateur actress in her youth, and had been keen to see the pantomime. Fred, who had been an aircraft engine designer for Rolls Royce was just happy spending time with his wife, and if she was happy, he was happy.

Bumping shoulders with her to catch her attention, he said, 'So, what do you think?'

'It's fun,' Beryl replied. 'But it makes me feel old when they use all these modern words. And I'm not entirely sure all of them are appropriate for younger ears, but I guess we need to move with the times.'

'Good, glad you're enjoying it. But they don't have a patch on you, darling.'

'Oh, Fred, what I wouldn't give to be back up on that stage again, singing my heart out.'

'You'd still give them a run for their money. Oh look, your turn for the ladies, see you in a bit.'

Waiting patiently in the queue for the snacks, sixty-seven-year-old Priscilla stood with her granddaughter, Harriet. She was treating her to her first pantomime and giving Harriet's parents a night to themselves.

Holding hands in the queue, Priscilla waggled Harriet's hand and looking down asked her, 'Are you enjoying it, Harriet?'

'Yes, gwanny, I love it,' came the reply, her eyes twinkling with excitement.

'Good. Which character do you like the best?'

Without hesitation, Harriet replied, 'Da cat! She is sooooo funny. She's bossing doze boys around, isn't she gwanny?'

'Yep, she's *certainly* doing that alright. Now, which flavour lolly do you want?'

'Chocolate please.'

'Ok, but if mummy and daddy ask, we had some fruit, ok?'

'Fruit? Yuck.'

Sat near the back, Tracy Fenton, head of the flower arranging committee, looked at the queue for the ice creams and decided against treating herself. If there had been a bar, she would have been on her second glass of Italian chardonnay by now. Instead, she took out her Kindle from its place in her handbag and carried on from where she had left off earlier in the afternoon – trying to block out what had just happened.

The vicar, who had been the first in line for refreshments, took his seat again with his polystyrene cup of tea. He glanced around, before unscrewing the top of his hip flask and pouring a healthy measure of whisky in and he took a quick gulp. Tea was definitely better with whisky in, rather than Polish Vodka.

Turning to face one of the parishioners as she sat back down next to him, he said, 'Well, that was good fun!'

Her glare made him quickly face the other direction and grin to himself.

Margaret and Will were two other retirees, who had also decided to brave the cold January weather to get out of the house and support the local entertainment. Both in their nineties, they normally spent most of their time playing Scrabble together, and watching antiques based programmes. A couple of years ago, Margaret had been convinced that she had a teapot that was worth a fortune, but when she had it valued, she was disappointed to learn that it was a mass-produced Woolworths one from the sixties.

As they sat carefully back down in their seats, with Will helping Margaret to sit down first, they soon got stuck into their choc-ices.

When they had finished, Margaret turned to Will, and asked, 'Why does the Cat keep calling Dick Whittington a banker?'

Backstage, Harry was reaching the end of reading Jessica and Ben the riot act.

'…and *if* you don't stick to the script in the second act, I will be *seriously* hacked off. Do you understand me? If there's so much as *one* single word missed, or replaced,' he said, looking at Jessica, 'then I will give your car number plates to my friends in the traffic division and ask them to stop your cars whenever they see them, and do a *thorough* inspection each time. And if they suspect that you have something about your person which you shouldn't have, they will take you to the police station and strip search you. Now, do I make myself *crystal* clear?'

Seeing him shake slightly, both Jessica and Ben nodded in unison at him.

'Good. Now go and get ready for act two. Remember, be warned.'

As they scuttled off, Harry leant back, not realising the props table was behind him instead of the wall, causing several items to crash to the ground. Muttering obscenities to himself, he picked them up and replaced them on the table.

Darren walked around the corner, and seeing Harry, did a prompt U-turn, and headed off in the opposite direction.

Spying the retreating figure, Harry hissed, 'Oi,' to catch his attention, but Darren was long gone.

Deciding he needed some fresh air for a few minutes, Harry made his way to the door, avoiding as many people as he could along the way.

Reaching the sanctuary of the peace and quiet of the outside, he looked around him at the snow that was still on the ground, and tried to calm his breathing down. Taking some deep breaths in and out, he felt his blood pressure starting to return to normal.

The door from the hall opened, and one of the A level students, Harry couldn't remember which one, stuck his head out. 'Oh, there you are, Mr Berwick. We should be starting again in a few minutes and your wife sent me to find you.'

'Right, thanks,' Harry replied. Taking his wallet out from his back pocket he produced a ten-pound note. 'Do me a favour, will you? Nip over to that shop and get me a little bottle of whisky?'

'Sure. Oh, but I'm only seventeen?'

'You're a student, I'm sure you've got a fake ID on you somewhere,' said Harry, waving the ten-pound note at the youngster.

'Err, right,' said the student, looking shifty and taking the money. 'Leave it with me,' and thumbing through his wallet, the student made off in the direction of the little shop.

Praying that aliens would swoop down and abduct him; or at the very least, zap the power grid with their ray guns, Harry went back inside and up to his perch.

Sixty-Two

Act Two

The bright main lights were once again extinguished, plunging everyone into a sudden darkness that was punctuated this time by the scraping of ice cream tubs.

Against his better judgement, Harry reluctantly brought up the front stage lights.

The red stage curtains opened again, and he opened his eyes. He saw everything as it should be for act two scene one. He cheered in his head and took a swig from the small whisky bottle that the greasy student had given him a couple of minutes earlier. Harry hadn't failed to notice that he wasn't given any change, but considering he'd just sent an underage teenager to fetch him whisky, he was in no position to complain.

Taking another sip, he remembered that Ben and Jessica weren't in too many scenes together in the second act, so all might just go according to plan.

He hoped.

Unless he had been *really* bad in a past life. In which case, he was in big trouble.

As the first scene melted away into the second and as Andrew delivered his lines as the Ship's Captain perfectly on stage, backstage, all was not plain sailing.

Leo was in the process of having a meltdown, as several of the props for the upcoming 'island feast' scene had gone missing. He had spent hours making papier-mâché steaks, chickens and turkeys for the act two banquet scene and now they were nowhere to be found.

'Well they were here earlier, so where the fuck are they now?' Leo snarled, his blue eyes darting about like a cornered cat looking for an escape route.

'Leo, language,' Helen whispered, pointing at a couple of nearby rats who were nibbling at a bag of crisps.

'I couldn't give a damn about my language. Where the hell is all the food?'

'It's got to be here somewhere. I'm sure I saw it earlier. Let me see if I can find a torch.'

'We've got about ten minutes until the scene, what are we going to do?' Leo said, putting his head in his hands.

'Don't worry. If it comes to it, they can just mime eating food, so it's not the end of the world,' Helen said, trying to reassure him.

'Oh, I'm so glad I spent all that time making the props then.'

'I'm going to look for a torch now, before I slap you,' Helen glared at him and shuffled off.

Andrew was enjoying himself. His lines were flowing easily, the set hadn't fallen down and Jessica seemed to be mostly sticking to her lines. He'd always fancied treading the boards and now his dream had been fulfilled. He had been in a couple of plays when he was at school, his favourite being Sweet Charity, but this was now more years ago than he cared to remember. He had enjoyed the last few months, despite all the ups and downs and not to mention the bloodshed. Going over his next few lines in his head, Andrew mentally prepared himself.

The storm scene was about to finish and Andrew and all the other actors on stage were holding onto parts of the ship, pretending to be thrown backwards and forwards in the waves of the storm. As the storm-sounding music was faded down over the speakers that were sat either side of the stage, the stage lights stopped flashing dramatically and returned to normal. The music died out completely, and Andrew stood up from where he had been crouched behind the big wooden ship's wheel. He looked around, imagining the wreckage, carnage and devastation before him. Opening his mouth to deliver his line, his thunder was stolen by the sound of a tremendously long, and loud, bottom burp coming from behind the set.

Quite a few of the children in the audience laughed, Andrew just about able to make out their little hands covering their mouths as they did so. Deciding to just go with it, Andrew said, 'I think the storm has moved on behind us. And I'll be surprised if it hasn't blown someone's pants off!'

Mercifully, the audience chuckled and Andrew carried on with the scene.

Backstage, one of the rats was having an asthma attack from trying to muffle his laughter.

'Has anyone seen his inhaler?' Helen's question was met with shaking heads from some of the other rats.

'I think he left it on the minibus, Miss,' one spoke up.

'Ok, well not to worry, everything will be fine. Darren?' She looked around. Darren was sat with his head between his knees, taking deep breaths. 'Darren!'

'What?' he said, glancing up at her, looking as white as a ping-pong ball.

'Ask around for an asthma inhaler, will you?'

316

'I don't need one, I'm just feeling faint with nerves, it'll pass in a bit.'

'Not for you, for him,' she said, pointing at the kid in question, who had now also started hiccupping from trying to stop his earlier laughter.

'Where am I going to get one of those?'

'Just ask people, someone must have one.'

'Sure, ok.' He got to his feet.

Helen turned back to attend to the wheezing rodent. Seconds later there was a soft thud and several muffled squeaks. Spinning around, Helen saw that Darren had passed out, but his fall had been softened by several of the children.

'Marvellous.'

Sometime later, back on stage, the current scene was going well for Andrew. He had just reached the point where during the feast on the island, they are suddenly overrun with rats.

'My island kingdom is not quite perfect, as you can see we have a rat problem,' exclaimed the tubby Island King, as the swarm of upper class rats ran amok around the stage, with one of them putting his foot through one of Leo's papier-mâché cooked, free-range, corn fed chickens, which had been found in the nick of time by Helen.

'Don't you worry about that, I know just the thing. Our feisty Ship's Cat will be able to sort out these pesky rats in a jiffy,' Andrew said, getting to his feet. 'Patch, we need your help catching these rats.'

'What rats?' said Jessica as the Cat, getting to her feet and facing the front of the stage, whilst the rats ran wild behind her. 'Can you see any rats anywhere, boys and girls?'

With some prompting and encouragement from the older members of the audience, Patch the Cat found out that the rats were "behind her". With that she was off, chasing the rats all over the stage, with the accompanying shrieks and squeaks, as all the rats eventually ran off the stage – one pausing to take a puff from something – followed by Jessica.

'You've done it,' said the Island King, looking dramatically happy.

'All in a day's work, my good fellow,' Andrew replied.

'You must let me reward you for the use of your moggy, I have some fi-,' the Island King stopped mid-sentence, as Chelsea ran onto the stage looking fearfully behind her.

Andrew looked at her in puzzlement. Chelsea's character was that of the rich merchant's daughter, whose house was supposedly back in London and *not* on the island.

'Err, hello, err, young lady. What are you doing here?' he asked her. Opposite him the Island King looked on blankly.

'I, um, had to, um, escape from someone,' she said, turning red.

'I see. But, err, how did you get onto this remote island?' Andrew said, his foot starting to tap nervously on the stage floor.

'Oh, is this not Butlins at Minehead?'

There was laughter from the auditorium.

Feeling a little braver, Andrew replied, 'Ah, I fear your satnav has led you astray. Minehead is several thousand miles that way,' he said, pointing across the stage.

'Lovely, thanks,' Chelsea said and hitching her skirt up a couple of inches, she ran off the stage.

Up in his perch, Harry was now halfway down his bottle of whisky.

318

Sixty-Three

The Two Cleaners

The Next Day

A hacking cough came from between two rows of chairs somewhere in the middle of the auditorium section of the hall. Sitting a couple of rows back, Jenny threw a discarded yellow Skittle that she had found on the floor in the direction of the coughing.

'Sounds like you're coughing up a lung, my love,' she said loudly.

'Too many fags last night. Urgh. Those Slovak fags are like double, double strength, or something',' replied Kelly, standing up and placing the black bin bag on one of the seats. She stretched her arms above her head and yawned. 'Are you just going to sit there all morning?'

'I'm directing operations, aren't I,' Jenny said, popping a sweet in her mouth.

'Need an operation more like, transplant some brains into that gert thick head of yours.'

'You're a little charmer today, aren't you, my little thistle bush,' Jenny said, throwing another abandoned sweet in Kelly's direction.

'I'm surprised you're chucking all this food at me, rather than eating it,' came the reply, as Kelly easily dodged the projectile she'd just thrown.

'I was going to share this bag of Maltesers that I found with you, but I think I've changed me mind now.'

'I think you've just proved me right,' Kelly muttered.

'Mmm?' Jenny said, with her nose in the bag of chocolates.

'I said, did you see the show last night?'

'Uh-huh.'

'And?' Kelly asked, sitting down on one of the chairs.

'And what?'

'God you're dense sometimes. Was it any good? I'm seeing it tonight.'

'It was alright. Don't get your hopes up though, Ben wasn't wearing tights.'

'Gutted. What was he wearing?'

'Some crappy outfit. Nothing tight though, so you couldn't see nothing.'

'That's rubbish,' Kelly replied to her, starting to pick up bits of litter from between the chair legs.

'Yep. The only half-naked bloke was some chubby fella, who was on for a bit in the second half.'

'Oh.'

'I know. And to think we changed Ben's name on that list to the main character as well. He should have at least worn tights.' she said, scratching her ear and crunching down on the last Malteser.

'I'm not sure I'll bother going now.'

'That reminds me,' she said, throwing yet another abandoned sweet in the direction of Kelly's backside as she bent over to pick something up. 'Why didn't you come with me last night? I was surrounded by children and oldies.'

'Oi! Will you stop it. I'm trying to tidy up here. Like you should be doing, so get off your arse and help.'

320

'Alright, my love, calm yourself, I'm getting up. And you didn't answer my question.' Jenny said, getting to her feet and looking around for the roll of bin bags.

'I told you already, I think old age is setting in already.'

'No, you didn't.'

'Oh, I thought I'd said. Well, I was on a date if you must know.'

'You found someone to go out with your mug?'

Jenny ducked as a sweet was lobbed in her direction. Followed by an empty ice cream tub, which, with its aerodynamic qualities, was only airborne for about six feet.

'Less of your cheek thank you. And yeah, he's well fit.'

'Where's this one from?' Jenny asked, knowing her friend's fondness for European men with chiseled cheekbones and floppy hair.

'Yeovil.'

'Oh right. Go well did it?'

'Yeah, just went to the pub and had a few civilised drinks.'

'Successful night then. Would you believe how much mess this lot left behind? There's sweet wrappers everywhere.'

Kelly put some more rubbish in her sack. 'I know, messy sods. Still, think of the extra money we're getting this week, clearing up after every night.'

'True, my love. Very true. Still, it looks like they were just chucking their rubbish about everywhere. Oh look. Half a bag of toffees,' she said poking her finger around inside the sweet bag.

'You're not going to eat them, are you?' Kelly said, her face a picture of disgust.

'Of course I am. They're wrapped up. Besides, there are people starving in the world, so you shouldn't let food go to waste.'

'God, you sound like my old mum.'

'Clever woman,' she said, popping a toffee in her mouth and chewing noisily.

They both meandered around the hall, which instead of its usual cold, dusty smell, emitted a sweet fragrance, like Willy Wonka's factory might.

'Were there a lot of people here last night then?' asked Kelly, tying a knot in the rubbish bag which now looked full.

'Yeah, it was. Gert loads of people there was. Mostly families and that.'

'Quite tame, was it?'

'Mostly, although the field mouse was well feisty.'

'Yeah? What was she doing?'

'She kept making comments to our Benny boy.'

'Like what?' Kelly asked, giving Jenny her full attention, hands on hips.

'She kept calling him *little Dick* and most of the time she looked like she was about to knee him in the goolies.'

'Not her happy usual bundle of joy then.'

'Most definitely not happy,' said Jenny, pulling her tights up. 'Not that I've seen many emotions on her face in the past. She normally just stands there giving people evil looks. Like some sort of ginger serial killer.'

'They say it's always the quiet ones you have to watch.'

'We're safe with you and your big gob then.'

'Everyone else is safe. It's just you that needs to worry. Especially if you don't get a move on. I want to get to the bingo at two, so shift it.'

Sixty-Four

The Book Club

Polly waited for Harry impatiently outside of the Tesco Express. The show had finished at the weekend, and as the local paper came out on a Thursday, they had decided to move their regular Wednesday night Book Club meeting to tonight, so that they could all hear the review at the same time. They had all promised that they wouldn't sneak a read of the review beforehand; even Leo with his limited attention span had agreed to abide by this rule.

Even though technically it was Darren's turn to host the Book Club this week, they had all decided that they should meet at Helen's house to read it, as this is where the idea to write, and then put on the pantomime had been conceived a few months back. This seemed like a lifetime ago now.

Polly tapped her foot impatiently and slid another carrot stick out of the packet that was tucked inside her multi-coloured handbag. Harry had been in the shop for what felt like an eternity now, when all he had gone in for was the newspaper.

Looking around her, she saw that most of the snow had disappeared now and it was starting to feel quite mild for the middle of January. Spring was still a long way off, but at least the bitter cold of the last few weeks was easing.

Harry finally came out of the shop and was met by Polly's impatient glare. He waved the newspaper at her, before tucking it under his arm. They trudged off in silence up the road, the anticipation preventing them from even whispering a word to each other.

After a tense ten-minute walk, they were outside of Helen's cottage, which was tucked away from the main road. The glow from the lit window lamp gently warming the sides of the curtains that were drawn across the living room window.

Standing outside the front door, Harry turned to her and raised an eyebrow. In turn she, after the smallest of pauses, nodded. Harry gently pushed on the doorbell with his gloved finger.

Milliseconds later, the door was snatched open by Helen, with the rest of the Book Club members peering from their seats to check it was Harry and Polly arriving at long last, even though they were only a few minutes late.

'Come in,' Helen welcomed them, quickly standing out of the way so that they could enter.

Wiping her feet on the mat as she crossed the threshold into the warm and snug living room, Polly looked around at the faces. Two empty chairs awaited them in the cramped circle and people nearest the door picked up their mugs of tea off the floor, to prevent the possibility of them being accidentally knocked over as the newcomers took their seats.

Like a reluctant king and queen ascending their thrones for the first time, Polly, along with Harry shuffled their way over to the vacant chairs and took their places.

Polly watched as Harry looked around the room at all the expectant faces. Valerie and Gerald were sitting on the sofa, Valerie with her hands placed delicately on her knees and Gerald holding his together on his lap. Leo was jiggling his knees up and down and chewing his lip. Helen was still standing by the door, as if she were ready to make a quick getaway if the news was bad. Darren and Ben were sat next to each other on the smaller sofa, with Andrew perched on the arm of the sofa. Chelsea and Patricia were on chairs that had been brought in from the kitchen. Chelsea was tapping her fingers on her leg as if an invisible keyboard rested on them and Patricia looked like she was about to deliver a eulogy. Jessica stood in the doorway to the kitchen, arms folded and looking defiant.

Polly heard Harry letting out the breath he must have subconsciously been holding in. 'Right then, cheer up you lot, you look like you're at a funeral,' he said, his confident voice dancing around the room, stirring up the quietness, causing the cat to open one eye.

There was a cough. 'I see that you've purchased the newspaper, Harry. Would you be so kind as to enlighten us as to its contents?' Valerie said.

'Yeah, come on Harry, put us out of our misery, eh?' said Andrew.

Now Polly held her breath.

'Righty-ho,' said Harry, opening the newspaper and thumbing his way through the pages. 'Oh,' he said stopping at one page. 'There's a car boot sale this Sunday at the Castle School.'

Polly nudging his knee and Harry looked up and realised that everyone was glaring at him. 'Sorry. Ah, here we are. Ok. I'll read it out.'

Harry cleared his throat and read slowly, making sure his diction was clear.

'"St. Jude's Book Club's performance of Dick Whittington was certainly an event that will be remembered for some time. This was the Book Club's first outing in the land of show business and they managed to stand their ground, despite the storm that raged in the second act.

I have never before seen a livelier and more energetic performance, from the Grumpy Cook to the hordes of rats, or from the Ship's Captain to the confident Cat. The performance was fresh and appeared to be spontaneous, regardless of what must have been several months of rehearsals, which is a testament to the two writers, Valerie Makepeace and Polly Berwick and the director, Harry Berwick (yes, a relation).

Playing Dick Whittington and his Cat, young Ben and Jessica's interaction was certainly unique and perhaps it should have been called 'The gutsy Cat and Dick Whittington', as she clearly wore the trousers in that relationship.

The boisterous young rats brought an interesting twist to the performance, which complemented the pace and style of this contemporary showpiece and the all-round well-acted scenes.

Full of many local references and humour, this pantomime succeeded at including everybody in the audience, from young to old; with hopefully only audience members over the age of eighteen understanding some of the jokes and language.

Well done, St Jude's Book Club, an attention-grabbing and noteworthy performance." '

Harry put the newspaper down and looked about the room.

'So, does that mean they liked it?' asked Darren.

'I think it does,' beamed Andrew. 'Well done everyone, we did it!'

There were cheers of delight from all corners of the room. Even Patricia managed to smile and nod her head.

'I always knew it would be a success,' said Valerie. 'And of course, the review does mention my writing.' Polly looked over at Valerie and raised an eyebrow. 'Apologies, you contributed your part as well, Polly.' Valerie said, and Harry placed his arm around Polly's shoulders in support.

'Well done to you all, you all performed spectacularly, and you did yourselves proud. Thank you to each and every one of you for your help, support and dedication,' Harry proclaimed, waving the newspaper above his head with his free hand.

'And well done to you, too, Harry. Expertly directed,' said Andrew, saluting his friend with his mug of tea. The rest of the group joined in with Andrew's sentiment, all thanking Harry for his calm direction and crisis management skills.

'Did we make any money in the end?' said Helen.

Harry turned to Chelsea and asked, 'Chelsea?'

'Yep,' she replied, pulling out a small notebook from the pocket of her coat that she was sat on. 'After all the costs were taken off, for flyers, costumes and the parking ticket that Polly got, from stopping on double yellow lines to deliver the advert to the newspaper, we raised just under five hundred pounds.'

'Excellent work,' said Harry above the noise of the clapping. 'The vicar will be pleased with that.'

'Think of all the whisky he can buy with that!' said Leo.

'I'm sure it will go to a good cause,' Harry quickly jumped in, as Valerie squinted her eyes questioningly.

'All in all, a good result,' said Helen.

'So then,' said Andrew casually. 'What shall we do next year?'

As the last person shut the door behind them, Helen settled down into the worn arm chair. Mr Darcy came over and rubbed against her legs and then jumped up onto her lap. He turned around three times, and then settled down, closing his eyes on his little black face as Helen gently stroked him a few times. She then picked up and opened her new book and smiled.

Acknowledgements

Thank you for reading my first book, and I hope you enjoyed it as much as I did writing it – it's certainly been a learning curve for me.

My love, thanks and gratitude go to my partner, Dominik, who kept encouraging me to finish the book; your support has been a terrific boost, thank you.

One of the first people I would like to thank is my good friend (and fellow author) John Marrs. Ever since John published his first book and I mentioned to him that I had always fancied giving writing a go, he's been there to encourage, guide and support me; as well as very kindly tell me when something wasn't working (even if I did momentarily sulk about it). So, John, thank you! Also thank you to his partner, John Russell, who whenever we all met up for lunch wouldn't object when I monopolized the conversation by asking John Marrs millions of questions relating to writing and publishing. Our next lunch outing is on me.

My heartfelt thanks to those of you that read sections and gave me some helpful feedback along the way, especially Tracey Morrow (your feedback right back at the beginning helped tremendously), Cherry Hibbert (for spotting my many, many spelling mistakes. I think 'custardy suit' was my favourite) and to my family (Mike, Priscilla, Ed, Hannah, Chris, Ella and Harriet), who put up with me asking them questions about book covers and what TV programmes two year olds watch.

Also thanks to all my fellow bookworms at THE Book Club on Facebook – your advice, guidance and humour is amazing!

Thanks also needs to go to Edward Reisner, who helped me with some music questions (at one point, Mr Darcy the cat was playing a jazz beat with his paws on a bedside cabinet).

And thanks needs to go to my cat, Monty, who gave me the idea for this story when I was watching him beat up one of his toy rats.

Thank you also to Andrew Shore, Martyn Bradley, Matthew Woods (your ideas helped a lot), Adam Brett and Pete Croft for your help and suggestions into various sections of the book.

And lastly but most importantly, thank you to you, dear reader, for buying this book and putting your trust in an unknown author. I truly hope you've enjoyed this story, and if so, I would be very grateful if you would be kind enough to leave a review for me.

You can follow me on Instagram: @Jim_Ryan_Author
Or on Facebook: www.facebook.com/authorJimRyan

21329063R00186

Printed in Poland
by Amazon Fulfillment
Poland Sp. z o.o., Wrocław